A CHANGE
of
FORTUNE

A CHANGE of FORTUNE

JEN TURANO

BETHANYHOUSE
a division of Baker Publishing Group
Minneapolis, Minnesota

Published by Bethany House Publishers
11400 Hampshire Avenue South
Bloomington, Minnesota 55438
www.bethanyhouse.com

Bethany House Publishers is a division of
Baker Publishing Group, Grand Rapids, Michigan

Printed in the United States of America

Library of Congress Cataloging-in-Publication Data
Turano, Jen.
    A change of fortune / Jen Turano.
      p. cm.
    ISBN 978-0-7642-1018-1 (pbk.)
    1. Man-woman relationships—Fiction. 2. Socialites—New York (State)—
New York—Fiction. I. Title.
PS3620.U7455C63 2012
813'.6—dc23   2012028887

This is a work of fiction. Names, characters, incidents, and dialogues are products of the author's imagination and are not to be construed as real. Any resemblance to actual events or persons, living or dead, is entirely coincidental.

Cover design by John Hamilton Design

Author represented by The Seymour Agency

12   13   14   15   16   17   18   7   6   5   4   3   2   1

In Memory of
Evelyn Gerdts Turner

*You would have gotten a
kick out of this one, Mom.
Miss you every day.*

*All my love,
Jennifer*

1

New York, 1880

*M*iss Eliza Sumner turned the page of the book she was reading aloud, glancing up and biting back a smile at the unusual sight of her two charges, Grace and Lily, listening attentively to her. She lowered her gaze and continued reading, raising her voice dramatically when she got to a riveting passage regarding a motley band of pirates.

"There you are, Miss Sumner," a voice exclaimed from the doorway.

Eliza set the book aside and hurried to her feet as her employer, Mrs. Cora Watson, advanced into the room.

"I've been searching everywhere for you," Mrs. Watson proclaimed.

As it was a normal occurrence for Eliza to spend her evenings in the schoolroom, she was a bit perplexed by Mrs. Watson's statement, but felt it best to keep that particular thought to herself.

"Here," Mrs. Watson said, thrusting a bundle of silk into Eliza's hands, "I need you to put this on immediately."

"I do beg your pardon, Mrs. Watson, but am I to understand you've taken issue with my gown?"

"Certainly not. Your gown is completely acceptable for the schoolroom, but I need your services at dinner."

"You wish me to serve the meal?"

"Don't be ridiculous," Mrs. Watson said.

Eliza eyed the massive amount of fabric in her hand and cautiously shook it out, unable to suppress a shudder as yard after yard of hideous color unfolded before her eyes. "Is this . . . a dinner gown?"

"It is."

"Mother, surely you don't expect Miss Sumner to wear that," Grace said, scurrying to Eliza's side. "Why, it's the most revolting shade of . . ." She paused and looked up at Eliza. "What color would you call that?"

"I believe the proper term would be puce," Eliza supplied.

"I think the proper term should be ugly," Lily piped up, joining her sister with her nose wrinkled. "It'll clash with her red hair, Mother."

"I know," Mrs. Watson said, "but it's the only gown I have on hand at the moment." She turned to Eliza. "Please don't take offense at this, Miss Sumner, but you're rather stout in build, and the only member of my family possessed of a similar figure is my aunt Mildred, who just happened to leave this gown the last time she visited."

As Eliza's "stoutness" was the result of layers of linen wrapped around her middle, she took no offense at all over Mrs. Watson's remark. Before she could formulate a suitable response, Grace let out a snort.

"Aunt Mildred only left that gown because she knew it was awful and not of the current fashion. Poor Miss Sumner will barely be able to walk, seeing as how the skirt is so long."

"She'll simply have to make the best of it unless she has a dinner gown of her own to wear."

Eliza bit her lip. While it was true she possessed more than her fair share of dinner gowns, they were currently back in England, and now was hardly the time to ponder that particular subject. She could not allow Mrs. Watson to discover the pesky little fact that she was in actuality Lady Eliza Sumner, not plain Miss, nor could she divulge the fact that her father had been the Earl of Sefton. She cleared her throat. "I'm sorry to say I have no formal attire at my disposal."

"Hmm, pity that," Mrs. Watson replied. "You'll have to wear Aunt Mildred's gown."

"May I be so bold as to ask what you require of me at your dinner?" Eliza asked.

"Oh, forgive me," Mrs. Watson said, wiping her brow absently with the back of her hand. "Agatha's developed spots. You need to take her place at the table."

Eliza stifled a groan. One of the main reasons she'd sought out employment as a governess was so she could remain inconspicuous, and attending a dinner party hosted by one of the upcoming social leaders of New York City was not exactly what she had had in mind when she accepted the position.

"But, Mrs. Watson," Eliza began, "surely you don't believe . . ."

"I cannot have an uneven number at the table," Mrs. Watson interrupted. "I finally received an acceptance from the Trumans, and Mr. Watson would not be pleased if I did anything to embarrass him, such as sitting down to dinner with an odd number of guests."

"Father must want to sell Mr. Truman a huge vat of soap," Grace declared.

"It's hardly proper for a young lady, Grace, to discuss business," Mrs. Watson said before turning back to Eliza. "I expect you downstairs in thirty minutes."

"Don't you believe your guests will consider it bad form for me to attend your dinner party?" Eliza asked, wincing when she heard the clear note of desperation in her voice.

Mrs. Watson narrowed her eyes. "Did your letter of reference not state you were proficient in the subject of etiquette?"

"Well, yes, certainly, but . . ."

"And did it not also state you are a distant relation of the aristocracy?"

Eliza nodded, knowing perfectly well her "distant relation" to the aristocracy was not very distant.

"Then I would have to assume you've attended a formal dinner in the past."

"I have not attended a formal dinner in quite some time."

"Has that caused you to forget your manners?" Mrs. Watson asked.

"Ahh . . . I don't believe so."

"Then there is absolutely no reason for you to balk at my request. I would have to believe you are well equipped to handle the silver."

"I am the governess," Eliza muttered.

"No one needs to know that, dear."

"I would have to believe someone at the dinner table will ask me my name," Eliza said.

"I suggest you tell them you're Miss Sumner."

"What if they ask me more questions?"

Mrs. Watson released a sigh. "My dear, I don't wish to cause you distress, but quite frankly, you are not the type of woman with whom one wishes to enter into conversation at a dinner party."

Eliza swallowed a laugh. Apparently her attempt at disguising her appearance and her true identity could be deemed a success.

"I really must get back downstairs," Mrs. Watson continued, seemingly unaware of the fact that she'd delivered Eliza an insult and a compliment in the same breath. "I have numerous details left unresolved, and I want everything to be perfect." She sent Eliza a nod. "I'll try to find a maid to help you into that gown."

Eliza watched Mrs. Watson walk through the door before shifting her gaze to Grace and Lily. "Our story will have to wait for another day."

"We were just getting to the good part," Grace complained. "I'm sorry my mother is being so demanding. She used to be somewhat fun."

"I don't remember her being fun," Lily remarked.

"That's because you were born after Father's business became successful," Grace said. "Mother wasn't responsible for hosting so many parties, and I'm afraid it's given her a bit of an edge." She sighed. "Agatha remembers a time when even Father was fun."

"Speaking of Agatha," Eliza said, "what type of spots do you think she has at the moment? Should someone send for a physician?"

"She hardly needs a physician," Grace said with a grin. "Agatha is only suffering from rebellious spots because Mother invited gentlemen tonight who are known to be eligible bachelors."

"Am I to understand there's nothing wrong with her?" Eliza asked.

"She's a bit crazy, but honestly, Agatha's always been that way."

Eliza felt her lips twitch. "Maybe I should pay Agatha a visit and call her on her ruse so I won't have to don this gown and make a complete cake of myself."

"You talk funny sometimes," Lily said.

"I imagine it comes from being British."

"Your accent is charming," Grace said. "I bet if I spoke like you all the boys would fall in love with me."

"As you are too young to even contemplate boys, being all of eleven years old, I think we'll return to the subject at hand. Where is your sister?" Eliza asked.

"She's gone into hiding and won't turn up until after dinner," Grace said.

"Wonderful," Eliza muttered before she walked over to the discarded book, picked it up, and handed it to Grace. "You may continue reading this to your sister, and you'll have to fill me in on the story line when we meet again two days from now. Tomorrow is Sunday, my day off, but I'll be waiting with bated breath to discover what happens with the pirates."

She turned on her heel and strode into the hallway, making her way to her room. She closed the door and allowed her shoulders to slump as she gulped in deep breaths of air, the reality of her situation setting in.

This was a disaster.

She moved to her bed and dropped the dinner gown on top of the covers, spreading the fabric out even as her eyes narrowed. There was no way she would be able to fit into it, no matter how "stout" Mrs. Watson claimed her aunt to be, because the gown had a cinched waist, a waist that would balk if she tried to squeeze her stuffing into it.

She unbuttoned the front of her serviceable gown and shrugged out of it, her hands moving immediately to the front ties of her specially made corset. She made short shrift of unlacing the ribbons and began unwinding one of the strips of linen she'd used to pad her figure. She dropped the cloth to the ground, retied her corset, and then snagged the gown off the bed, wrestling it over her head. It got stuck halfway down her body.

She squirmed out of it, unlaced her corset, and unwound another strip of cloth, her fingers moving rapidly as she suddenly recalled that Mrs. Watson was supposed to send a maid to assist her. She squeezed into the gown and buttoned it up the best she could before she scooped the abandoned linen off the floor and stuffed it beneath her mattress. She struggled to button the last few buttons, but finally admitted defeat when she simply couldn't reach them.

She could only hope the maid didn't notice anything unusual. She grinned. Honestly, if she didn't look unusual at the moment, she'd eat this gown. She moved to the mirror, grabbing hold of a chest of drawers when she tripped on the hem. She twitched the fabric out of her way and straightened, her grin widening when she got a good look at her reflection.

She looked like an opera singer.

Large blue eyes stared back at her out of a pale face, which had a smattering of freckles marching along the bridge of her nose. Her grin turned into a smile, showing straight white teeth and causing a dimple to pop out on her right cheek. Her smile faded as her eyes lifted to her hair, which she had pulled tightly away from her face and secured in a matronly bun and which in no way resembled the intricate styles of her past. She shook herself. There was no time for reflection just now.

Her gaze traveled the length of her body, and her mouth dropped open. Although she'd managed to get the gown over her middle, it now gaped around the neckline and she was at a loss as to how to fix that little problem. She tugged the material up only to have it slide back down the moment she let go.

"Pins," she declared, spinning on her heel and stumbling over to a table, which held a battered jewelry box some former governess had apparently left behind. She rummaged around in it for a minute and managed to locate a few pins. She jabbed them into the fabric and moved back to the mirror.

"That's hardly better, but it will have to do," she told her reflection.

Would anyone be able to recognize her? Her gaze lingered on the dumpy and unusually shaped woman staring back at her. Who would ever believe she'd once been the most sought after woman in London? What would her friends think if they could see her now?

"You don't have any friends," she muttered, turning away from the mirror as a knock sounded on her door.

"Come in."

The door opened, and a maid by the name of Mary entered the room. "Mrs. Watson asked me to assist you, but it seems you managed nicely on your own."

"I still have a few buttons I can't reach."

Mary stepped to Eliza's side and quickly buttoned her up. "What an interesting color."

"Lily thinks it clashes with my hair," Eliza said.

"It does at that, but I must say, it's not all horrible. The color draws attention to your eyes."

"That will never do." Eliza moved back to the jewelry box and pushed the contents around, delighted when she located an old pair of spectacles. She shoved them on her face and then promptly lost her balance as the room swam out of focus.

"I didn't know you wore spectacles," Mary said.

Eliza thought Mary might be frowning in her direction, but as she couldn't clearly see her face, she wasn't sure. "I only wear them on very rare occasions, dinners mostly. Spectacles make it easier to see the silver."

"I've never heard of such a thing, but if you can't see the silver, I suppose you should keep them on," Mary said. "Pity though, seeing as you have such lovely eyes and Mr. Hamilton Beckett is expected tonight." Mary lowered her voice. "He's the most sought after gentleman in New York."

"Then I would have to believe it would be difficult for me to garner his attention with or without my spectacles," Eliza said wryly. "I am the governess, and the only reason I've been pressed into service is because Agatha has developed spots."

Mary made a *tsk*ing noise under her breath.

Eliza frowned. "Do you know about Agatha's spots?"

"The entire house knows about the spots."

"Does Agatha make a habit of refusing to attend her mother's dinners?" Eliza asked.

"No, but I believe the poor dear has finally had enough of her mother's schemes. I overheard them earlier today, and they were engaged in a bit of a tiff. I don't believe Miss Agatha appreciated the fact that Mrs. Watson was forcing her to sit next to Mr. Beckett at dinner."

"I thought you said Mr. Beckett was the most sought after gentleman in New York?"

"He is, but I think Miss Agatha finds him too old," Mary said.

"How old is he?"

"He might be thirty."

"Thirty is hardly old."

"Not to you."

Eliza stifled a laugh. Here was further proof her disguise was a success, seeing as how she was only twenty-one years old, not much older than Agatha. She sent Mary a smile and then headed for the door. "Thank you for your help, Mary."

"Maybe you should say some extra prayers to help you get though the evening," Mary suggested.

Since Eliza was less than pleased with God at the moment, seeing as how He had not helped her sort through the mess she currently found herself in, she ignored Mary's statement.

"Would you like me to help you down the stairs?" Mary asked as Eliza ran smack-dab into the doorframe.

"That won't be necessary," Eliza said as she sailed through the door, ruining the effect by tripping on the trailing fabric of her gown.

"I'll say those prayers for you," Mary called as Eliza straightened and slowly walked down the hall.

The steps proved to be quite the obstacle, and she finally had to push the spectacles down her nose in order to navigate them. She paused on the first landing to tug her hem out from under her feet, and as she did so, she saw a pair of eyes peering at her through a crack in a door.

"Agatha," she muttered.

The door shut with a snap.

Eliza considered marching over to the door and demanding Agatha take her rightful place at the table, but the arrival of another maid distracted her. She shoved the spectacles back up her nose.

"Miss Sumner, Mrs. Watson is asking about you," the maid said. "My, don't you look . . . fetching."

Eliza released an unladylike snort. "I think hideous would be a more appropriate word."

"You might have a point," the maid said. "Do you need help getting down to the dining room, since you seem to be dragging a large amount of skirt behind you?"

"I'll be fine," Eliza said, sending the closed door one last look before she continued on her way, vowing to herself she would have a few words with Agatha if she survived the evening.

After what seemed like hours, but was only minutes, she finally managed to reach the end of the stairs and cautiously made her way to the dining room.

"Miss Sumner," Mrs. Watson exclaimed, appearing at Eliza's side. "What took you so long?"

"I apologize, Mrs. Watson, but I had a bit of difficulty maneuvering down the steps."

Eliza couldn't be certain, but she thought she saw Mrs. Watson's lips quiver.

"Oh dear, that gown is worse than I imagined," Mrs. Watson declared as she took Eliza by the arm and peered into her face. "I must say, those spectacles are the perfect accessory. They make you look eccentric, which will go far in explaining the gown."

As Eliza was trying for inconspicuous, the last thing she wanted to hear was that she'd managed "eccentric."

"This is a horrible idea," she mumbled.

"Nonsense," Mrs. Watson said, steering Eliza through a crowd of people and coming to a halt in front of an incredibly long table.

"How many guests did you invite?" Eliza sputtered.

"Only fifty-two, well, fifty-three now that we've had an unexpected guest show up."

Hope blossomed.

"That's wonderful," Eliza exclaimed. "Now you won't need me to attend."

"I still need you, seeing as how the unexpected guest is a gentleman. Mr. Zayne Beckett, to be exact. The family is railroad money, so please, be polite when you sit next to them at dinner."

"I'm sitting next to Mr. and Mr. Beckett?"

"I know, it's a bit unseemly to have someone of your station sitting next to my most honored guests, but I didn't have time to rearrange the seating chart, and I'm hopeful we can use this to our advantage."

"I'm afraid I'm not following," Eliza said slowly.

Mrs. Watson's voice dropped to a mere whisper. "I have high hopes of the elder Mr. Beckett and my Agatha forming an alliance. All you need to do to assist me is bring Agatha into the conversation often and speak of her in glowing terms."

Eliza blinked. "Mrs. Watson, I barely know your daughter,

and I'm not certain I'm equipped to discuss her with gentlemen I've never met. What would I say?"

"You can tell them how sweet and demure Agatha is and how she would make the most biddable of wives."

Eliza arched a brow. "Are we discussing the same Agatha who made up a case of the spots to escape your dinner party?"

Mrs. Watson ignored Eliza's statement. "Good heavens, old Mr. Sturgis is sitting beside Mrs. Costine. That will never do. They loathe each other." She spun around and darted away.

Eliza squinted at the table, unable to see the writing on the small place cards set on each plate. She tipped her glasses down the bridge of her nose and moved slowly past the chairs, looking for her name. She sighed in relief. There she was, just two chairs down. She shifted away from the table and didn't even have a moment to gasp as her feet got tangled and she lost her balance. Falling toward the table, cutlery sprang ever closer and the strange thought came to her that Mrs. Watson was definitely going to relieve her of her post after she wrecked the table, but before her face found purchase amongst the china, an arm snagged around her middle and pulled her to safety.

She stood still for a moment to allow her nerves a chance to settle before she forced her gaze upward to acknowledge the gentleman who had saved her from a most unpleasant fate.

All the breath left her in a split second as his features swam into view.

He was the most compelling man she'd ever seen, possessed of sun-kissed brown hair and blue eyes the exact shade of the sky. His face, with sharp angles and a strong jaw, was rugged in a manner quite unlike the faces of the gentlemen she had known in England. His lips were firm and unsmiling at the moment, but from the small creases at the corners, she could tell he was a man who was accustomed to smiling. Her eyes traveled over his broad shoulders, but then the promise she'd made to herself regarding the avoidance of handsome gentlemen sprang to mind, which had her pushing her spectacles back into place. His features turned hazy as resolve straightened her spine.

"Thank you," she muttered.

"You're very welcome," the man said, his voice causing the hair to stand straight up on her arm. "May I assist you into your chair?"

"That will not be necessary," Eliza replied as she stepped past the man to take her seat.

She heard a sudden telltale rip of fabric and realized her skirt was stuck around the legs of the chair. A yelp escaped her lips before she plunged to the floor.

2

Mr. Hamilton Beckett blinked and then blinked again as his gaze settled on the lady who was currently sprawled at his feet, her unfortunate choice of a gown spread out in a billowing cloud around her.

"What did you do to that lady, Hamilton?" Zayne sputtered, causing Hamilton to jolt out of his momentary stupor and realize the poor woman might be in need of his assistance. He crouched down next to her.

"Excuse me, miss, are you all right?"

The lady stirred and started to nod, but then stilled and emitted a sharp hiss.

"Have you been injured?"

"Pins," the lady muttered.

"I'm sorry?"

"I'm being stabbed by pins."

"What did she say?" Zayne asked.

"I think she said she's being stabbed by pins," Hamilton replied as the lady's eyes shot open, and he encountered lovely blue eyes. "May I help you to your feet?"

Her eyes closed, and she shook her head.

"Is there some injury, other than the pins, you're suffering from at the moment, Miss . . . ?"

"Sumner," the lady said. "I'm Miss Sumner, and no, I'm not suffering any other injury, well, except to my pride."

Hamilton bit back a grin. "Well, Miss Sumner, it's a pleasure to meet you, although not a pleasure to meet you under this dire circumstance. I'm Mr. Hamilton Beckett, and this is my brother, Mr. Zayne Beckett."

"Of course you are," Miss Sumner murmured.

That was an odd response. He chanced a glance at Zayne and found his brother grinning back at him. There would apparently be no help from that end. "Please allow me to help you from the floor, Miss Sumner. I fear, given the fact that there are numerous guests milling around, you're in danger of being trampled."

A muffled snort met his request before Miss Sumner began to mumble something undetectable under her breath.

"Do you think she's been . . . drinking?" Zayne asked.

The mumbling stopped as Miss Sumner's eyes flashed opened, and she glared at Zayne.

"You're not helping matters," Hamilton said, even though he was rapidly coming to the same conclusion. He'd never dealt with an inebriated woman at a dinner party before and, quite honestly, he had no idea how to proceed. "Let's get you to your feet."

"I prefer to remain here."

It would seem she was a stubborn drunk. "I don't think that's a viable option considering dinner is about to be served," he said.

Miss Sumner released a dramatic sigh, her face turning an interesting shade of purple, which was at complete odds with the color of her gown. "The pins have come out of my dress. I fear if you lift me up, it might stay behind."

Perhaps he was mistaken regarding her sobriety or lack thereof, given the fact that her speech was somewhat eloquent.

"We can't have that," he finally said, relieved when a pair of women's shoes appeared next to Miss Sumner's head. He looked up and discovered Mrs. Watson peering down at them.

"Miss Sumner, may I inquire as to why you're lounging on the floor?" Mrs. Watson asked.

Miss Sumner uttered something which sounded very much like "it should be obvious" before she lifted her head. "You really must compliment your staff, Mrs. Watson. This floor is remarkably clean."

Hamilton choked back a laugh, got to his feet, and smiled at Mrs. Watson. "I believe Miss Sumner tripped on her hem, and she's currently suffering an unfortunate dilemma." He lowered his voice. "It would seem she's in imminent danger of losing her gown due to some unruly pins."

"Oh . . . dear," Mrs. Watson said before she looked at Miss Sumner. "Perhaps it might be best to see if you can sit first without any repercussions before you attempt to get to your feet."

Miss Sumner gave a brief nod, pushed herself up to a sitting position, and then winced and pulled a pin out of the neckline of her gown. Hamilton stifled another laugh when the lady calmly shoved the pin back into the bodice of her gown as if it were an everyday occurrence to have pins popping out of one's clothing. His amusement increased when she rooted around under her voluminous skirts, pulled out a pair of sadly mangled spectacles, and pushed them onto her face, her eyes blinking behind the lenses.

"Ah, Mr. Beckett, so good to see you could make it," a jovial voice said behind him, drawing his attention.

Hamilton turned and recognized Mr. Watson beaming back

at him. Beaming, that is, until the gentleman shifted his gaze to Miss Sumner.

"Miss Sumner, what are you doing here, and why are you on the floor?"

Hamilton noticed a trace of what could only be described as unease cross Miss Sumner's face, which was rather unusual considering Mr. Watson was known to be a likeable sort, if somewhat overly ambitious. He cleared his throat when he realized Miss Sumner seemed to be at a loss for words.

"Miss Sumner suffered a small accident, Mr. Watson. I was just about to help her to her feet."

"But . . . what is she doing here?" Mr. Watson asked.

Mrs. Watson stepped forward, placed her arm on Mr. Watson's, and seemed to give it a good squeeze, since Mr. Watson emitted a grunt.

"Miss Sumner graciously offered to take Agatha's place this evening, dear," Mrs. Watson said.

"Should I ask why?" Mr. Watson questioned.

"It would be better for your digestion if you didn't know all the pesky little details," Mrs. Watson said before she smiled at Hamilton and Zayne. "It's so lovely to see you both here, Mr. and Mr. Beckett. I do hope you'll enjoy your dinner. Thank you for seeing to Miss Sumner, and now, Roger and I must take our seats. I wouldn't want to incur Cook's wrath by allowing the meal to grow cold." She sent Hamilton one last smile before pulling Mr. Watson rapidly away.

"This is turning out to be a very strange evening," Zayne said.

"Indeed," Hamilton replied before he bent down next to Miss Sumner, who was still blinking furiously behind her spectacles. "Shall we try to get you off the floor?"

Miss Sumner gave her neckline a sharp tug and nodded. Hamilton took her arm and carefully hoisted her to her feet, keeping his hand on the top of her back to allow her a moment to ascertain her gown would stay in place. When it became apparent the lady was in no danger of standing in the dining room suddenly dressed only in her undergarments, he dropped his hand and pulled out her chair, grimacing when his foot trod on her gown and Miss Sumner tilted to the left.

"This dress is a menace," he said, steering her into her chair and pushing it into place. A loud ripping noise met his efforts, and he was surprised to see a flicker of a grin tease Miss Sumner's lips. He took his seat, waited for Zayne to sit down on the other side of Miss Sumner, and then turned his attention to the servant who was waiting patiently by his side, a bottle of wine in his hand.

"May I offer you some wine?" the servant asked.

Miss Sumner lifted her head. "That sounds delightful." She reached for her glass, but instead of picking it up, her hand somehow landed on the mold of butter shaped like a dove, and to Hamilton's amazement, her fingers tightened around it before her mouth dropped open and she stilled, apparently in a quandary about what to do next.

Hamilton raised his hand to stop the servant, who was about to start pouring the wine. "Would you happen to have some lemonade instead?" he asked.

"I do not care for lemonade," Miss Sumner proclaimed as she pulled her hand out of the butter and promptly dropped it to her lap.

Hamilton was fairly certain she was wiping the last vestiges of butter on her skirt, although why she wasn't simply using her napkin was beyond him. He reached over and handed her his napkin, earning himself a cheerful smile from her in the process.

"Oh, there it is," she said as she took his offering and promptly wiped her hands with it. "I wonder if butter leaves a stain," she said to no one in particular.

"About that lemonade?" Hamilton asked the servant.

"I prefer wine," Miss Sumner stated.

"Apparently, but I'm not certain it prefers you," he muttered.

Miss Sumner looked up and tilted her head, studying him for a moment before she released a breath and whipped off her spectacles. "I'm not drunk." She held up the glasses. "I decided to wear these this evening in order to detract attention from this truly repulsive gown I've been forced to wear, but unfortunately, the lenses are incredibly powerful, and instead of allowing me to remain unnoticed, they've caused me to draw undue attention to myself, given the fact that I've been less than graceful."

"Why were you forced to wear that gown?" Hamilton asked as he nodded to the servant, and the man began filling their glasses.

"It's complicated," Miss Sumner mumbled before she bit her lip, the motion drawing Hamilton's attention to her mouth. His gaze lingered as the thought came to him that her lips were lovely, especially the way they were pouting at the moment. A loud cough from Zayne caused heat to flood his face.

What was wrong with him? He was fairly certain his brother had caught him gawking at Miss Sumner, and he was beyond disconcerted to realize the lady had somehow garnered his interest—interest he found downright alarming, given the fact that there was an air of mystery surrounding her and he'd sworn off mysterious women forever. He took a sip of wine and forced himself back to the conversation at hand.

"You were saying?" he asked Miss Sumner.

"I wasn't saying anything," she replied before her gaze darted around the table and then returned to his as she leaned forward and lowered her voice. "If you must know, I'm not actually a guest."

"You're an imposter?" Hamilton asked.

Miss Sumner laughed, the sound somewhat delightful. "I'm the governess."

"You're a governess?" Zayne asked loudly, which caused several of the surrounding guests to stop their conversations and stare at them.

"Shh," Miss Sumner whispered, "I don't believe Mrs. Watson wanted that to become common knowledge, but I didn't see the harm in letting you two know." She sighed when titters began running down the table. "It seems the secret's out of the bag now, or whatever that American expression is." She sent Zayne a smile. "That's why I'm in this gown. I was pressed into service when Agatha . . . well, best not get into that at the moment, except to say Miss Watson was indisposed, and Mrs. Watson did not have time to secure another guest. I do hope the two of you won't be too disappointed you're stuck with me."

Instead of being disappointed, Hamilton found he was intrigued. The longer Miss Sumner spoke, the more obvious it became she was no mere governess. There was something about her manner, something about the way she enunciated every word while tilting her chin with an almost haughty attitude, that made him realize she was more than what she seemed.

For some odd reason, he found himself longing to discover her secrets, including exactly why she was attempting to pass herself off as a governess.

❧

Eliza suppressed a shiver when she realized Mr. Hamilton Beckett was watching her as if she were a bug caught under the glass. Was he doing so because she'd admitted to being a governess? Was he appalled by the fact that he had to share a meal with her? She bit her lip. No, Mr. and Mr. Beckett did not lend her the impression they were snobs.

Why wouldn't he drop his gaze?

Her thoughts were distracted when a bell rang out and a

handsome gentleman stood up, introduced himself as Reverend Fraser, and proceeded to deliver the blessing.

"Tell me, Miss Sumner," Hamilton said after the blessing was finished, "how long have you been in this country?"

"Not long," Eliza admitted, thankful the conversation came to a halt when servants appeared and began placing platters of food around the table. She didn't care to discuss her situation, especially not with Mr. Hamilton Beckett, who seemed to find something very interesting about her. It set her nerves to jingling, as she could not afford to attract anyone's interest.

She took a bite of salmon, swallowed, and then directed the conversation to the city of New York, pleased to discover Mr. and Mr. Beckett were extremely knowledgeable regarding their home and the people who occupied it. She was relieved when Mr. Hamilton Beckett stopped watching her and settled into his meal, seemingly content to spend the dinner telling her about the many guests sitting around the table.

"You need to watch out for that lady over there," Hamilton said with a discreet nod to a woman sitting six guests away. "Her name is Mrs. Hannah Morgan, and she's a wealthy widow with high social expectations."

"I don't believe I'll have much of an opportunity to socialize with the woman, Mr. Beckett," Eliza said. "I'm the governess, not a guest."

"Your manners are very fine for a governess," Hamilton said. Apparently she'd been mistaken in thinking he'd stopped watching her.

She set down her fork. "A governess is responsible for teaching her charges proper deportment, Mr. Beckett. Mrs. Watson would not have hired me if I was less than proficient at the dinner table."

Hamilton leaned forward, causing an odd tingle to race down Eliza's spine. She scooted back in her seat, ignored the sound of ripping fabric, and returned her attention to her meal.

"I wasn't accusing you, but complimenting you," Hamilton said softly. "I didn't mean for you to take offense."

Eliza raised her gaze, and her mouth ran dry when she noticed the sincerity lingering in Mr. Beckett's eyes. For a brief, insane moment, she wished for nothing more than to once again become the witty, beautiful woman she'd been in England, if only to see his reaction to her. She knew it was a ridiculous wish—after all, she was not in the market for a gentleman friend—but even knowing this, she couldn't discount the fact that she was having a very strange reaction to Mr. Beckett. He fascinated her—there was no other explanation—but she was also annoyed by him, annoyed that he was causing her to suffer tingles all over her body.

She'd never met a man who caused her to tingle.

She bit back a snort. Honestly, why was she even allowing her thoughts to travel in such a ridiculous direction? Before she could contemplate that to satisfaction, a conversation on the opposite side of the table suddenly caught her attention.

". . . and Lord Southmoor is to be in attendance tomorrow."

All thoughts of remaining inconspicuous disappeared as Eliza set her sights on the woman who'd uttered that earth-shattering remark.

"Forgive me," she said loudly, causing the woman to look her way, "did you just mention Lord Southmoor?"

The woman narrowed her eyes. "Aren't you the governess?"

Obviously they'd been overheard. Eliza forced a smile. "I am the governess, ma'am. Miss Sumner at your service."

"Miss Sumner," the woman replied with a regal nod. "I'm Mrs. Amherst."

"Pleased to make your acquaintance," Eliza said. "You were remarking on Lord Southmoor?"

"Are you acquainted with him?" Mrs. Amherst inquired.

"I would not be so presumptuous to believe I know all the

members of the aristocracy, but his title does sound familiar. May I be so forward as to inquire whether he is a rather tall gentleman?"

"He is, and very slight of frame," Mrs. Amherst said.

Rage mixed with triumph raced through her. She'd found him at last, the man she'd been searching for, the man who'd stolen everything. She reined in her emotions, realizing she needed to make absolutely certain. "Does he have a wife?"

"You mean the countess?"

"His wife is a countess?" Eliza sputtered.

"Lord Southmoor is an earl, which does make his wife a countess," Mrs. Amherst said.

Not only had the man stolen her father's fortune, it would appear he'd taken liberties with his title as well.

"Would you happen to know Lady Southmoor's given name?" Eliza asked once she was able to form a coherent sentence.

"I hardly enjoy an intimate relationship with the woman, but I believe her name is Salice," Mrs. Amherst said.

Eliza swallowed the grunt she longed to emit. It was almost too much to comprehend, the idea that this so-called countess was claiming the name Salice when Eliza knew perfectly well her given name was Sally and she'd once been Eliza's governess before she'd married Bartholomew Hayes, a man who'd been employed by Eliza's father as his man of affairs. It was ironic, if truth be told, given that Eliza now found herself a governess and Sally, alias Salice, was prancing around New York as an English aristocrat.

"Miss Sumner, are you all right?" Hamilton asked, pulling her from her thoughts.

"Perfectly fine."

Hamilton sent a pointed look to the crushed dinner roll in Eliza's hand.

"Oh," Eliza said, relaxing her fingers and dropping the roll to her plate before she realized Mrs. Amherst was speaking to her once again.

"Are you familiar with the Southmoor estate?" Mrs. Amherst asked. "Lady Southmoor was describing her country manor the other evening and it sounds enchanting."

The only Southmoor Eliza was familiar with was her father's old hunting lodge in the wilds of Scotland, which her father had laughingly dubbed Southmoor because it was south of the moors. It suddenly became clear to her exactly where Bartholomew had gotten inspiration for his fictitious title and, apparently, an entire country estate.

"I'm afraid I'm not familiar with Southmoor Manor," she finally said.

Mrs. Amherst sent her a sympathetic smile. "Tell me, dear, who are your relations in England? Do you count any aristocrats as family?"

"I'm distantly related to the Earl of Sefton," Eliza said before snapping her mouth shut. How could she have let that escape?

Mrs. Amherst's eyes sparkled. "Why, Lady Southmoor remarked on your family just the other day. She said she was great friends with Lady Alice Sumner."

Eliza began to seethe. Her mother, Alice, had been dead for over ten years, and it was beyond a stretch for Sally to make the claim they'd been "great friends," considering Sally had been the governess. Eliza drew in a deep breath and slowly released it. "Do you know where Lord and Lady Southmoor are currently residing?"

"I've heard they recently purchased a remarkable house on Park Avenue. It's three stories with all of the latest amenities." Mrs. Amherst shook her head. "I also heard that Lady Southmoor was quite put out over the location. She wanted to purchase a home here, on Fifth Avenue, but her husband insisted on the Park Avenue mansion." She lowered her voice. "He had the funds available to purchase it outright, which had the owners willing to quickly vacate the premises in order that Lord and Lady Southmoor could move in immediately."

"How lovely for them," Eliza muttered between gritted teeth.

"We'll see Lord Southmoor tomorrow evening," Mrs. Amherst said. "Would you care to have me send him a greeting from you?"

"No," Eliza said, forcing another smile when she saw Mrs. Amherst's startled expression at her vehement denial. "That is a very kind offer, Mrs. Amherst, but since I am only a governess, I fear I am beneath his notice and he might become confused as to why you are mentioning me to him in the first place."

"Then I will remain mum on the subject," Mrs. Amherst said. "It would not do to inadvertently confuse the man, especially as Mr. Amherst is hopeful of furthering his acquaintance with Lord Southmoor and Mr. Daniels."

Eliza heard Mr. Hamilton Beckett draw in a sharp breath of air. She shot him a glance and found him leaning forward in his chair, his eyes gleaming.

"Mr. Eugene Daniels?" Hamilton asked.

"Yes," Mrs. Amherst agreed. "Mr. Daniels is holding a dinner tomorrow night at his home in honor of Lord and Lady Southmoor."

Eliza wasn't certain why Mr. Beckett was emitting tension in waves, but the only logical explanation was that it concerned this Mr. Eugene Daniels, the man who just happened to be hosting a dinner party in honor of the very man Eliza had crossed an ocean to find. She opened her mouth to inquire exactly who Mr. Daniels was, but her words died on her tongue when Mrs. Watson interrupted.

"Ladies, please follow me. I believe it's time to leave the gentlemen to their brandy and cigars."

It was just her luck that her services for the evening were

seemingly at an end just when things were getting interesting. She pushed back her chair before Mr. or Mr. Beckett had an opportunity to help her, sighing in resignation as a loud rip met her ears.

"I do believe this dress has seen its last dinner," Zayne remarked as he rose to his feet and then bent over to tug some fabric from under the leg of the chair. "What's this?"

Eliza yelped. "Stop that."

"I do beg your pardon," Zayne exclaimed as he dropped the cloth and straightened. "Was that part of your gown?"

Eliza decided it would be best not to respond, as there was not much she could say that would make any sense. She rose to her feet and felt more of her stuffing slide down her legs, her oversized corset obviously unable to keep up with the task of holding it all in. She dipped into a quick curtsy and spun on her heel, stopping when Mr. Hamilton Beckett laid an arm on her sleeve.

"You forgot your glasses," he said, snagging them off the table and handing them to her.

"Thank you," she said as her finger glanced against his skin, the contact causing her heart to race.

"Will you be back for dessert?" Hamilton asked.

It was nearly impossible to concentrate, seeing as she felt like an entire herd of horses had taken to galloping through her veins. What was the question?

Ahh . . . yes . . . dessert.

"My services were only required for dinner," she managed to get out. "Please accept my appreciation for allowing me to share the meal with you. It was a true pleasure."

"You were most entertaining," Zayne replied.

"That was unintentional," Eliza muttered.

"You were delightful," Hamilton said. He took her hand and lifted it to his lips.

Heat seared through Eliza at his touch. She'd had her hand kissed numerous times before, but not once had a simple grazing of a gentleman's lips against her knuckles caused her to react this way. She tugged her hand out of his grasp, mumbled one last "good evening," and stepped away from the table, this last action causing the remainder of her bindings to roll down her legs. Gathering what little dignity she had left, she turned and moved as quickly as she could out of the room.

3

The following afternoon, Eliza looked around the crowded omnibus and wondered how a person was supposed to make the conveyance stop. She'd never ridden in a public coach, as she was accustomed to personal coaches back in England, but her funds were limited at the moment, so here she was, shoved up against a window, trying to remember to breathe through her mouth because the man sitting next to her smelled like fish and seemed to enjoy belching every few minutes. To distract herself from the unpleasantness at hand, she looked out the window and tried to make sense of everything she'd discovered over the past day.

Mr. Bartholomew Hayes was in New York, currently passing himself off as English aristocracy. He was also making excellent use of her money, living in a mansion that was beyond spectacular, and outfitting it with the latest furnishings evidenced by the numerous delivery wagons that had pulled up with annoying frequency while Eliza lurked on the opposite side of the street. She'd watched with mounting rage as everything from beautifully appointed furniture to a huge fountain in the form of a swan passed into the house before her eyes.

It had taken every ounce of self-control she possessed to refrain from storming through the front door and confronting the man who'd been her father's most trusted employee, a trusted employee who'd turned out to be nothing more than a lying, thieving, no-good scoundrel who'd managed to systematically divert her father's vast fortune into his own accounts sometime during the months surrounding her father's death.

A loud snort from the man now pressing a beefy arm up against her side forced Eliza from her thoughts as she edged closer to the window. Perhaps it would be for the best if she got off the omnibus and simply walked the rest of the way to the Watsons' house because, at the rate the man kept shifting, he would soon be sitting on top of her.

Eliza shuddered at that idea, the notion coming to her that gentlemen of all stations in life were certainly more trouble than they were worth . . . although Mr. Hamilton Beckett seemed as if he might be worth the trouble.

She blinked at that bothersome idea. Now was hardly the time to become distracted, even if the distraction was one incredibly handsome gentleman who was possessed of amazing eyes and . . .

"Put him out of your mind," she muttered.

"You say something?" the man beside her asked, his expression a bit wary.

The poor man most likely believed he was sitting next to a crazy person, and who could blame him? She cleared her throat and tried to think of something sane to say.

"I was wondering how to get the omnibus to stop," she finally replied.

"You have to pull on that there rope," he said, gesturing down by his feet. "It's attached to the driver's leg and when he feels it tug, he stops."

There was no possible way Eliza was going to lean over the man to pull on the rope. She decided to stay put for the moment and turned her face back toward the window.

Her temper began to simmer when she realized she wouldn't be in her current predicament if Mr. Hayes had refrained from taking her very last pound. If he would have left her a smidgen of her father's fortune, she would still be in London, basking in the admiration of her friends and her fiancé, instead of residing in New York without a single friend and possessed of an ex-fiancé.

The memory of Lord Wrathshire, or Lawrence as he'd insisted she call him in private, caused her temper to go from simmering to boiling in a split second.

Who would have thought a gentleman could turn from his intended simply because said intended suddenly found herself without funds?

She felt her face grow warm when their last conversation sprang to mind.

She'd gone to Lawrence as a last option when it became clear her situation was desperate, intent on asking him for a small loan to see her and her cousin, the new Earl of Sefton, through until the next harvest.

Unfortunately, events did not go as planned.

Lawrence listened to her pretty pleas and then informed her he'd heard the rumors about her father wasting his fortune away, and since there was now an insurmountable blemish staining her family name, he could no longer remain engaged to her. After making that proclamation, he'd turned and walked out of the room without saying another word.

Apparently he'd been more enthralled with her fortune than her sparkling personality.

He'd also apparently been more than willing to listen to the lies Mr. Hayes had spread about her father, lies Eliza knew Mr. Hayes had spread to cover up his own perfidy.

The omnibus slowed to a stop, and Eliza realized they were on Fifth Avenue. Unwilling to waste an opportunity to not have to reach over the man to pull on the rope, she struggled to her feet and breathed a sigh of relief when the man lumbered out of his seat and allowed her to pass. She moved to the door, jumped to the ground, and took a moment to get her bearings. She set her sights in the direction of the Watsons' home and began walking quickly, arriving back at the house in less than ten minutes. She entered through the back door which led to the kitchen, took a few moments to exchange pleasantries with the cook, and then made her way to her upstairs room, shutting the door behind her. She walked to her bed and plopped straight back onto it, too tired to even bother taking off her shoes.

She closed her eyes, intent on taking a short nap, but sleep would not come.

Her nemesis was residing close at hand.

Mr. Hayes most likely never imagined she would have the gumption to follow him all the way across an ocean, or even attempt to seek out his whereabouts in the first place. She'd been forced to assume the role of investigator once it became clear the authorities were convinced society had the right of it and her father had simply been a wastrel who'd left Eliza destitute. No amount of arguing could convince them to help her, so she'd rolled up her sleeves, took to the streets, and through chatty men at the docks, discovered Mr. Hayes was on his way to New York, so New York was where she'd decided to go.

Her cousin, a likeable gentleman who'd assumed her father's title, seeing as how Eliza's one and only brother was no longer alive, tried to convince her she'd lost her mind, but necessity forced him to acknowledge their dire situation and agree to

help with her plans. He'd penned a lovely letter of recommen-
dation, and armed with the funds she'd obtained from selling
her engagement ring, she bought a ticket to New York and set
sail for America.

Knowing her meager funds wouldn't last long, she'd sought
out an employment agency, and to her delight, Mrs. Watson had
walked into the agency a mere five minutes after Eliza. When the
woman had discovered Eliza was from England, she'd hired her
on the spot, barely glancing at the reference letter the agency
had pressed into her hand.

The sudden squeaking of a door caused her eyes to flash
open, but she quickly shut them when she realized it was Agatha
strolling into her room.

"I know you're awake," Agatha said.

"I'm not."

Agatha laughed. "I came to apologize for last night and to
bring these back to you."

Eliza opened one eye. "Bring what back to me?"

Agatha crossed the room and placed a wad of fabric on the
bed. Eliza recognized her stuffing and refused to groan out loud.

"What is that?" she forced herself to ask.

Agatha arched a brow. "The fabric you use to pad your figure.
I must admit, I've been wondering all day what you would use
in its place."

"Obviously you have too much time on your hands and . . .
I don't pad my figure."

"You're not a rotund woman," Agatha said. "Your face is
very thin."

"I carry my weight in my middle."

Agatha's other brow rose to meet the first one.

Eliza blew out a breath. "I might enhance my figure just a
touch."

"I'm waiting with bated breath to hear why," Agatha said.

The conversation was turning tricky. Eliza knew it wouldn't be prudent to blithely admit she'd assumed a disguise in order to perpetuate a fraud, especially as she was currently a governess to Agatha's sisters. "I didn't care to attract unwanted attention from my employer," she settled on saying.

"My father is hardly the type to chase the staff."

"I wasn't aware of that when I accepted the position." She sent Agatha what she hoped was an innocent smile. "We governesses have a hard lot in life."

"You may be many things, Miss Sumner, but you're no governess."

The conversation was disintegrating rather rapidly. "I'll have you know, I came to this country with a very fine letter of reference from Lord Sefton, who happens to be a high-ranking member of British society."

"He's probably a relative," Agatha said.

Eliza decided it was in her best interest to change the subject. "What happened to your spots?"

A shifty expression crossed Agatha's face. "To my amazement, I woke up this morning and found not one spot on my face."

"Were there actually any spots on your face last night?"

Agatha ignored the question. "I was even able to attend church this morning, since I was spot free, although I hardly found an opportunity to become uplifted by the sermon, because Father scowled at me the entire time."

"He was most likely scowling at you because he wanted you to entertain Mr. Beckett last night."

"Father would love nothing more than to see me married to the man," Agatha said as she took a seat on Eliza's bed before she kicked off her shoes and tucked her feet underneath her.

"You have an issue with Mr. Beckett?" Eliza asked.

"Not really. The man is fascinating and extremely handsome."

A touch of something that felt almost like disgruntlement sliced through Eliza. "If you're so intrigued with the gentleman, why would you refuse to attend the dinner?"

"I didn't say I was intrigued with him," Agatha corrected before her gaze turned crafty. "Did you find him intriguing?"

"Of course not."

Agatha frowned. "That is unfortunate. I thought the two of you might suit, although there is his brooding nature to consider."

"He didn't appear brooding to me," Eliza said before she snapped her mouth shut when Agatha sent her a knowing smile. She cleared her throat. "Why do you find him brooding?"

Agatha shrugged. "If truth be told, he has every reason to brood. His wife died over two years ago, leaving him with two slightly difficult children. Then, there have been rumors swirling around town that someone is out to ruin his railroading company, and finally, his mother has put it about that he's in desperate need of a new wife, which has every society miss following him everywhere. From what I've heard, he hasn't been amused."

"He was fairly amusing last night at dinner," Eliza said. "I must say he and his brother kept me well entertained."

"Zayne was there?" Agatha asked with a note of what sounded like disappointment in her voice.

Eliza eyed Agatha for a moment. "This certainly explains your lack of interest in Mr. Hamilton Beckett or any of the other gentlemen your parents have selected for you. Although, to give your mother credit, the minister she brought in to say the blessing last night was remarkably handsome and seemed to be a rather pleasant sort."

"Reverend Fraser is a divine-looking gentleman, but alas, he's set his sights on Miss Julie Hampton."

"You don't seem overly distressed by that," Eliza said.

"Although I am a woman of strong faith, it was never my dream to marry a man of the cloth. I would hardly be an appropriate role model, considering I have a tendency to get into mischief."

"You also seem to have a tendency to switch uncomfortable subjects with remarkable ease," Eliza said. "We were discussing Mr. Zayne Beckett."

"I'm certain I have nothing more to say regarding the gentleman."

"You hold him in affection," Eliza said.

"That's completely beside the point," Agatha muttered, "and that's not what we were discussing at all. To refresh your memory, we were talking about the brooding Mr. Hamilton Beckett."

"And I said he was hardly brooding last night," Eliza said. "I find myself curious, though, as to why Mr. Beckett is annoyed with his mother's efforts to find him a suitable wife. May I assume he was so in love with his first wife that he can't bear the thought of marriage to another woman?"

"I don't believe he was in love with Mary Ellen," Agatha said. "She was beautiful, and I would imagine he might have thought himself in love with her at first, but—" she lowered her voice—"she was giving attention to gentlemen other than Hamilton while they were married."

"How in the world did you discover that information?" Eliza asked.

Agatha began toying with the edge of the bedcover. "I've always been observant. In fact, my life's ambition is to become a journalist and write about the observations I make."

"Are your parents aware of this ambition?"

"I'm afraid I have yet to mention it to them, although, considering I sent an article to the *New York Tribune* two weeks ago, I might need to get around to broaching the subject, especially if my story is accepted."

"And you believe your father will readily embrace the sight of his daughter's name in print?" Eliza asked.

"I wouldn't write under my real name," Agatha said. "I chose Polly Ponders as my pen name because I certainly didn't want to draw undue attention to myself, considering my first article deals with the deplorable conditions in the clothing mills. Do you have any idea how nasty the men are who own those places?"

"You've been visiting the clothing mills?"

"It would be best if I didn't answer that," Agatha said before she scooted farther back on the bed, stuffed a pillow behind her, and frowned. "I've been meaning to ask you something."

"This should be good."

"Now, there's no need to take that tone," Agatha admonished. "We are of a like age and should try to be friends."

"I can't imagine your parents would approve of your forming a friendship with the governess."

"As we've already discussed, you're not a governess, nor do I believe you'll be with us long, so that isn't an issue."

"Why would you want to pursue a friendship with me?" Eliza asked.

"You're obviously an interesting woman, and I thought it would be nice to have someone to confide in, seeing as how I've only recently returned from boarding school and find myself at loose ends, with none of my friends left here in town."

Eliza smiled as she thought how lovely it would be to have a friend. All of the ladies she'd believed were her friends back in London had presented her with their backs the moment whispers of the scandal began to swirl. Her smile widened. "I would be honored to become better acquainted with you."

Agatha grinned. "Wonderful."

"I believe you mentioned you've been meaning to ask me something?"

"Indeed," Agatha said. "This morning, after I rescued your

stray bindings, I tried to track you down to relieve your mind, but you weren't in attendance at church today. That's when I realized I've never noticed you at church on any given Sunday."

"Truth be told, I'm not in accord with God at this particular point in my life."

At Agatha's confused look, Eliza allowed a brittle laugh to escape. "If you must know, Miss Watson, in the span of a year and a half, I lost my father, my fiancé, and my fortune, which made me quite aware of the fact that God rarely bothers to listen to prayers and certainly doesn't grant the requests made."

"You lost your father and your fiancé? Did they die in some tragic accident?"

She really needed to be more careful with what she let slip. "My father died of a long illness, and I prefer not to speak of my ex-fiancé, as the gentleman turned out to be nothing but a cad."

"I see," Agatha said slowly before she nodded. "That's why you've come to America. You're searching for your missing fiancé."

Eliza rolled her eyes. "He's most likely still in London, searching for another heiress. Obviously he was more enthralled with my fortune than he was with me, and when it went missing, well, he did the same."

"How does one's fortune go missing?"

"Mine went missing because my family trusted a rather cunning man of affairs, Miss Watson."

"Please, call me Agatha."

"Very well, Agatha. You may call me Eliza, but only when we're alone." Eliza shot a glance to the window, frowning when she noticed the darkness. "Now, I do so hate to break up our little chat, but it's getting late."

"You're kicking me out?"

"Not at all, I'm simply telling you I need to retire for the evening, since I need to be well rested to deal with your sisters."

"Very prettily said," Agatha grouched as she rose from the bed, "but you're still kicking me out."

Eliza went to the door and held it open, unable to hide her grin.

"I have more questions for you," Agatha warned as she quit the room.

"I'm certain you do," Eliza replied before she shut the door, her thoughts immediately going to the plan she was determined to carry out—a plan she was unwilling and unable to share with Agatha.

4

*T*hirty minutes later, Eliza stole down the hallway, her boots in her hand, trying to be as quiet as possible. She tiptoed down the back stairs and slipped out the door, hurrying over to a garden bench, where she sat down and quickly laced up her boots.

She stood and twitched her dark skirt into place before she set her sights on the far side of the garden, moving across the lawn as stealthily as possible before struggling through a bothersome row of hedges which, thankfully, led her to a back alley. She headed for the main street and lingered for a moment in the shadows in order to allow a group of people to pass.

"Are you lost?"

Eliza bit back a scream and, with a hand to her throat, glared at Agatha, who, for some unknown reason, was standing right behind her. "What are you doing?"

"Following you," Agatha said.

Eliza narrowed her eyes. "Why?"

"It's obvious you're up to something. I thought I'd offer you my assistance."

"That is out of the question. You have no idea where I'm going or what I'm about to do. For all you know, I could be a mass murderer intent on finding my next victim, which just might happen to be you, seeing as you're convenient."

"Good thing I have my trusty pistol with me, then," Agatha said as she lifted her hand and revealed a gun.

"Put that away," Eliza hissed. "You could hurt yourself."

Agatha stuffed the pistol into her pocket. "Don't tell me you're not armed."

"Where, pray tell, would I have been able to procure a pistol?"

"I got this one from a fellow on Thirty-Second Street."

"Of course you did," Eliza muttered. "This is a very bad idea."

"I look at it as a great opportunity to expand my investigating skills," Agatha said.

"This is not a game. There's danger involved."

"You know," Agatha replied, ignoring Eliza's statement, "I might have been mistaken regarding your suitability for Mr. Beckett. I can't imagine him embarking on an adventure like this, nor do I believe he'd appreciate a woman with such a daring nature."

"I don't have a daring nature, and I don't wish for an association with Mr. Beckett."

Agatha began whistling under her breath.

"Listen, I know you may find this exciting, but I must plead with you to return home," Eliza said. "I'm not a woman prone to an adventurous way of living; I simply have no choice in this matter."

"Perhaps if you explained the situation, I would be better equipped to decide if I should get involved."

"It's not your concern."

"I thought you said we could be friends."

"I would never request assistance in what I'm about to do from one of my friends. I could very well end up in jail tonight."

"I wasn't aware you were prone to dramatics, Eliza."

Eliza took a deep breath and counted to ten. "I am not prone to dramatics, Miss Watson."

"Agatha," she corrected.

"For tonight, you are Miss Watson and I am Miss Sumner, your family's governess. Now I must insist you leave me here and return home."

Agatha folded her arms across her chest and began tapping her foot against the cobblestones.

"You are exceedingly annoying," Eliza huffed.

"Thank you."

"It was not a compliment."

Agatha grinned. "Where are we going?"

Eliza blew out a breath and edged into the street, Agatha sticking remarkably close to her side as if she feared Eliza would suddenly bolt away and leave her behind. "I'm heading to Park Avenue," she finally admitted.

"Why do you want to go there?"

"Is that a note of disappointment I detect in your voice?"

"The danger level of our excursion has diminished considerably."

Honestly, the woman was apparently a bit deranged. Eliza slowed her pace and glanced at Agatha. "I do believe breaking into a house constitutes danger."

"We're going to break into a house?" Agatha asked, her eyes gleaming with anticipation.

"No, *I'm* going to break into a house. You're relegated to standing watch."

"That's hardly fun," Agatha said.

"I didn't promise you fun," Eliza replied, increasing her stride, only to come to an abrupt stop when Agatha tugged on her arm. "What?"

"If our destination is Park Avenue, you're going the wrong way."

"Oh," Eliza said, spinning on her heel and heading in the opposite direction.

Agatha suddenly gave a shrill whistle, causing Eliza to pause and turn as a hired carriage rumbled to a stop a few feet away from her.

"Come on," Agatha called as she hurried to the carriage, opened the door, and jumped in.

Eliza followed and plopped down on the seat. "I don't have funds readily available for such a luxury."

"Hiring a carriage is hardly a luxury, and I assure you I have more than enough funds available to cover the cost."

"I don't accept charity," Eliza muttered.

"It's not charity when I've foisted myself on you."

"True," Eliza agreed, relaxing as she settled into the seat.

Agatha leaned out the window. "Park Avenue, if you please." She pulled her head in as the carriage began to move. "So, tell me exactly what we're about to do. Are we intent on robbing someone?"

"I'm not a thief," Eliza said. "I never said anything about robbing a house, especially since what I'm after is already mine."

"You're going after your fortune," Agatha said with a nod. "Are we looking for your missing fiancé as well?"

"You're forgetting our last conversation. It was not my *ex-fiancé* who stole my fortune; it was my father's man of affairs, Mr. Hayes. My *ex-fiancé* wouldn't have sullied his hands with something as common as theft. He's more the type who would hire someone to do his dirty work."

"He doesn't sound very appealing."

"He's not, but London society caters to his every whim, given the fact that he bears an old title and has vast holdings."

Agatha's eyes widened. "You're more than simply Miss Sumner, aren't you?"

Seeing no point in denying the truth, Eliza nodded. "My father was the Earl of Sefton, and as the daughter of an earl, I hold an honorary title. My formal address is Lady Eliza Sumner."

"Why isn't it Lady Eliza Sefton?" Agatha asked.

"Sefton denotes our estate, whereas Sumner is our surname. Honorary titles use a person's surname."

"You have an estate?"

"Unfortunately, no, I do not. England has very strict laws regarding entailments, and my father's estates and his title went to my distant cousin."

"You're an only child?"

"I am now. My brother is deceased; hence, a distant relation inherited the lands."

Agatha looked out the window for a moment and then turned her head, a frown marring her beautiful face. "Why didn't you just let it be known you were an aristocrat the moment you stepped foot in New York? Everyone would have fallen all over you, fortune or no fortune, and you wouldn't have had to seek out employment. There are more than enough people in town who would have loved to extend you hospitality."

"I never had any intention of entering New York society. My only purpose in this country is to recover my fortune and then return to England to restore my father's good name."

"Recovering your fortune will accomplish that?"

"Money does wonders, although I have been wondering how I will deal with all of my so-called friends who gave me the cut direct once my money went missing and Mr. Hayes spread dreadful rumors around town regarding my family," Eliza said. "I'm hopeful I'll be able to graciously accept their apologies, but quite honestly, I'm not certain I have it in me." She glanced out the window. "Oh look, I think we're almost there." She tapped on the roof, which caused the carriage to grind to a stop before she jumped out with Agatha right behind her.

Agatha handed the driver his fare before she blinked. "Why did you have him let us off in front of a shop?"

"I thought it would be less suspicious," Eliza said.

"Yes, because there's nothing suspicious about two women lingering around a shop in the middle of the night," Agatha said.

Eliza grinned, took Agatha by the arm, and steered her up the street, coming to a sudden stop, which caused Agatha to stumble against her. "Sorry, I should have warned you," she said before nodding toward the other side of the street. "There it is."

Agatha began to sputter. "We're going to break into Lord Southmoor's home?"

"You're acquainted with him?"

"Hardly, but Mother pointed out this house last week. She has high expectations of being invited here one day."

"Yes, well, as the gentleman in question is a fraud, I hope she won't be too disappointed if she doesn't receive an invitation to one of his dinners. My fondest desire is to see the man residing behind bars soon because, you see, Lord Southmoor is actually Mr. Bartholomew Hayes, my father's old man of affairs."

"Are you certain?" Agatha asked.

Eliza nodded. "Absolutely, and to top matters off nicely, his wife used to be my governess."

"Good heavens," Agatha whispered.

"Indeed. It's my hope to find evidence of their deceit or better yet, my fortune."

"And you believe your fortune is what, stashed under the mattresses?"

"Of course not. I'm certain a large amount of my fortune is currently residing in a bank. However, I received interesting information while I was still in London concerning the rather large chest Mr. Hayes had in his possession when he left England. I was told it took four men to get this chest on board the boat, and Mr. Hayes would not allow it out of his sight. I have since come to the conclusion that Mr. Hayes most likely converted some of my fortune to cash and perhaps gold, and that is what I'm looking for tonight."

"But . . . you just said it took four men to carry that chest."

"I did say that, didn't I?"

"This is a bad idea," Agatha muttered.

"I told you that from the start, and there is still plenty of time for you to change your mind and return home."

"I have never backed down from a challenging situation before, and I don't intend to start now," Agatha said as she lifted her chin, sent Eliza a glare, and then began stomping her way across the street.

"We have to go around to the other side, where I spotted an open window earlier today," Eliza said, catching up to Agatha and taking a firm hold on her arm to slow her down. She steered her to the right and grinned. "You might want to work on the whole subtle aspect of your demeanor if you truly plan on pursuing a career in journalism."

Agatha's steps slowed to a mere crawl. "Better?"

"Hardly, but now is not the moment to squabble with you," Eliza said as she stepped around a gentleman who was standing in the street, gawking at Lord Southmoor's home. She couldn't say she blamed him. It was a most spectacular building, purchased with her funds, of course. Her jaw clenched and she tightened her grip on Agatha's arm, causing her new friend to emit a yelp.

"Is something the matter?" Agatha asked as she shook out of Eliza's hold and rubbed her arm.

"Nerves must be getting to me," Eliza muttered as they

reached the sidewalk. She turned to Agatha. "This is the tricky part. We need to slip through the side yard without being detected, and then there's a low wall we'll have to jump over that will lead us straight into the garden. I'll go first, and you follow me in a minute."

"Why do you get to go first?" Agatha grouched.

Eliza ignored Agatha's complaint and hurried into the shadows, locating the stone wall within a few seconds and making short shrift of jumping over it. She turned when Agatha slipped up beside her. "I don't think you waited the full minute."

"I was afraid you'd break in without me," Agatha said with an innocent smile.

"You still have time to turn back."

"Not on your life."

"I was afraid you'd say that," Eliza said before she moved up to the house and pushed on the window she'd noticed earlier. To her relief, it opened at her slightest touch, and to her further relief, the room they were about to enter was dark, the only source of light coming from the moon. She took a deep breath and pulled herself over the sill, landing lightly on the floor. She moved out of the way and waited as Agatha's head appeared above the sill and then her body dropped from the window and plopped on the floor with a thud. Every muscle in her body froze as she cocked an ear and listened for any sound of people in the house, people who might have heard Agatha's less than graceful fall from the window.

The only sound was that of Agatha struggling to get off the floor.

"Sorry about that," Agatha whispered as she finally found her feet and pushed her skirt down. "By the way, you might have told me you were planning on wearing trousers under your skirt tonight. I would have done the same."

"As you weren't supposed to be with me tonight in the first

place, you can't chastise me for not informing you of what I was wearing. Now, where should we start our search?"

"If I were attempting to hide a chest filled with treasure, I'd hide it on the second floor, seeing as it would be harder to steal from up there," Agatha said. "What are we going to do if we run into anyone, namely Mr. Hayes or that old governess of yours?"

"They're attending a dinner party hosted by some fellow named Eugene."

"Have you given any thought to the servants?" Agatha asked.

"I did give them a thought, especially after your fall, but since no one came shouting an alarm, I would have to believe the servants have either retired for the evening in their quarters or have left the house in search of their own frivolity. Honestly, Agatha, everyone knows servants can rarely be found when their employers are gone for the night."

"It would add a dash of excitement if we were discovered," Agatha muttered.

"There's that disappointment again," Eliza said, surprised to feel a bubble of amusement tickle her throat. "Come on, we'd best get this over with before we are discovered."

She slipped out into a hallway and glanced around, the darkness making it difficult to find the stairs. "You'd think with the amount of money Bartholomew stole from me, he'd leave a few lamps lit," Eliza grumbled as she tripped over a small statue, righted it before it fell, and then felt what seemed to be a railing right past the statue. She moved to it and smiled. "I found the stairs," she said as she reached out and grabbed Agatha's hand in order to pull her up the steps behind her. She stopped at the top. "Which way should we go?"

"I say we try every door and split up in order to cover more ground."

"Good thinking," Eliza whispered before she dropped Agatha's hand and moved forward, keeping her hands in front of her to aid her balance. She finally managed to locate a door and was just about to open it when Agatha let out a soft whistle.

"I found something over here," Agatha whispered.

"Over where?"

"Just follow my voice."

Thankfully, Agatha was opening the door wider and a sliver of moonlight flooded out, lighting Eliza's way. She moved into the room and shut the door, her gaze traveling over a large desk, rows of books lining the walls, and . . . she blinked and then blinked again.

There was a large chest sitting bold as brass right in the middle of the room.

Surely it was not going to be this easy, was it?

"Eliza," Agatha hissed before Eliza could take a single step toward the chest, "someone's been here before us."

"What?"

"Shh," Agatha said as a loud thump came to them from the other room. "I think they might still be here."

"Come on," Eliza said, her heart thudding wildly. The moon chose that moment to disappear beneath a cloud, and the room went pitch-black. She made her way toward the door, lurched into a table she didn't see, and froze as the table crashed to the ground.

"Run," Agatha squealed.

Eliza needed no second urgings. She jumped over the table and raced for the door, but before she could do more than open it, a strong arm encircled her waist as a hand clamped over her mouth, stifling her scream.

"Be quiet."

Eliza's mouth would have dropped open in surprise if a hand hadn't been pressed over it. She relaxed and the hand moved away.

"Mr. Beckett?" she whispered, knowing the answer before he had a chance to reply. The hair on her arm was standing straight up, an odd occurrence which had also happened the last time she was in Mr. Beckett's presence.

"Miss Sumner?" Hamilton asked as his hand fell from her waist.

A match hissed and dim light filled the room.

"Mr. Beckett," Agatha exclaimed.

"Miss Watson?" Zayne questioned as he shut the door before his eyes narrowed. "What are you doing here?"

"I could ask you the same question," Agatha returned.

Eliza suddenly found herself pinned under Zayne's glare. "I don't understand what could have possessed you to involve your charge in this madness. Breaking and entering is against the law," he snapped.

Before Eliza could respond, Agatha marched up to Zayne and swatted him on the arm, causing him to drop the match. The room plunged into darkness.

"I am not a 'charge' of Miss Sumner," Agatha growled. "I have not had a governess in years, and as for us breaking the law, well, the pot really shouldn't call the kettle black."

Zayne struck another match and stepped closer to Agatha. "Didn't you just make your debut?"

"Three years ago," Agatha snapped.

"While Miss Watson's age is certainly of some concern," Hamilton said, "there are more pressing matters to discuss. I insist the two of you explain what you're doing here."

"I don't believe you're in a position to insist on anything," Eliza replied.

"I disagree," Hamilton said. "My brother and I are here on a personal matter, which begs the question whether you're involved in what we're investigating."

"I can assure you we're not," Eliza returned. "Now, as we have limited time left to us, I really must get back to the business at hand."

"And what business is that?" Hamilton asked.

Eliza ignored him and returned to the chest.

"There's nothing in there except books," Zayne said as the match sputtered out and the room returned to darkness.

Disappointment washed over her. "Did you happen to notice another chest?"

"I can't say I did," Zayne said.

"Eliza, we'll have to try somewhere else," Agatha said as she stumbled forward and grabbed on to Eliza's arm to steady herself.

Eliza walked carefully out of the room, using her hand against the hall wall to guide her way. She felt the molding of a door and fumbled for the knob, turning it quickly and pushing it open before she pulled Agatha into the room. Thankfully, this particular room did not have a curtain over the window and the moon was cooperating, giving them more light.

"This looks like the master suite," Eliza said. "I'm going to check the dressing room." She strode across the room and pulled open the dressing room door. "There's another chest."

"What did you find?"

Eliza jumped and then released a breath when she realized it was only Zayne, apparently without any more matches at his disposal, standing behind her. The hair on her arm remained flat, and she found it very curious indeed that she only seemed to experience that unusual sensation when Hamilton was around.

"Grab the end and pull this chest out for us," she said, taking a step back.

"You want me to help you rob Lord Southmoor?" Zayne asked.

"As what hopefully resides in that chest is mine to begin with, it's hardly robbery."

"What do you mean, Miss Sumner?" Hamilton asked as he

melted out of the darkest part of the room and sent what she knew was a glare in her direction.

The hair on Eliza's arm stood to immediate attention.

"Shh," Agatha hissed. "I hear someone."

Eliza stood frozen in place as she heard the sound of feet climbing up the stairs. A flicker of light shone under the door and then traveled past.

"We need to get out of here," Hamilton whispered.

"I'm not going anywhere without that chest . . ." Eliza said, her voice trailing off when someone suddenly raced down the hallway on pounding feet. Seconds later the sound of shouting reached her ears.

"Come on," Hamilton ordered, grabbing Eliza's hand and propelling her to the door.

"Not without my chest," Eliza snapped, swallowing a gasp when Hamilton dropped her hand, picked her up, and slung her across his shoulder. She couldn't get another word out of her mouth as he ran out of the room and down the hallway, her head banging against his back as he bolted down the stairs. He hit the ground floor and rushed into the first available room, dropping her abruptly as he moved to a window and threw it open. He gestured for Eliza to join him before the shrill sound of a whistle drifted to them on the breeze.

"It's the police. Hurry," he said, taking her by the arm and pushing her through the window.

Her skirt snagged on the windowsill and she felt a flash of irritation as she tumbled out the window, leaving her garment behind. She scrambled out of the way as Agatha came hurtling through the air, landing with a soft *oof* beside her. A loud crash had her turning back to the window.

"What happened?" Eliza called.

"Zayne fell, but I'll get him," Hamilton called back. "Don't wait for us. Climb over that stone wall past that big tree. Our horses are there, and we'll join you shortly."

Eliza grabbed Agatha's hand, running as fast as she could toward the wall. She climbed to the top with Agatha by her side, both of them careening over the edge to land in the dirt. She scrambled to her feet and glanced around, letting out a grunt.

"I don't see any horses," she managed to get out, her breathing ragged from the run.

"We must have jumped over the wrong wall," Agatha said. "Come on, we need to get out of here."

"What of Mr. and Mr. Beckett?"

"They'll be fine. They know where their horses are; we're on foot."

"Good point," Eliza said before she found herself running after Agatha down a dirt alleyway. She skidded to a stop at the edge of the main street. She leaned forward and peered around. "It's clear."

They strolled into the street, and Eliza could only hope they didn't look too guilty, both of them covered in sweat and her wearing trousers of all things. Before she could point that particular issue out to Agatha, a man's voice sounded behind them.

"Stop right there, ladies."

Eliza stumbled to a halt and then slowly turned, appalled to discover a policeman standing a few feet away from her.

"May I ask why you ladies are roaming the streets this time of night?"

"Good evening, sir," Agatha said pleasantly. "My friend and I are simply out for an evening walk. Beautiful night, isn't it?"

"It won't be beautiful where you're heading," the officer returned.

"I beg your pardon?" Agatha asked.

"You'll be begging the pardon of a judge soon," he said. "Let's get you over there with your friends."

Good heavens, Hamilton and Zayne must have already been apprehended, but . . . why was the officer gesturing to a group of ladies who were huddled together and wearing the most outlandish garments Eliza had ever seen?

Realization set in and she couldn't help herself; she laughed as relief swept over her. "Sir, I fear there has been a grave mis-understanding. My friend and I aren't, well, you know . . . ladies of ill repute."

"I don't think there's any 'misunderstanding' about it," the officer said, his eyes lingering on Eliza's trousers.

Before she could even formulate a response to that, she was taken by the arm, hustled over to a large covered wagon with bars over the windows, and promptly thrown inside, Agatha following a second later. The door slammed shut with a re-sounding thud, and the wagon lurched forward, causing Eliza to topple to the floor.

"This is a disaster," she grumbled as she accepted Agatha's offer of a hand up. She plopped down on the bench beside her friend and frowned when she noticed Agatha grinning back at her. "What could you possibly find amusing in all this?"

"This is wonderful fodder for a story. I could do an entire feature on how soiled doves are treated in the city."

"This is serious."

Agatha shrugged. "Mr. and Mr. Beckett will soon set it to rights."

"How can you be so sure? They'll risk detection if they come to rescue us."

"Eliza, we're not in here because the police think we broke into that house. We're in here because they mistook us for pros-titutes. They must have been doing some type of roundup. But enough about our current circumstances; I've been dying to find out what you thought about Mr. Beckett flinging you over his shoulder in that manly way and carting you out of that house."

Eliza did not wish to dwell on Mr. Hamilton Beckett at the moment. If she was truthful with herself, she would admit she'd definitely been affected by his nearness as he hefted her down the stairs. It hadn't escaped her notice that the gentleman had not suffered any difficulty with her weight. Good heavens, he'd barely broken into a sweat and his breathing had been anything but labored. The railroad business was apparently good for a gentleman's health.

It was beyond disconcerting.

She took a deep breath and forced a smile. "I would much rather discuss the reasoning behind your disgruntlement regarding the fact that Mr. Zayne Beckett didn't realize how long you've been out of the schoolroom."

Agatha's grin slid off her face, and to Eliza's relief, the subject swiftly changed to the weather.

5

"Where are Miss Sumner and Miss Watson?" Zayne asked as he landed on the ground beside Hamilton and looked around.

Hamilton gestured up the road. "They're in that police wagon."

"Why?"

"I would have to think there was an officer waiting for them when they jumped over the wall," Hamilton said.

"That's strange, considering we weren't the cause for the ruckus back at the house after all," Zayne said. "Before I followed you out the window, I overheard one of the servants shrieking something about finding his lady love being a touch too friendly with another gentleman."

"That's what caused all that commotion?"

"It was quite riveting, all the nasty accusations and innuendos being shouted around. I was almost disappointed I couldn't stay to hear more, but considering we were more than fortunate to not have any of the servants see us as we raced out of the house, I wasn't willing to press my luck."

"If the police weren't summoned because of our presence, why do you suppose Miss Watson and Miss Sumner were apprehended?"

Zayne tilted his head. "Did you notice anyone else being shoved into the police wagon?"

"There were quite a few ladies of ill repute being tossed in after them."

"There's your answer then. I would assume the police were making one of their roundups this evening, and poor Miss Watson and Miss Sumner stumbled into the midst of that madness."

"They look nothing like prostitutes."

Zayne held up a wad of what appeared to be fabric. "Miss Sumner is currently without her skirt."

"Why in the world would she take off her skirt?"

"I think the blame for that rests solely with you," Zayne said with a grin. "You probably should have taken greater care when you shoved the woman out the window. Lucky she was wearing those trousers."

"I see nothing lucky about it. She's currently trundling off to jail."

"But at least she's not in her undergarments. That would be hard to explain."

Hamilton laughed. "Let me see that," he said, gesturing to the skirt. Zayne tossed it to him and he held it up. "Doesn't it seem as if Miss Sumner has miraculously shed a good thirty pounds or so to fit into something this small?"

"I thought she looked a bit trimmer."

"Do you think she's purposefully disguising her figure?" Hamilton asked.

"I think she's disguising a lot of things, given the fact that we just encountered her breaking into Lord Southmoor's home," Zayne said dryly. "I must say, she's very intriguing."

"Intriguing is an apt word for her."

Zayne smiled. "You like her."

Hamilton let out a snort. "Whether I like Miss Sumner or not is a moot point. There's something mysterious surrounding her, and after everything I went through with Mary Ellen, I have no interest in becoming better acquainted with a woman I can't trust."

"Miss Sumner is no Mary Ellen."

Hamilton shrugged. "She could be; we only met her last night."

"True, but she seems to possess a great deal of character. It couldn't have been easy for her to attend that dinner last night, and yet she rose to the occasion and persevered throughout the meal. Mary Ellen would never have agreed to place herself in such an uncomfortable situation."

"My wife wasn't one to do anything she didn't want to do," Hamilton said, "but enough about Mary Ellen and my interest or lack thereof in Miss Sumner. We need to fetch our horses and head off to jail. Hopefully we'll be able to convince the officers on duty tonight that there's been a serious misunderstanding. It shouldn't be too difficult to get the ladies released, considering that no one knows they were dabbling in a bit of breaking and entering."

Hamilton made his way to where he'd left his horse, stuffed Eliza's skirt into his saddlebag, and then pulled himself up into the saddle, waiting for Zayne to do the same before edging his horse down the alley and into the street. He turned to his brother. "I still can't believe Miss Watson was in attendance tonight with Miss Sumner. I always took her for a more subdued young lady."

"She wasn't very subdued when she was taking me to task about my impression she'd only just left the schoolroom," Zayne said.

"I got the distinct impression she . . . liked you."

Zayne blinked. "As in romantically likes me?"

"Liked," Hamilton corrected. "She was definitely insulted concerning the fact that you thought she was still a child. Her interest in you might have waned."

"She took me by surprise," Zayne said. "She's turned out to be a very attractive young woman—headstrong, but attractive."

"Maybe you should tell her that when you see her, not the headstrong part, but the attractive bit. It might appease her wounded pride," Hamilton said.

"I can't do that, it might give her false hope," Zayne said. "Besides, from what you've said in previous conversations, I was under the impression her father has his eye on you as a potential suitor."

"Mr. Watson has been annoyingly persistent in that regard," Hamilton admitted. "His desire to see his daughter well wed is only eclipsed by his desire to become associated with our railroad business to increase his capacity to distribute his soap. It's no wonder Miss Watson found an excuse to avoid the dinner last night."

"You've become awfully cynical in your old age."

"You'd be cynical too if parents continuously placed their unmarried daughters in your path. Your association with Helena has led everyone to believe you're firmly off the market," Hamilton said.

"I am firmly off the market, which brings us back to the subject of Miss Watson and her indignation over my thoughtless remark. I can't very well soothe her feelings because she might form unrealistic expectations, and you know perfectly well I'm completely committed to Helena."

Hamilton steered his horse around a lumbering carriage and waited for Zayne to rejoin him. "I hope you won't take this the wrong way, but I've been sadly negligent in voicing my opinion where Helena is concerned. I think the only reason you've stayed with her all these years is because of her fragile health."

"Honestly, Hamilton, this is hardly the time to get into a discussion regarding my future wife. If you've forgotten, we're in a bit of a pickle at the moment."

Hamilton knew perfectly well Zayne was deliberately changing the subject, seemingly unwilling to discuss the many faults of Helena. He pushed aside the opinions he longed to express, knowing there was still time to make his brother see reason, and nodded. "Fine, for now we'll set all talk of Helena aside and concentrate on formulating a plan. What do you think about storming through the doors of the jail and demanding the ladies' release?"

"That's a wonderful idea, especially since I've always wanted to spend a night in a dreary cell."

"Do you have a better idea?"

"Not really."

Hamilton blew out a breath and steered his horse past an obviously intoxicated gentleman who was weaving in place in the middle of the street, holding a rousing conversation with himself. "We could always pay one of the officers," he finally said once they'd traveled sufficiently away from the now-bellowing gentleman and his words could be heard. He turned when he realized Zayne was no longer by his side, but was sitting on his horse a few yards behind, his expression one of disbelief.

"You cannot be serious, Hamilton. We can't bribe an officer of the law. We really will end up in a cell right beside the ladies."

"I think we should look at it as an incentive, not a bribe."

"It's the same thing," Zayne grouched as he nudged his horse forward. "Bribery is hardly honorable."

"Neither was breaking into Lord Southmoor's house," Hamilton pointed out.

"We had a reason for that."

"And we have a reason for bribery if all else fails. We can't leave Miss Sumner and Miss Watson languishing behind bars. I shudder to think what type of trouble they'll get into if they're left to their own devices for too long. Besides, I feel a bit responsible for them getting apprehended in the first place. I was the one who told them to jump over that wall, and unfortunately, amidst all the chaos, I have the uncanny feeling I might have pointed to the wrong wall," Hamilton said.

"You weren't the one who suggested they go on a madcap adventure and steal into Lord Southmoor's home."

Hamilton grinned. "Maybe we should let them stew a bit. It might cause them to refrain from getting into this type of mischief in the future."

"Sadly, I don't think even a night in jail will curb Miss Watson's and Miss Sumner's apparent appetite for adventure," Zayne muttered.

"You might have a point, but no time to ponder the ladies' many deficiencies right now, because the jail's just ahead." He brought his horse to a stop in front of a hitching post, jumped to the ground, pulled his saddlebag off the horse, and waited for Zayne to join him. "Ready?"

"I still don't think we have a viable plan," Zayne said.

"Probably not, but we can't dither around out here. The damsels in distress are waiting for their knights in shining armor to come rescue them," Hamilton said.

"You should probably keep that particular notion to yourself. I have the sneaky suspicion Miss Watson does not see herself as a damsel in distress and will most likely take offense at the mere suggestion she needs a knight to come to her aid."

"Remember when ladies wanted a knight in shining armor?" Hamilton asked with a shake of his head as he led the way up the steps and walked through the door of the jail.

"I think most ladies still want that, just not Miss Watson and definitely not our sister," Zayne said.

"Arabella would certainly be offended if she'd heard my comment," Hamilton replied as he glanced around and released a groan. "The place is filled to the brim, and it appears as if we need to join that group of people waiting in line over there."

"They look like criminals," Zayne said.

"Then we should feel right at home," Hamilton remarked dryly, walking over to take his place behind a red-eyed gentleman who was rocking back and forth on his heels and muttering something that sounded like threats under his breath. Hamilton allowed the man his space, thankful that the line moved rapidly, and it only took a mere twenty minutes for them to reach the front. They were directed to an officer sitting at an adjacent desk.

"What may I assist you with, sir?" the officer asked.

"I'm here to retrieve two young ladies who were apprehended by mistake," Hamilton explained.

The officer blew out a breath. "They were apprehended by mistake?"

"Indeed, the women in question were only out for an evening stroll and somehow ended up here."

"You don't say," the officer said. "Are you here to post bail?"

"I'm of the belief there's no need for bail, seeing as the women are innocent," Hamilton said.

"We don't arrest innocent women," the officer snapped. "Every single person I've spoken with this evening has made the same claim."

"These particular ladies really are innocent," Hamilton said. "It is my assumption that the ladies might have been mistaken for women of the night. You see, one of them suffered an unfortunate accident, which resulted in the lady becoming parted from her skirt."

"A likely story."

"I have the skirt in question right here," Hamilton said, dropping the saddlebag to the ground as he bent over to release the fastenings. He stilled when the officer shot to his feet, and the next thing Hamilton knew, a gun was pointing in his direction. He slowly straightened and held up his hands. "I'm not armed. I'm just trying to show you the skirt as proof to the validity of my story."

The officer watched warily as Hamilton bent over again, flicked the saddlebag open, and pulled out Eliza's skirt.

"This is most unusual," the officer said as he resumed his seat.

"You have no idea," Zayne muttered, stepping forward. "Have you seen the ladies in question?"

"A lady wearing trousers and her companion were taken to a cell a short time ago, where they're waiting to be processed," the officer admitted.

Hamilton reached into his pocket and didn't allow himself a moment to reconsider what he was about to do. He slid some bills across the desk and leaned over as he lowered his voice. "Would that help get the ladies released without being processed?"

The officer eyed Hamilton for a long moment, pushed the money back to him, and surged to his feet. "Follow me."

"Now you've done it," Zayne muttered. "I told you bribery was a bad idea, but did you listen? No, you just had to go and try your hand at it."

Hamilton didn't have a chance to respond because, before he knew it, he found himself in a nicely appointed room with a gentleman who was buried in a newspaper and sitting behind a desk. A nameplate with *The Honorable Judge Silverman* engraved on it was resting right at the front of the desk.

This was a fortunate turn of events. He was acquainted with Judge Silverman, which was certainly going to make the nasty business of getting the ladies released relatively easy. He stepped up to the desk and cleared his throat, the noise causing Judge Silverman to peer over the paper and then lower it when recognition seemed to set in.

"I say, is that you, Mr. Beckett?" Judge Silverman asked before he rose to his feet and held out his hand. "What in the world are you doing here this time of night?"

Hamilton shook the hand and grinned. "I could ask you the same thing."

"Behind on my paper work as usual, so I volunteered to stay a few extra hours in case my services were needed." Judge Silverman smiled. "The end of the weekend is always a bit of a strain on the department. People find themselves getting involved in all sorts of trouble."

"Isn't that the truth?" Hamilton mumbled.

Judge Silverman shook his head. "What brings you here, son?"

Before Hamilton could reply, the officer stepped to his side. "This man apparently believes it is acceptable to offer bribes in order to hasten the process of getting someone out of jail."

Judge Silverman made a *tsk*ing noise as he nodded to the officer. "You may go. I'll settle matters with Mr. Beckett."

The officer sent the judge a nod, turned on his heel, and strode from the room, closing the door behind him.

"Care for a drink before you explain what possessed you to attempt to bribe an officer of the law?" Judge Silverman asked.

"I'm really beginning to dislike that word," Zayne said as he moved around Hamilton and shook Judge Silverman's hand.

"Ah, the other Mr. Beckett," Judge Silverman exclaimed. "I'll have to tell my youngest daughter you're still in town." He winked. "She's been devastated over the fact that you're supposedly moving west to join that young lady of yours."

"Please tell me my response to that will not affect my future," Zayne said.

Judge Silverman laughed and walked to a side table, pouring three drinks and handing them around before he gestured to two chairs. He resumed his position behind the desk. "Why don't you start at the beginning?"

Hamilton took a sip of his drink. "It's a tad difficult to put into words exactly what happened, Your Honor, but from what I can surmise, two ladies, Miss Watson and Miss Sumner, were apparently mistaken for ladies of the night. When Zayne and I discovered they'd been carted off to jail, we decided a grave injustice had occurred, seeing as how these ladies are not what we think they've been accused of being and . . . that's why we're here, to see them released as quickly as possible."

"Explain the bribe," Judge Silverman demanded as he eyed Hamilton over the rim of his glass.

"I suppose I can only plead insanity," Hamilton said. "Events have been disturbing to say the least, and I really only wanted to expedite the process of getting two innocent ladies out of jail."

Judge Silverman sat forward. "You mentioned one of the ladies is a Miss Watson. She would not happen to be a member of the soap family Watsons, would she?"

"The very one," Hamilton said.

Judge Silverman blew out a breath. "And you swear to me these ladies are innocent of all wrongdoing?"

How could he possibly answer that with a straight face?

"I assure you these women are not prostitutes," he settled on saying.

Judge Silverman rustled around his desk and pulled out a plain piece of paper. He scribbled something on it and handed it to Hamilton. "You'll need that to get the ladies released, and I can only hope Mr. Watson will be in an understanding frame of mind when he discovers what happened tonight. He is one of the most generous patrons of the department."

"I have a sneaky suspicion Miss Watson won't be keen to share the details with her father," Zayne said.

Judge Silverman laughed. "She's a delightful minx, isn't she?" he said as he stood and moved to the door, opening it and speaking with a man on the other side. He turned back to Hamilton. "Officer Whitman will escort you to your ladies, gentlemen. I would love to chat longer, but I fear it's urgent to get these ladies released, seeing as how they're innocent and have been unjustly held."

"I truly appreciate your assistance in this matter, Your Honor, and I'll be certain to send over a donation for the force tomorrow," Hamilton said.

Judge Silverman smiled, and Hamilton shook his hand once more before walking into the hallway with Zayne. Officer Whitman led the way, taking them down a steep flight of steps and through another long hallway before he stopped in front of a closed door. He rapped on it and a rather surly-looking officer poked his head out.

"These gentlemen are here to pick up two women," Officer Whitman announced, tipping his hat before turning and striding away.

Hamilton handed the officer the paper, watching as the man scanned it and suddenly lost all hint of surliness.

"Thank the good Lord," the officer exclaimed as he ushered them through the door and closed it behind them. "These women are enough to drive a man to drink."

"What have they done?" Hamilton asked cautiously.

"The one with the red hair and trousers, she's been all right, but the other, she's been an absolute nightmare, very vocal with her displeasure. From this paper, it would appear the ladies have been maligned, but I can honestly claim I don't feel much sympathy for them at the moment, not with the pounding in my head that shrieking caused."

"I don't hear any shrieking," Zayne said.

"That's because the young lady has resorted to prayers.

You should have been here ten minutes ago; the noise was deafening."

Hamilton increased his pace until he came to the cell the officer indicated. He leaned forward and peered through the bars, locating Miss Sumner immediately. She was more than a bit disheveled as she slouched against the wall, her hair straggling about her shoulders and her expression forlorn. For some odd reason, he found her incredibly appealing. He moved aside so the officer could unlock the door, completely unprepared for what happened next.

6

*E*liza blinked and then blinked again as recognition set in.

It was Mr. Hamilton Beckett.

He'd come for her.

Her feet flew into motion, and before she knew it, she was throwing herself into his arms, his warmth seeping through her. Tears she'd been holding back for what seemed like forever spilled from her eyes, and all she seemed capable of doing was burrowing closer to him.

She felt safe in his arms, safe in a way she hadn't felt in months.

"Are you all right?" Hamilton asked.

Good heavens, what must he think of her?

She was clinging to him and drenching the front of his coat with her tears.

The night had apparently been too much for her normally steely nerves.

She drew in a deep breath and slowly released it, ordering her tears to cease falling before taking a step back even as a trace of disappointment swept through her when Hamilton's arms fell away. She forced her chin up in order to meet his gaze and found herself unable to respond when she noticed the concern in his eyes. She managed a brief nod.

"Are you certain you're all right?" he pressed.

"I wasn't sure you'd come," she finally whispered.

"Did you think Zayne and I would leave you and Miss Watson in jail?"

Eliza gave one small hiccup. "I don't put much trust in people."

"If it makes you feel any better, Miss Sumner, neither do I."

Before Eliza could respond to that telling statement, Zayne appeared by her other side.

"What happened to your hair?" he asked.

Eliza lifted her hand and encountered a tangled mess. "I was told some women try to hide weapons in the most unlikely of places. They made me take out all my pins and then refused to give them back to me." She felt tears dribble down her cheeks.

Hamilton muttered something under his breath, pulled out a handkerchief, and began dabbing at her face.

"Come now, Miss Sumner, there's no need to cry," Hamilton said. "I think your hair looks lovely." He frowned and rubbed his handkerchief more diligently against Eliza's face, causing her to wince. His hand stilled. "Did someone strike you?" He touched her cheek with one finger, causing a shiver to run down her spine.

"I fell getting into the wagon."

"Did you suffer any other indignities?" he asked.

"I was ogled by criminals."

"Ogled?" Hamilton hissed.

Eliza nodded. "And there was whistling involved."

"Oh . . ." Hamilton said, his lips twitching ever so slightly. "Perhaps it would make you feel better if you put on your skirt." He dropped a saddlebag she hadn't realized he was carrying and pulled out her skirt, handing it to her.

She was oddly touched when he and Zayne presented her with their backs, their broad shoulders lending her privacy.

It was refreshing to learn chivalry was not dead, at least in regard to the two gentlemen blocking her from view. She slipped into the skirt, made short shrift of fastening it, and then smiled. "I bet this will put an end to the ogling."

Hamilton and Zayne turned and looked at her before Zayne laughed and shook his head. "Please don't take offense at this, Miss Sumner, but I don't believe the only reason you were 'ogled' was because you were wearing trousers. You've been hiding your looks quite effectively."

"I'm sure I have no idea what you're suggesting," she said.

"There will be plenty of time to discuss that particular issue after we've secured Miss Watson," Hamilton said.

"Good heavens, I forgot Agatha."

Zayne grinned and gestured with his hand. "If it's any consolation, I don't think she noticed."

Eliza swallowed a laugh. Agatha was sitting on the floor, joined by women of the night, all of them bowing their heads as Agatha whispered prayers under her breath.

"Is she . . . praying?" Zayne asked.

Eliza nodded. "She started that after her threats to the guard began to wear on the man's nerves." She took a step forward. "Agatha."

Agatha raised her head and jumped to her feet. "See," she proclaimed to the women, "my prayers were answered. Help has arrived."

"Help has arrived for you, but what about us?" one of the women asked.

"Good point," Agatha said as she turned to Eliza. "Do you have any money on you?"

"I'm a governess; I never have any money on me."

Agatha set her sights on Hamilton. "Could you extend me a loan to bail these ladies out of jail?"

"I'll do it," Zayne said, speaking up.

Agatha sent him an appraising look, sniffed once, and turned her back on him as she addressed the prostitutes.

"This *fine* gentleman is going to post your bail, which means you'll soon be free. I know it's not my place, but I must encourage all of you to attempt to find another line of work. There's a wonderful church off Broadway, and the minister there is always willing to help a soul in need. You may tell Reverend Fraser that Miss Watson sent you."

"You've been very kind, Miss Watson," one of the woman said.

Agatha smiled, assured the women once again they would soon be released, and strode out of the cell.

"I told you there was power in prayer," she said to Eliza.

"You also told me you were certain Mr. and Mr. Beckett would come to our aid," Eliza reminded her.

"Yes, but my prayers guaranteed our release and also sent help for those poor women."

Eliza glanced to the prostitutes and wondered if Agatha was right. She pushed the thought away, unwilling to dwell on the power of prayer at this particular moment. She looked at Hamilton. "Are we free to leave now?"

Hamilton turned to the guard, who nodded and said, "You'll need to stop by the office to retrieve their possessions."

"You had possessions?" Zayne asked.

"Agatha had her gun," Eliza explained. "She put up a bit of a fight when it was confiscated."

"I still don't understand why they wouldn't let me keep it," Agatha grouched. "Jail is a dangerous place."

"Yes, I see your point," Zayne said. "I don't know what these officers were thinking, divesting a criminal of her weapon."

Eliza smothered a laugh when Agatha sent Zayne a glare and stomped off ahead of them. It took only a few minutes to retrieve their belongings, but after Agatha reclaimed her gun and small bag, she opened her bag, pulled out some bills, and thrust them into Zayne's hands.

"I don't think this is enough to cover the cost of the bail for those women, but I'll send the rest to you at my earliest convenience."

"There's no need for you to repay me," he said.

"I have no desire to be in debt to you," Agatha said. "It's become crystal clear to me that you are *not* the man I thought you to be. I can't believe I spent so much time harboring an infatuation for you."

"But . . . I had no idea you felt that way about me," Zayne said slowly.

Eliza felt the distinct urge to yell at the man to cease talking.

He unfortunately didn't hear her unspoken plea and continued on.

"You must know I'm committed to Helena."

Agatha muttered something that sounded very much like "you *should* be committed" before she smiled. "There's no need for any distress, Mr. Beckett. I'm not going to fall to pieces over your lack of affection. I made a momentous decision as I languished in jail this evening, and I fear I won't have any spare time to pursue an attachment with any gentleman. I'm more determined than ever to devote my life to writing articles, which I hope will shed light on the appalling circumstances of those less fortunate than I."

"That's hardly a suitable profession for a woman of your social status," Zayne said with a snort.

"Further proof I was spot on regarding your character," she

said before she spun on her heel and marched out of the room, leaving Eliza to deal with two befuddled gentlemen.

"Well," she finally said, "there you have it."

"There I have what?" Zayne asked.

"I'm not actually certain, but thought I should say something to fill the silence," Eliza said with a grin as she accepted Hamilton's arm and allowed him to direct her out of the room and down a hallway.

"Do you think Miss Watson will be waiting for us?" Zayne asked.

"Since she gave you all of her money, I don't think she has any other option," Eliza said before she walked through another door and nodded. "There she is."

Agatha took that moment to look up from what appeared to be an intense discussion with an officer and gestured for them to join her.

"Would someone care to explain why we were released from jail without bail being paid?" Agatha asked.

"You may thank Judge Silverman for that favor," Hamilton said. "When he learned you'd been unjustly arrested, he signed an immediate form of release and wanted me to extend to you his deepest apologies for such a grave misunderstanding."

"Judge Silverman knows I was here?" Agatha sputtered. "What possessed you to divulge that information to a gentleman who is personally acquainted with my father?"

"It just slipped out," Zayne said.

Agatha narrowed her eyes.

"I think I'll go post the bail for those other ladies," Zayne muttered before he hurried away in the opposite direction of where bails were paid.

"Coward," Agatha called after him.

"We need to get you out of here," Eliza said, taking Agatha

by the arm and pulling her toward the door, pausing as Hamilton opened it for her.

"So, Mr. Beckett," Agatha said as they walked out into the cold night air and stood on the steps of the jail, "how much did it cost you to get us released?"

"Again, there was no need to post bail, but to answer your question truthfully, I did offer to make a donation to the department."

A flicker of unease swept through Eliza. "I don't have funds available at the moment to repay you for your donation, Mr. Beckett."

"I don't expect you to repay me, Miss Sumner. If I'd been more specific regarding what wall I wanted the two of you to jump over, you might not have landed here in the first place."

Eliza knew he was simply being kind, but before she could utter another protest, Zayne rejoined them.

"You'll be happy to know those women are now free to go about their business," Zayne said cheerfully. "I have a bet with one of the officers that at least some of them will end up back in jail before the night is through."

"You really are a horrible man," Agatha said.

"I think I'll go get the horses," Zayne said, ambling down the steps without a backward glance.

"Zayne, wait," Hamilton called.

Zayne turned around and quirked a brow.

"I'm going to hire a carriage to see the ladies home," Hamilton said. "I'll need you to take my horse."

"Why do you get to ride in a nice warm carriage?" Zayne asked.

Hamilton sent a pointed look to Agatha that resulted in Zayne spinning on his heel and striding away.

"There's a carriage," Hamilton said. He hurried down the steps, and Eliza couldn't resist watching him. He was such a handsome gentleman, strong and possessed of a long gait, which seemed to eat up the distance to the carriage with remarkably little effort. She heard something that sounded very much like a chuckle and turned to find Agatha watching her with an annoyingly knowing look on her face. Luckily, Agatha didn't appear to have any words to match the look at the moment, but, not wanting to give her an opportunity to find the words, Eliza set her sights on Hamilton and began walking his way.

Two minutes later, she was settled into her seat, thankfully traveling in the opposite direction of the jail.

"Are you up for some questions?" Hamilton asked.

"That depends on what you want to know," Eliza said.

"I need to know why you were at Lord Southmoor's tonight. Were you there because of Mr. Eugene Daniels?"

"I don't personally know a Mr. Eugene Daniels," Eliza returned.

"That complicates matters," Hamilton said. "I was certain we shared a common problem."

"It's unlikely your problem is anything like mine unless you've had reason to entrust Bartholomew Hayes with a large sum of money," she said.

"Who is Bartholomew Hayes?" Hamilton asked.

"He's the man currently posing as Lord Southmoor, but I really don't think I should say anything else about my situation. It wouldn't be fair to involve you in it."

"Miss Sumner, I'm already involved."

"Eliza, just tell him," Agatha said. "We could use some assistance."

Realizing Agatha was right, Eliza took the next few minutes to explain matters to Hamilton. He said not a single word as she told her tale, but sat perfectly still on the seat, an unreadable expression on his face. When she was done, he turned his head and looked out the window. She began to fidget as silence filled the carriage. "Don't you have anything to say?" she finally asked.

"I can't believe you traveled across an entire ocean to try and track down a criminal on your own."

That was all he could say?

Eliza's temper flared. "It's not as if I had any choice in the matter, and besides, I found him, didn't I?"

"Well, yes, but don't you have male relatives or a gentleman friend who could have handled this problem?" Hamilton asked.

"My only living relatives are my cousin and his wife, but they have problems of their own, seeing as how my cousin inherited my father's estates, but has no money to run them."

"Miss Sumner did have a fiancé at one time, but he turned out to be a scoundrel," Agatha said.

"Yes, thank you for that," Eliza muttered.

"You conveniently left out any mention of a fiancé," Hamilton said.

Was it her imagination, or was there an odd tone in his comment, a tone that seemed almost . . . annoyed? Eliza shook the thought away. No, that was ridiculous. Mr. Hamilton Beckett surely was not bothered by the fact that she'd once possessed a fiancé, or . . .

"Your fiancé?" Hamilton prompted, pulling her from her thoughts.

She forced a smile. "If you were listening, Mr. Beckett, you would have heard Agatha mention the small fact that I used to have a fiancé. I no longer have one, as the gentleman in question seemingly only valued my rather large dowry, and when that disappeared, so did he."

"I find that hard to believe," he said.

Eliza inclined her head. "Thank you for that, Mr. Beckett." Her eyes met his, and oddly enough, the world around her simply melted away. There was something quite lovely in his eyes, something . . .

Agatha coughed loudly, causing Eliza to blink and realize an unusual silence had descended over the carriage while she'd been trapped in Hamilton's gaze. Honestly, it was a touch embarrassing, but how was a lady supposed to form a coherent word when a gentleman such as Mr. Beckett was watching her with such blatant—could it be interest—in his eyes?

"I could get out," Agatha muttered.

"No need for that," Eliza said before she shook herself ever so slightly to clear her head. "Where were we?"

"We were discussing your situation," Agatha said, "and I, for one, must insist you allow us to help you sort out this mess."

"Excellent suggestion," Hamilton said. "Since it appears you no longer have a male relative at your disposal, Miss Sumner, I will assume that role and do everything in my power to assist you."

The last thing Eliza wanted was for Hamilton to assume the role of older brother, as her reaction to the gentleman was certainly not sisterly. She pushed the thought to the farthest recesses of her mind and gave what she could only hope was an appreciative smile. "You are too kind, Mr. Beckett, and I fear I might actually be forced to take you up on your offer. It does seem we're both embroiled in something disturbing. You mentioned a Mr. Eugene Daniels. What part does he play in all of this?"

"For the past two years, Mr. Daniels has been systematically underbidding business deals my family has been pursuing. I know relatively little about the man, but Zayne and I are determined to bring his shenanigans to an end. He's cost our company thousands of dollars, and when I heard he was acquainted with Lord Southmoor, or rather, Mr. Hayes, I couldn't resist trying to learn more about their association."

Eliza frowned. "I'm not certain how there could be an association between the two men. Mr. Hayes only recently entered this country, and I never heard him speak of a Mr. Daniels while he was in England."

"It seems to me as if there were many things you didn't hear Mr. Hayes speak about," Agatha said before she glanced out the window and turned back to Hamilton. "You can have the driver set us down here, Mr. Beckett. I don't think it would be wise to stop in front of my house."

Hamilton tapped on the roof and the carriage began to slow. He leaned forward and placed his hand on top of Eliza's before she had a chance to get out. "I'll call on you tomorrow morning so we may finish our discussion."

Eliza discovered she was unable to respond. The warmth of his hand was distracting, to say the least, and his touch was causing little jolts of something disturbing to rush through her.

"Mr. Beckett, you can't call on Eliza during the day," Agatha said. "She's the governess, and my father is intent on persuading you to form an attachment to me. You'll have to come tomorrow evening after seven. My parents are planning to attend the theater."

"Seven it is," Hamilton said as he removed his hand from Eliza's and swung out of the carriage. He helped Agatha out and then offered his arm to Eliza. She took it and refused to allow herself the luxury of a shiver.

"I'll see you tomorrow," Hamilton said, giving her arm a gentle squeeze before he released it and jumped back into the carriage before it began to roll away.

Eliza felt her knees wobble ever so slightly, but forced them to straighten when Agatha let out a laugh.

"Still going to claim you have no interest in Mr. Beckett?" Agatha asked as she took Eliza's hand and pulled her toward the house. "Did you notice how he couldn't seem to keep his eyes off of you?"

"Ahh . . . no, I didn't notice that."

Agatha arched a brow before her stride suddenly slowed.

"What is it?" Eliza asked, directing her gaze to where Agatha was staring in horror.

Light spilled from the Watson house.

"There they are," a voice called from down the street.

Agatha took that moment to bow her head.

"What are you doing?" Eliza sputtered.

"Praying."

"Pray quickly because . . . it looks like your father is coming our way."

7

*H*amilton leaned back against the seat, smiling when an image of Miss Sumner barreling out of the cell and directly into his arms came to mind. She'd been so soft and warm and . . . he blinked when Zayne's face appeared at the window and the carriage rolled to a stop.

"I have your horse," Zayne said.

"I forgot about my horse."

"No doubt your thoughts were on the enchanting Miss Sumner."

Hamilton certainly wasn't going to admit the fact that his thoughts had indeed been with Eliza. He ignored the calculating look on Zayne's face, climbed out of the carriage, and took his time paying the driver, wanting to prolong the conversation he knew his brother was dying to broach. He watched the carriage amble away and accepted the reins his brother threw him before he pulled himself up on his horse.

"So," Zayne began, "about Miss Sumner?"

Hamilton ignored the question and urged his horse into a trot.

Unfortunately, Zayne soon caught up. "This unusual turn of events might put a damper on your plan of remaining single."

Hamilton pulled his horse to a stop. "I'm hardly contemplating marriage at the moment, especially to Miss Sumner. I barely know the lady."

"True, but she's certainly managed to capture your attention."

"Her life is a mess."

"Mary Ellen was a mess, and yet you tried to sort her out."

"Yes, and that turned out well for me," Hamilton replied.

"It's not your fault she was killed, Hamilton," Zayne said softly. "You had no way of knowing she would try to run from you."

"I should have known. She'd grown increasingly secretive right before she died."

"And those secrets are what had her fleeing into the night in the midst of a horrible storm and getting thrown from her horse," Zayne said. "Any fault resulting from Mary Ellen's accident lies solely with her."

"I still wonder whom she was running to that night and if—" Hamilton stopped speaking when loud shouting pierced the air. He turned his head in the direction of the noise. "Please tell me that's not Miss Sumner and Miss Watson down there."

Zayne released a groan. "I think they've been discovered."

"Of course they have; their luck is horrendous," Hamilton said. He turned his horse and looked over his shoulder. "Are you coming?"

"Maybe we shouldn't get involved in this, Hamilton. It might make matters worse for the ladies."

The yelling suddenly escalated, drawing Hamilton's attention. He peered down the street and settled his sights on four dark figures in the distance. There were three slight figures and one large one, obviously a man. He narrowed his eyes. From what he could see, it appeared as if the man was looming over one of the women, and Hamilton instinctively knew it was Eliza who was bearing the brunt of the tirade. He urged his horse forward and reached the group in less than a minute, jumping off his horse and striding in the direction of the man, who turned out to be Mr. Watson.

" . . . fact that there was no note, no Agatha and . . ." Mr. Watson's voice trailed off when Hamilton reached his side. The finger Mr. Watson had been shaking in Eliza's face paused in mid-shake as the man opened and closed his mouth, then smiled a smile that was less than amused. "Mr. Beckett, fancy seeing you out and about this time of night."

"Mr. Watson," Hamilton said before he allowed his gaze to travel over to Eliza, who was apparently holding up well under what could only be considered trying circumstances. Not one tear could be found in the lady's eyes, and his respect for her rose. Nevertheless, he couldn't let Mr. Watson continue ranting at her. She wasn't solely responsible for what had happened tonight. He turned to the gentleman, but was distracted when Mrs. Watson stepped forward and beamed at him.

"Mr. Beckett, it's delightful to see you again so soon. I do hope you enjoyed the dinner last night."

"It was lovely, Mrs. Watson," Hamilton said.

"I'm just sorry you weren't able to enjoy Agatha's company," Mrs. Watson continued. "She was feeling poorly, but as you can see, she seems to have recovered."

Hamilton shot a glance to Agatha, who looked positively alarmed at being brought into the conversation. He watched her edge closer to Eliza.

"Well, we don't want to keep you," Mr. Watson said.

Hamilton decided there was no point in avoiding the reason he was currently standing in the freezing night air, making polite conversation. "I was wondering what all the shouting was about."

"No need for your concern," Mr. Watson said. "It's a family matter, and I wouldn't want to bother you with all the pesky little details."

"You were yelling at Miss Sumner, and I'm concerned about her welfare."

All appearances of affability disappeared from Mr. Watson in a split second. "Mr. Beckett, as I said before, this is none of your business, and I'll thank you to stay out of it. Miss Sumner has behaved in an irresponsible manner this evening, and I'm perfectly within my rights to discipline her as I see fit."

"I told you, Father," Agatha said, speaking up, "it wasn't Miss Sumner's fault. I'm more to blame than she is, seeing as how it was my idea to join her in the first place."

"She is the adult in this situation, so she receives full blame for the fact that you left the house without even the courtesy of a note," Mr. Watson snapped. "Do you have any idea, young lady, how frantic your mother and I were when we returned home to find you missing? Not to mention the fact that Mr. Truman and his upstanding son, Stanford, were appalled to discover you're the type of lady who would show such little consideration for your parents."

Hamilton watched as Agatha began to sputter. He actually felt a small trace of sympathy for Mr. Watson, but it disappeared when he glanced to Eliza and found her nibbling on her lip, seemingly more upset than he'd first thought. Agatha's sudden screeching had him wincing and returning his attention to the argument at hand.

"Honestly, Father, I have had enough," Agatha railed. "For one, I'm nineteen, which makes me an adult, and for two, I'm tired of the constant parade of hopeful gentlemen you've put before me, each of them—well, except for you, Mr. Beckett," she said with a nod to Hamilton, "only interested in me because of the huge price you've put on my head. I've tried to be patient, but I'm at the end of my rope. I have no intention of marrying anyone in the near future."

Mr. Watson stared at his daughter for a full minute before he swiveled his head and glared at his wife. "This is your fault. You've been too lenient with the child."

"Honestly, Roger," Mrs. Watson whispered, "you're embarrassing me quite dreadfully. What must Mr. Beckett think of us?" She sent Hamilton a smile. "I fear we're a bit overwrought at the moment, Mr. Beckett. You simply must forgive us. Agatha is certainly not the hoyden she's currently portraying. I can only believe her behavior is the result of spending time with Miss Sumner. When I hired her, I had no idea she would lead my children astray."

Eliza began sputtering, much like Agatha had done only moments before. Hamilton watched as she drew a deep breath, and when she obviously believed herself to be somewhat under control, opened her mouth.

"When I set out this evening, Mrs. Watson, it was not my intention to lead your daughter 'astray.' Unfortunately, Miss Watson and I incurred a small bit of trouble, but truly, it was a big misunderstanding, and as there was actually no harm done, I hope we can put this matter firmly behind us."

"No harm done?" Mrs. Watson asked. "Of course there was harm done. Why, just look at the two of you. I've never seen Agatha's hair and clothing in such a state, and I haven't even started on your appearance." Mrs. Watson's eyes took on a dangerous glint. "Where, pray tell, have you left your girth?"

"Yes, good point, Cora," Mr. Watson exclaimed as he took a step closer to Eliza and looked her up and down. "I would have to believe, given the circumstances of this evening and the fact that you have obviously taken steps to disguise your true appearance, that you must be a criminal of some sort and have entered into employment with my family under false pretenses."

"I'm not a criminal," Eliza said.

Mr. Watson ignored her statement. "I would bet that accent of yours is as misleading as your appearance. Tell me, what is your true purpose regarding my family?"

"I think this conversation is getting completely out of hand," Hamilton interjected as he casually placed himself in front of Eliza. He'd detected a slight trembling of her lips and knew she was a hair away from dissolving into tears. For some reason, that bothered him more than he cared to admit. There was just something about her that tugged at him. Perhaps it was because he'd discovered she was carrying the weight of the world on her exceedingly slim shoulders. Or maybe it was because even though both Mr. and Mrs. Watson were screaming at her, she'd never once tried to throw the blame for their misadventure at Agatha, who, he was convinced, hadn't given Eliza any choice about letting her tag along. "I'm certain the ladies are beyond exhausted, and I think it might be for the best if this conversation waited to take place until the morning."

Mr. Watson drew himself up. "I won't have that woman under my roof another minute. I have three daughters at home, Mr. Beckett, and as you have a daughter of your own, I'm certain you'll understand my reasoning. Would you allow a woman of questionable character to mingle with your child?"

"Miss Sumner does not have a questionable character," Hamilton said. "If you only knew who—"

"There's no need to get into that," Eliza said, speaking up and cutting off Hamilton's statement. "Mr. Watson is perfectly within his rights to dismiss me, although I would appreciate being allowed time to pack my bags."

"That's ridiculous," Agatha snapped. "You've done nothing wrong, Eliza."

"Good evening," Zayne said as he materialized out of the darkness and strode to Hamilton's side. "I do hope I'm not interrupting."

"About time you got here," Hamilton muttered.

"I had to run down your horse," Zayne said out of the side of his mouth. "I don't think the animal appreciated all of the screaming and seemed to be intent on leaving without you." He turned to Mrs. Watson and sent her a charming smile. "Now, what did I miss?"

"There is no need for you to trouble yourself with this nasty business, Mr. Beckett," Mrs. Watson said with what appeared to be a forced smile. "My husband and I are more than capable of dealing with that woman, a woman who, I might add, took it upon herself to encourage my daughter to get into some type of mischief."

"I understand the reasoning behind your anger," Zayne said in a soothing tone. "Since I have no children of my own, I can't say I've ever experienced quite what you've gone through this evening, but, seeing as the lovely Miss Watson has been safely returned to you, there was no harm done and all's well that ends well."

Mrs. Watson ignored Zayne's remark as a crafty gleam entered her eyes. "Why were you and your brother riding down our street in such close proximity to our home at this unusual hour?"

Zayne shot a look to Hamilton as if to ask how he was supposed to answer. Hamilton shrugged, having no idea how Zayne should respond.

"You might as well tell them the truth," Agatha said.

Mr. Watson narrowed his eyes. "Am I to understand the four of you were together this evening?"

"In a manner of speaking," Hamilton replied. "We didn't start out that way, but Zayne and I . . . encountered Miss Sumner and your daughter . . ."

"Yes?" Mrs. Watson prompted.

"They had to rescue us from jail," Agatha blurted.

Silence descended. Hamilton was almost afraid to look at Mr. Watson, knowing without a doubt the gentleman was not going to react well to that piece of information. A mere second later, this was confirmed.

"You were in jail?" Mr. Watson thundered in Agatha's direction.

"I was, but in my defense, it was all a complete misunderstanding. It could have happened to anyone," Agatha said.

"Yes, but it didn't happen to just 'anyone,' it happened to you," Mr. Watson raged before spinning to Eliza. "Explain yourself."

"Uhh . . ."

"Never mind," Mr. Watson snapped. "You're hardly likely to tell me the truth." He stared at her for a moment and then nodded. "You may consider yourself dismissed, effective immediately."

"Father, again, it wasn't her fault," Agatha said. "I insisted on joining her tonight, even though she tried to protest. Besides, you know Reverend Fraser was just saying this morning we should show our fellow man compassion. I highly doubt God would look kindly on your tossing Miss Sumner into the streets."

"My compassion only goes so far," Mr. Watson said between gritted teeth before he looked at Eliza. "I will send your belongings to you after you find a new place to stay. Given the fact that my daughter is partly to blame for this situation, I will include your wages along with your possessions. I will not, however, include a letter of reference. Heaven forbid you move to another family and put them through the same distress you've caused mine."

Hamilton stepped forward. "You may send her possessions to my house."

Eliza sucked in a sharp breath of air, but before he had an opportunity to reassure her that everything would be fine, Mr. Watson interrupted.

"You're not thinking clearly, Mr. Beckett. Society will be all atwitter if it becomes known you've extended your hospitality to this . . . this . . . woman."

"As my mother is currently in residence at my house, there will be no reason for any talk," Hamilton said. "We often entertain guests, and that is exactly how we're going to treat Miss Sumner."

"But . . . what about Agatha?" Mr. Watson asked.

Hamilton wasn't certain what Mr. Watson was suggesting. He released a sigh. "If you're determined to throw her out in the streets as well, then by all means, she's more than welcome to come along with Miss Sumner."

Mr. Watson began to sputter. "That's not what I meant at all, Mr. Beckett. I was referring to the fact that I thought you and my daughter shared a common affection for one another."

"He has not listened to a word I've said," Agatha grouched, sending Hamilton a look of apology before turning back to her father. "Mr. Beckett is a lovely gentleman, to be sure, as is his brother, but there's no affection shared between any of us. You need to accept that." She turned to Eliza. "You should go with Mr. Beckett for now, Eliza. He'll look after you and help you with . . . you know."

Eliza looked as if she didn't know what she should do. She bit her lip and then lifted her gaze, her somewhat forlorn expression causing Hamilton to feel an odd jolt run through him. "You don't have to do this," she whispered.

"You're wrong," he said.

"I could stay in a hotel."

"You don't have any money," Agatha said.

"It's settled, then," Zayne said briskly, before he turned and made his way back to his horse. "Shall we go? I, for one, am anxious to return home."

"Now, just one minute," Mr. Watson said. "I don't understand what's going on here." He looked at Hamilton. "You're making a big mistake. She's not to be trusted."

Hamilton glanced at Eliza and felt a smile tug his lips. She was gazing back at him, her eyes wide and somewhat wary, and he knew in that instant Mr. Watson was wrong; Eliza was completely trustworthy, and he needed to take her home with him.

She was a damsel in distress, and for some odd reason he knew he was the man who was supposed to rescue her.

He took Eliza by the arm and guided her to his recently returned horse, nodding once to Mr. and Mrs. Watson, even as the thought came to him that his life was becoming stranger by the second, and for some reason, it didn't bother him in the least.

8

*I*s she dead?"

Eliza was having the loveliest dream regarding a dashing hero who just happened to look exactly like Hamilton, but it seemed somewhat odd to have that particular question interrupt it. A sudden sharp pain in her arm dispersed the last vestiges of sleep as her eyes flashed open and she bolted straight upright in bed. She was met by the sight of an angelic-looking boy with black hair peering over the edge at her.

"Did you just bite me?" she demanded.

The little boy nodded.

"We thought you were dead."

Eliza shifted her attention to a beautiful little girl with golden curls.

"Why would you think I was dead?"

The little girl shrugged. "You weren't moving."

"I was asleep."

"But you could have been dead," the little girl proclaimed.

"Obviously, I wasn't," Eliza pointed out as she rubbed her arm where a welt was developing. She glanced to the boy. "It's never permissible to bite another person."

The boy's lower lip began to tremble. "Sorry," he muttered, his large hazel eyes filling with tears.

Eliza swallowed a sigh as her heart melted. She couldn't very well stay angry at the child, given that he was seemingly distressed over his actions. She patted the edge of the bed. "Perhaps you would feel better if you sat down."

The little boy's tears disappeared as he scrambled up on the bed and beamed back at her, revealing a mouth full of sharp little teeth. Eliza resisted the urge to scoot away from him. "What's your name?"

"Benjamin," he said before he plopped his thumb in his mouth.

"Well, Benjamin, I can only hope it was an uncommon occurrence for you to bite my arm, and I'm hopeful you've learned your lesson and will refrain from sinking your teeth into any other unsuspecting target."

"He goes by Ben," the little girl said. "He bites people all the time. Grandmother doesn't know what to do about it. She keeps saying he'll grow out of it, but I told her not to get her hopes up. I'm Piper."

Eliza smiled. "I don't think I've ever met anyone by the name of Piper. It's a very pretty name."

"It's not my real name. My real name's Penelope, but I don't know what my mother was thinking, naming me that."

"I see," Eliza said, suddenly realizing she was almost certainly in the presence of Hamilton's children, given that they bore a marked resemblance to him. Well, mostly Ben bore a resemblance. Piper was possessed of a delicate face with beautiful bone structure, and Eliza could only assume she took after her mother. Hamilton's deceased wife must have been absolutely stunning if Piper had gotten her looks from her. That thought caused an annoying twinge of something that felt almost like jealousy to stir.

"Am I interrupting?"

Eliza let out a yelp when she noticed Hamilton lounging in the doorway. She snagged the counterpane and pulled it up to her neck. Unfortunately, her action had poor Ben tumbling off the bed and landing with a soft thud on the floor.

"Good heavens, Ben, I'm so sorry," she exclaimed, fighting to untangle herself from the counterpane before jumping off the bed and kneeling beside the child. "Are you all right?"

"Why is she wearing trousers, Daddy?" Piper asked.

Eliza glanced down and discovered Piper was right. She'd forgotten the fact that she'd pulled off her skirt before she'd collapsed on the bed and now . . . honestly, she felt more than embarrassed. To avoid looking at Hamilton while she was so rattled, she settled her attention on Ben, who was still lying on the floor, gazing back at her with clear reproach in his little eyes. "May I help you up?"

He shook his head.

"I'll do it," Hamilton said as he moved past her and scooped Ben up into his arms. He sent her a smile. "I'm sorry I wasn't here to perform proper introductions, seeing as how my children somehow managed to get out of the nursery undetected, but no need to get into that just yet. Piper, Ben, this is Miss Sumner. She's a guest of ours and will be staying with us for a few weeks."

"She knocked me off the bed," Ben said before he stuck his thumb in his mouth and buried his head in Hamilton's shoulder.

"She didn't mean to, Ben," Piper said. "Besides, now you're even, since you bit her."

Hamilton frowned. "We've talked about this, Ben. You promised me you weren't going to bite anymore."

"Dead," Ben muttered.

"I'm sorry?" Hamilton asked.

"They thought I was dead," Eliza clarified, the sight of Hamilton cradling his son doing strange things to her heart. There was something so sweet and yet masculine about his manner that she found herself longing for . . . she blinked and shook herself, relieved to discover Hamilton hadn't appeared to notice her distraction as his attention was directed at his children.

"Why did you think Miss Sumner was dead?" he asked.

"Miss Brighton read us a story about a dead lady, and the lady in the book was not moving at all, just like Miss Sumner," Piper said.

Hamilton narrowed his eyes. "Your nanny was reading you a story about a dead lady?"

Piper nodded and took a seat on the edge of the bed. "It was a great story, Daddy. There was a murder and a mad scientist."

"I think I'll have to have a little chat with your nanny. Stories about murder, dead ladies, and mad scientists are hardly appropriate for a five- and a three-year-old," Hamilton said.

"You can't have a chat with her because she's . . ." Piper's voice faltered as she suddenly jumped off the bed and edged her way to the door. "I'm starving. I think I'll go find some breakfast."

"What did you do to the nanny, Piper?" Hamilton asked, causing Piper to stop in her tracks and release a rather dramatic sigh. She suddenly brightened. "Hello, Grandmother."

"Ah, I thought I heard voices," a woman said from the doorway. "What are the three of you doing . . . I wasn't aware we had a guest."

"Daddy brought her home last night," Piper explained.

The woman arched a brow.

"Mother, don't jump to conclusions," Hamilton said. "This lady is a friend of mine, Miss Eliza Sumner. Miss Sumner, this is my mother, Mrs. Gloria Beckett."

"A pleasure to meet you," Eliza said, feeling her face flush under Gloria's sharp regard.

"You brought her home last night?" Gloria asked as she advanced into the room.

"It was really late, Grandmother. I saw them," Piper said.

Hamilton set Ben down before he turned to Piper. "Why were you out of bed in the middle of the night? Where was Miss Brighton?"

Eliza bit back a grin when she noticed a shifty expression cross Piper's face. She looked down in surprise and found that Ben had obviously forgiven her and was now pressing his small body against her leg as he peered from his sister to his father. It was rapidly becoming apparent the two children had gotten themselves into a bit of mischief.

"Miss Brighton is no longer in our employ," Gloria said.

"That's why I said you couldn't chat with her," Piper said. "She's gone."

"Why?"

"Well, you couldn't talk to someone who isn't here, Daddy."

"You know that's not what I was asking."

"Grandmother, did I tell you how really late it was when Daddy brought this lady home?"

Eliza turned her head away when a laugh took her by surprise. Piper was completely precocious and, if Eliza was not mistaken, more than a handful.

"Piper," Hamilton growled, "enough. You will explain to me exactly what happened to Miss Brighton."

"Why do you always think it's me?" Piper demanded, planting her hands on her slim hips.

"Because Ben is only three, and you've been responsible for the last four nannies leaving in high dudgeon."

"What does that mean?"

"Mad."

"Miss Brighton wasn't really mad," Piper said slowly.

"She was scared," Ben said.

"Scared?" Hamilton questioned.

"I didn't know she was afraid of spiders," Piper explained with a huff as if she could not understand that particular matter in the least. She turned to Eliza. "Are you afraid of spiders?"

The corners of Eliza's mouth twitched before she shook her head.

"See? Miss Sumner isn't afraid of spiders. Maybe she should be our new nanny."

"We're not speaking of Miss Sumner, Piper. We're speaking about Miss Brighton. What did you do to her?" Hamilton asked.

Piper bit her lip and then began to speak very quickly as though, by getting the words out fast, they wouldn't be as telling. "I tossed Herman to her."

"Herman?"

"He's my pet spider."

"You don't have a pet spider," Hamilton pointed out.

"Well, not anymore, since Miss Brighton squashed him." Piper summoned up a tragic expression earning a full-out grin from Eliza. "It was horrible, Daddy. Guts were everywhere."

"Guts," Ben proclaimed with a bob of his head.

Hamilton closed his eyes, and Eliza noticed his mouth moving, even though no sounds were coming out of it. He seemed to be silently counting.

"May I assume you retaliated against Miss Brighton for squashing your spider?" Hamilton finally asked.

A mulish expression crossed Piper's face. "I don't know what 'retaliated' means."

"It means you did something to get back at Miss Brighton."

"Oh."

"Well?"

"Piper threw Herman's body at Miss Brighton," Ben said, earning himself a scowl from his sister in the process.

"Please tell me your aim wasn't good," Hamilton pleaded.

"Herman landed on her face," Piper admitted rather reluctantly.

"Then I bit her leg 'cause Miss Brighton yelled at Pip," Ben explained, his lower lip trembling once again.

Hamilton squatted down next to Ben. "Did that frighten you?'

"Yep."

"Miss Brighton had a reason to yell, Ben. Piper did throw a spider at her, and that wasn't a very nice thing to do."

"It wasn't very nice of Miss Brighton to stomp on my Herman either, Daddy, and then she screamed at Ben for biting her, even though there wasn't any blood, and Ben started crying and that's when—" Piper suddenly stopped speaking and began once again to edge her way to the door.

"There's more?" Hamilton asked.

Piper stopped moving and her shoulders drooped. "I let Charlie out."

"You didn't," Hamilton said.

"Who's Charlie?" Eliza asked.

"Charlie's our neurotic dog. He took an immediate dislike to Miss Brighton," Hamilton explained. "Dare I ask what happened next?"

"Charlie chased her to her room, where she barely took any time to pack," Gloria said, speaking up at last.

"So we're short one nanny again?" Hamilton asked.

"I'm too old for a nanny anyways, Daddy," Piper said.

"I don't want a nanny either," Ben said. "Sometimes they spank me."

Eliza drew in a sharp breath. She patted Ben's head. "I could be their nanny."

"You're a nanny?" Ben whispered, sidling away from her leg before he sent her an accusing look.

"No, but I could learn how," Eliza said. "It can't be much different than being a governess."

"Out of the question," Gloria snapped. "I know nothing about this woman, not even the reason she's currently residing in our special guest room."

"'Cause she's special," Ben said, scooting back to Eliza's side. Eliza beamed at the little boy.

"Miss Sumner is too pretty to be a nanny," Piper remarked to no one in particular.

"She's not too pretty to be our mama," Ben said.

Eliza looked up, only to discover Hamilton watching her in a somewhat disconcerting manner. She felt heat rush over her face even as a tingle of something traveled through her, but she refused to acknowledge the tingle, knowing that, with a suspicious and annoyed mother in the room, she needed to keep her wits firmly about her. She dropped her gaze and settled it on Ben, wondering how to reply to his statement. She was spared a response when Hamilton stepped in.

"Miss Sumner is not here to be your mama, Ben. She lives in England and will be going back there soon, but until that time, I'm sure she'd love to be your friend."

Eliza felt a sliver of disappointment stab her at Hamilton's words. She bit back a snort. Honestly, what had she expected the gentleman to say? That Ben was right and Hamilton was going to immediately ask for her hand? She blinked back to reality when Gloria strode across the room and stopped right in front of her. Eliza resisted the urge to bolt.

"It is past time I got some answers," Gloria said. "I have no idea what's going on, but I fear something quite shady is transpiring."

"There is nothing 'shady' at all regarding this situation," Hamilton said. "May I suggest we allow Miss Sumner an opportunity to freshen up, and then we'll continue this discussion over breakfast?"

"She's staying for breakfast?" Gloria asked.

"Grandmother," Piper admonished, "you've forgotten your manners."

"There are some situations, my dear," Gloria returned, "where manners are overrated."

Eliza sighed and looked at Piper. "Maybe it would be best if you were to take your brother and go have your breakfast. Your grandmother obviously has questions for me, and some of those questions may not be appropriate for tender ears."

"My ears aren't tender," Piper protested, reaching up to feel her ears.

"Of course not, you're five," Eliza said, "but your brother is only three, and from what I can hear at the moment, his stomach is grumbling."

"We don't have anyone to watch out for us, and Grandmother always likes us to say a blessing before we eat, but I can't re-member all the words and then God will be mad at me, so we should just wait until everyone can eat breakfast together," Piper said with a nod.

"I thought you told your father you didn't need a nanny to watch out for you, and I'm certain God would understand if you didn't get the blessing exactly right," Eliza said.

Piper looked as if she wanted to argue, but then, to Eliza's surprise, she marched across the room, took Ben by the hand, and pulled him through the door without another word. Eliza chanced a glance at Hamilton and found him watching her with amusement dancing in his eyes.

"You might just make a good nanny, Miss Sumner," he said. "I've never seen Piper cooperate quite so easily."

"Since it appears you have no nanny readily available to care for your children, I really must reiterate that I would feel better regarding my situation if you would allow me to earn my keep. I'm not comfortable accepting charity."

"My hospitality is not charity," Hamilton said.

"What would you call it, then?" Eliza asked.

"Hospitality," Hamilton returned with a grin.

Eliza's breath caught in her throat. He was such an appealing gentleman, especially when he smiled, that she was having a very difficult time remembering the small fact that she wasn't in a position to lose sight of her more important goal. She forced her gaze away from him, only to discover Gloria watching her with what could only be described as confusion on her face.

"Would someone please explain to me what's going on here?" Gloria demanded.

Hamilton moved to Gloria's side and gestured her into a chair before he looked at Eliza. "Would you like me to tell her or do you care to do the honors?"

"I think you'd do a better job of it," Eliza muttered, moving to a chair by the side of the bed and taking a seat, suddenly coming to the realization that she'd forgotten all about the fact that she was currently garbed in trousers. It was little wonder Hamilton's mother was confused. A grin teased her lips when she also remembered the fact that her hair had been beyond untamed last night, and she shuddered to think what it looked like now after a long sleep. She folded her hands into her lap and hoped she presented a somewhat demure picture.

"I suppose I should start at the beginning," Hamilton said, taking a seat beside his mother.

"I always find that's the most prudent place to start," Gloria said.

9

One hour later, Eliza found herself at the mercy of a maid named Mabel, who apparently took every word Gloria said to heart and was now diligently applying herself to the task of making Eliza "appear her best." She winced when hot tongs nearly burned off a layer of her scalp, but she didn't utter a sound, still too amazed at the latest turn of events to even consider voicing a protest about the attention she was now receiving.

She'd been certain Gloria would show her the door after she learned all the particulars regarding her less than honest means of tracking down Bartholomew Hayes, including posing as a governess and taking advantage of the Watson family. Such had not been the case. Gloria had listened to her story, asking a few questions here and there, and when Eliza was finished with her tale, Gloria had sent her a rather alarming look before turning to Hamilton and ordering him from the room before she'd summoned Mabel.

Eliza was a bit concerned regarding the seemingly ever-present glint in Gloria's eyes, but with all the scrubbing, pulling, and curling, she'd not had a moment to contemplate the matter further.

"Ah, good, your hair is almost done," Gloria exclaimed, striding into the room with her arms laden with clothing. "I took the liberty of bringing you some of my daughter's gowns. They won't be a perfect fit, but seeing as how Mr. Watson has not yet had the common courtesy to send your possessions over, Arabella's gowns will have to do."

"Won't Arabella mind my absconding with her gowns?"

"Hardly, she has an entire wardrobe filled with gowns she's never worn," Gloria said. "Besides, Arabella isn't currently at home. She's traveling out west with my husband, Douglas, who needed to go to California to check on a railroading venture he's involved in at the moment."

"Did you not care to take the trip with them?" Eliza asked.

"Truth be told, I normally do accompany Douglas on his adventures, but since my grandbabies are without a proper mother, I decided it would be best if I stayed close to home for the moment."

The gleam in Gloria's eyes intensified, causing alarm to course through Eliza's veins.

The woman was up to something, and Eliza had a sneaky suspicion that something concerned a proper mother for Piper and Ben. She opted to change the subject and prayed Gloria was the type of woman to become easily distracted.

"What does Arabella do when she travels with her father?"

"She's a strong supporter of the women's suffrage movement and adores nothing more than attending rallies to spread the word. I'm sure the two of you will get along famously after she returns to town."

Eliza winced when Mabel took that moment to give a last

tug to her hair before she stepped aside and gestured to the privacy screen. Eliza rose from the chair, moved to where Mabel indicated, and accepted the clothes Gloria tossed over to her. She shrugged out of the dressing gown she was wearing, slipped into the soft undergarments, and waited for Mabel to lace her up before pulling the gown over her head.

"I don't want to disappoint you, Mrs. Beckett," she said as she stepped out from behind the screen, "but I'm not sure I'll still be around to make your daughter's acquaintance. I do need to return to England."

Gloria muttered something undetectable under her breath before she smiled. "Don't you look pretty as a picture in lavender? Hamilton will be completely delighted."

Obviously that had been a glint in Gloria's eyes, and apparently the woman was already scheming. Eliza took a deep breath, but before she could get a single statement out of her mouth, such as the fact that she was not in the market for a man, Gloria turned on her heel and strode out of the room.

Now, that was odd and more than a little abrupt.

"Aren't you coming?" Gloria asked, poking her head back through the door. "The morning is almost gone, and I, for one, am famished. We'll join Piper and Ben in the dining room."

She'd forgotten all about Piper and Ben. "Surely they won't still be there, will they?" she asked as she moved across the room and walked with Gloria down a long hallway.

Gloria smiled. "I have not heard any sounds of disaster, so I'm hopeful they are indeed still in the dining room."

"What if they're not?"

"It might be best not to even consider that idea," Gloria muttered.

They reached the bottom of the stairs, and Eliza took a moment to glance around, appreciating the tasteful, yet luxurious décor surrounding her.

"It is quite lovely here," she finally said.

"Could do with a woman's touch," Gloria said with a wide smile and a knowing wink.

"Then I suppose it is fortunate your son has you around," Eliza said with a wink of her own.

"I would not dream of offering Hamilton suggestions on décor," Gloria said. "That decision really should be left to a wife."

The conversation was becoming downright disturbing. Eliza opened her mouth even as her mind struggled to find a suitable reply, but her response was cut off when Piper took that moment to stomp into view.

"I thought everyone was going to join me and Ben for breakfast," Piper grouched as she came to a stop right in front of Eliza and sent Gloria an injured look. "We waited and waited, and then, well, we finally had to eat, but what if Ben or I'd choked? Who'd have been there to save us?"

"Do you and Ben make a habit of choking on your food?" Eliza asked.

"They've never once choked," Gloria said with a roll of her eyes.

"You always say it's better to be safe than sorry," Piper returned. "Food can be dangerous."

Eliza grinned. "I'm sorry we didn't join you, Piper, but your grandmother thought it best for me to freshen up before we left the room. Quite frankly, I wouldn't have felt comfortable sitting down to dine dressed in trousers."

Piper eyed her for a moment. "Do you only wear trousers when you're up to something shifty? Miss Brighton read me a book about ladies who were criminals, and it said they were shifty. I don't know what 'shifty' means, but I think it has something to do with women wearing trousers."

"Once again I find myself questioning the employment of

Miss Brighton," Gloria mumbled before she took Piper by the arm and began tugging her down another hallway, Eliza following a few steps behind. "Piper, Miss Sumner isn't a criminal, but a member of British high society. Her proper form of address is Lady Eliza Sumner, but she prefers, for the moment, to be called Miss Sumner." She stopped walking and frowned. "Speaking of criminals, I still don't understand why the London authorities didn't take any action against Mr. Hayes or help you find him, especially as you are indeed an aristocrat."

"Mr. Hayes was so convincing with his lies that even Scotland Yard dismissed my accusations." She heaved a sigh. "I was actually told they found me to be a touch delusional."

"What's 'delusional'?" Piper asked.

"Crazy," Gloria said.

"Miss Sumner doesn't seem crazy."

"Thank you, Piper. It's very reassuring to know someone finds me sane," Eliza said with a grin.

"I hope you won't think me too forward, Miss Sumner," Gloria began, "but I'm acquainted with quite a few people over in England, some of them involved in the highest levels of government. Would you mind if I wrote them regarding your situation? They might be able to lend some assistance in restoring your father's good name."

"I wouldn't want to put you through the bother, Mrs. Beckett."

"It wouldn't be a bother, my dear, and please, call me Gloria."

Eliza felt her eyes well with tears as she realized there were still people left in the world who were possessed of compassion, people who wished to help her for no other reason than wanting to extend her a kindness. Her world tilted on the spot.

"Thank you," she finally managed to say. "You must call me Eliza."

"Why is your voice all shaky?" Piper asked.

Eliza was spared having to respond when Gloria began

walking again, pulling Piper beside her. They entered the dining room and her gaze settled on Ben, who was slouching in a
chair. His head shot up and a smile that reminded Eliza exactly
of Hamilton's smile spread over his face. She moved to the chair
right next to him, waited until a servant pulled it out for her,
and then sat down, completely charmed when Ben pushed a
muffin in front of her, a muffin sporting what appeared to be
tiny teeth marks on one side.

"I saved this for you," he said before he plopped his thumb
into his mouth.

"Thank you, Ben," Eliza said before she picked up the muffin
and took a bite. She swallowed and smiled. "It's delicious, the
best muffin I've ever eaten."

Ben grinned around his thumb and edged a little closer to
her, his plump arm brushing against her sleeve.

"Ah, finally I've discovered everyone's whereabouts," Hamilton said as he strode into the room. He bent over when Piper
let out a squeal and rushed to his side, and Eliza's heart melted
when he scooped his daughter into his arms and placed a loud
kiss on her cheek. "Are you enjoying your morning, darling?"
he asked.

Piper shook her head. "We were abandoned until just now
and . . . Ben gave Miss Sumner a muffin. He never gives me
muffins."

"'Cause you're my sister," Ben stated as if that explained
everything.

Eliza shifted her attention back to Hamilton and discovered
him giving her a somewhat lingering perusal. She felt her pulse
gallop through her veins under his intense regard and wondered
what he was thinking.

"Doesn't Eliza look enchanting?" Gloria asked.

"She looks . . . lovely."

Although "lovely" could certainly be considered a compliment, there was a distinct note of what sounded almost like disgruntlement in his voice.

Did he find something lacking in her intricately styled hair, or could he not appreciate the way the lavender color of his sister's gown brought out the blue of her eyes?

Could he be comparing her with his beautiful, yet apparently troubled, deceased wife?

That was not something Eliza wanted to consider. To hide her discomfort, because his gaze was becoming more disconcerting by the second, she stuffed a piece of muffin into her mouth and promptly choked.

Hamilton set Piper down, strode to her side, and pounded her soundly on the back.

"I'm fine," she managed to gasp as he continued to pound.

"See?" Piper said. "I told you food was dangerous."

Eliza choked again when a laugh took her by surprise, accepted the glass of water a servant pressed into her hands, and took a sip, willing her pulse to settle. For some unknown reason, it was racing as if she'd just performed an exacting task.

If only Hamilton would move away from her, maybe she'd be able to collect her scattered wits.

It was beyond disturbing, this reaction she kept having whenever he was near.

She chanced a glance at Gloria and found her watching Hamilton with what could only be described as delight.

This was bad; Gloria seemed to have found something encouraging in her son's behavior, although what could be encouraging about a gentleman who was now glowering in Eliza's direction was beyond her. If she didn't regain control of the situation, Gloria would soon start planning a wedding, with or without her consent.

"Has there been any word from Mr. Watson?" Eliza asked when she finally recovered her voice, hoping that would put an end to all the pesky plots that were apparently swirling around her.

"We do not need to talk about him at the moment," Gloria said with a pointed look to Piper and Ben. "Besides, we have more important matters to discuss."

It was truly remarkable how innocent Gloria could appear, especially when she was clearly pursuing some ulterior motive.

"What important matters?" Eliza found herself asking.

"We need to take you shopping. Arabella's gowns will do well in a pinch, but you really deserve garments tailored to your own personal style."

That certainly wasn't what she'd expected to come out of Gloria's mouth. "I have no desire to go shopping," Eliza said slowly.

"Nonsense, Eliza, every woman adores shopping. I simply must take you to the Ladies Mile or Fashion Row, and we can take the El to get there," Gloria said with an innocent smile.

"I love the El," Piper said.

That explained the innocent smile.

Feeling decidedly outnumbered, Eliza released a huff. "What, pray tell, is the El?"

"It's a raised train," Hamilton explained. "It's one of the easiest ways to get around the city, and Piper enjoys traveling on it."

"Of course we would take Piper with us," Gloria said.

The woman apparently had no qualms about using her granddaughter as a pawn in whatever diabolical plot she was currently conceiving. "I don't want to disappoint Piper, but if you've forgotten, I'm trying to remain unnoticed at the moment."

"I highly doubt you'll be recognized on the crowded streets of New York," Gloria replied.

Eliza crossed her arms over her chest. "You may very well have a point, but I just remembered the small fact I have no funds available to me at the moment, seeing as how all of my belongings and wages are still back at the Watson residence. Besides," she continued when Gloria opened her mouth, "even if I did have my funds with me, they are relatively limited, and I do not have the luxury of wasting them on trivial purchases."

"Proper clothing is hardly trivial," Gloria muttered.

"I would be more than happy to provide you with funds," Hamilton said, speaking up as he smiled one of his devastating smiles in Eliza's direction.

It took her a few seconds to gather her thoughts, and when she finally collected them, she felt more confused than ever. Why was he being so pleasant when, mere moments before, he'd seemed rather distant and almost surly?

The only explanation that came to her was that gentlemen were obviously odd beings, and she should not even attempt to understand them.

"I do appreciate the offer, Mr. Beckett, but it would not be proper to accept money from you, considering I'm already accepting your hospitality," she finally said. "I'm not comfortable, as I've stated numerous times, accepting charity."

"It would have been fun," Piper said softly, drawing Eliza's attention. She couldn't help but notice the way Piper was standing a little away from the table, scuffing the toe of her shoe against the floor. As she continued to watch the child, a memory of her mother flashed to mind, a memory of shopping and the delight Eliza had felt as she'd accompanied her mother down Bond Street. Piper would never have such memories, as her mother was long dead.

Admitting defeat, she rolled her eyes. "Very well, I'll go shopping, but I'm not purchasing anything."

"Fair enough," Gloria said. "At least it will allow us an opportunity to become better acquainted. Do you have any plans for the rest of the day?"

"As long as we return by nightfall, I'm more than happy to go today," Eliza said.

Eliza blinked when Hamilton let out a grunt.

"What are you planning on doing after nightfall?" he demanded.

"I have to continue with what I was doing last night," Eliza said.

"That is out of the question."

"Oh dear," Gloria muttered as she jumped out of her chair, plucked Ben up in her arms, and took Piper by the hand, not speaking another word as she quickly ushered the children out of the dining room, leaving only a charged silence in her wake.

10

*H*amilton watched as Eliza pushed back her chair, got to her feet, squared her shoulders, opened her mouth, and then, to his surprise, snapped it shut. She leveled a chilling look filled with disdain in his direction, tilted her chin, which he absently noted was rather endearing, and then turned on her heel and stalked from the room without speaking a single word.

For a moment, he simply stood there, pondering what had just happened.

He knew perfectly well he was right regarding the fact that Eliza could not be let loose on the streets of New York. There was no telling what mischief the lady would find, and if she was even thinking about returning to Lord Southmoor's home, well, it didn't bear contemplating what disaster waited for her there.

Still, his reaction to her declaration might have come off a touch pompous, but surely she understood he only wanted to keep her safe?

He released a breath and made for the door, pausing in the hallway when he couldn't find a trace of her.

"She went that way," Piper said from the stairwell, pointing down the hall.

"Thank you, Piper, but I must remind you that you're not allowed to eavesdrop on people."

"What does 'eavesdrop' mean?"

"Listening in on conversations you're not meant to hear," he said before setting his sights on the corridor.

"But you didn't say anything," Piper called after him.

Hamilton swallowed a laugh and continued forward, sticking his head in every room without finding Eliza until he found himself in the kitchen. His cook and two maids were pressed up against the window, whispering something he couldn't hear. Their whispering came to an abrupt end when he cleared his throat.

"Mr. Beckett," Mrs. Whitehouse, his cook, exclaimed. "What are you doing in the kitchen?"

"I'm looking for Miss Sumner."

Mrs. Whitehouse gestured to the back door. "She went that way."

Hamilton nodded and strode across the room, stopping when Mrs. Whitehouse stepped into his path.

"You might take the poor dear a coat," she said. "Although, by the expression on her face, the lady is furious at the moment and might not even feel the cold."

Hamilton plucked a coat off the rack by the door, sent Mrs. Whitehouse a smile, and made his exit before his cook gave any other suggestions. He'd been surrounded by women all his life, and he was more than familiar with their ability to stick together. He reached the dirt path leading into the garden and made his way through the hedges, stopping when he spotted Eliza standing by the garden wall.

"I brought you a coat," he said.

"I'm not cold," she said even as she shivered.

"If it makes you feel any better, Mrs. Whitehouse is the one who suggested I bring this to you."

"Well, if Mrs. Whitehouse was so kind as to worry over my welfare, it would be churlish of me to refuse."

Hamilton refused to grin as he took a step forward, intent on placing the coat around Eliza's slim shoulders. He stopped when she made a sound like an angry cat, and he settled for holding it out to her. She snatched the coat from his hand and slipped it on.

"I would prefer to be alone," she said with a sniff.

"I'm afraid you'll have to suffer my company for a few more minutes, Miss Sumner. I owe you an apology."

"Too right you do," Eliza said. "You have no authority over me, Mr. Beckett, and it was not well done. . . ."

Hamilton found it difficult to concentrate on what Eliza was saying. Her lips were moving rapidly, but he couldn't actually decipher what the words coming out of her mouth were. It was such a lovely mouth, and he found it quite quirky, given the fact that it could assume different positions with alarming frequency. Like now, it was pursed in a most attractive manner, and now . . . it was moving again as if the lady could not get the words out fast enough. His gaze traveled upward, past eyes that were flashing, and settled on her hair. He couldn't help but appreciate the efforts of Mabel. The curls she'd been able to produce on Eliza's head, well, they were tantalizing. He had the strangest urge to reach out and touch them, to feel with his own hand if they were as soft as they appeared, something he'd been contemplating ever since he got a good look at her in the dining room. He pulled abruptly back to reality when Eliza poked him in the chest.

"Stop smiling."

"I'm not."

"Why are your lips curled up, then?"

Hamilton forced his lips into a straight line. "Better?"

Eliza let out a snort before she turned on her heel and strode to a stone bench. He wondered if she expected him to follow. He took one step, but paused when she sent him another glare. He watched as she plopped down and turned her head in the opposite direction.

She was adorable when she sulked.

"May I join you?" he asked a minute later, swallowing a laugh when she swiveled her head, sent him a sniff, and then returned to staring at something apparently riveting over her shoulder.

Deciding he might as well take his chances, he moved to the bench and sat down, his amusement increasing by the second when she inched away from him. "It was not well done of me to make that statement," he began.

"On that we can agree," Eliza said.

"I just want to keep you safe."

"That's not your problem."

"You're a guest in my home, and I feel responsible for you."

"I can leave."

Hamilton waited to continue until she finally turned her head. He released a sigh. "Have you ever felt you were in danger of repeating mistakes you made in the past?"

"I'm afraid I don't understand what you're saying."

"Have you heard anything regarding Mary Ellen?"

"Agatha told me your wife died. I'm sorry for your loss," Eliza said, her glare softening to a mild glower.

"I was to blame for her death."

Eliza tilted her head. "For some reason, I find that difficult to believe."

"It's the truth. That's why I said I was in danger of repeating the mistakes of the past. You see, when Mary Ellen and I began to drift apart, I reacted poorly. Instead of allowing her to explain why she felt the need to behave in an inappropriate manner, I began to forbid her access to the people I felt were leading her astray."

"How did that work out for you?"

"Not very well," Hamilton admitted. "Trying to control Mary Ellen was like trying to hold water in my hand. She became more distant and secretive. We were constantly at odds with one another, until one day, she apparently couldn't abide me any longer and ran away."

"And that is when she died?"

Hamilton nodded. "She was thrown from her horse, and her body was found along the Hudson River."

"Did her horse possess a questionable temperament?"

"She did. Mary Ellen chose Diamond, not because of her disposition, but because she was such an unusual horse. She was pure white and fairly glowed in the sunlight."

"You said 'was' an unusual horse. Diamond died in the accident as well?"

"Diamond was never found, but we came to the conclusion she most likely plunged into the Hudson River, given her agitated state, and drowned," Hamilton said.

"It seems odd her body never washed up to shore, although I suppose she could have washed out to sea, but . . . a horse is really heavy."

Hamilton smiled. "I see you've been reading the same types of books as the notorious Miss Brighton. I hate to disappoint you, but there's no intrigue to be had in this particular situation. It was a tragic accident, but that's all it was, an accident."

"How long has it been?" Eliza asked.

"Mary Ellen died a little over two years ago, and although her passing has gotten easier with time, I know I'll always feel responsible for what happened. I should have realized my prayers for her hadn't been answered and been more diligent in keeping her safe, no matter how much I'd come to despise her."

"I didn't realize you were a man of faith."

"I'm afraid my faith has been somewhat strained the past few years, given what occurred with my wife."

Eliza sent him a small smile and then frowned. "You said your wife died two years ago. Don't you think it's a bit of an odd coincidence that you began having difficulties with that Eugene fellow right around that time?"

Before Hamilton could reply, Zayne stepped out from behind a large tree where he'd obviously been lurking and grinned as he moved to join them.

"Lovely to discover everyone's still alive." He nodded at Eliza. "Piper told me all about what transpired. I was afraid I'd find the two of you engaged in a verbal skirmish."

"Piper notices entirely too much," Eliza said. "I'll have you know I didn't raise my voice one time to your brother while we were in the house."

"I see you've conveniently forgotten the tirade you directed at me out here," Hamilton muttered.

Eliza rolled her eyes before turning back to Zayne. "Your brother and I were just discussing a bit of an odd coincidence."

"And what was that, Miss Sumner?" Zayne asked.

"Please, call me Eliza. It seems a bit silly to remain so formal, doesn't it?"

"Eliza, then, and you must call me Zayne," he said as he stepped forward, stopped directly in front of Eliza, and reached out to take hold of her hand, raising it to his lips. "Forgive me, but I've completely neglected my manners. You look beautiful today."

Hamilton felt the unusual urge to snatch Eliza's hand out of his brother's grasp. He frowned when he realized the urge stemmed from the fact that he felt extremely possessive toward her. The thought left him uncomfortable. He took a steadying breath and ignored the feeling of relief that swept over him when Zayne finally let go of Eliza's hand.

"Getting back to the odd coincidence that Miss Sumner, or rather, Eliza, brought up," Hamilton said, shooting Eliza a quick glance to ascertain she'd included him in her request for informality. He smiled when she nodded and found he'd lost his train of thought. Her smile really was quite extraordinary.

"The odd coincidence . . . ?" Zayne prodded.

"Oh yes, quite right," Hamilton said. "You know, it is rather odd." He caught his brother's gaze. "Did you ever realize we began experiencing difficulties with our business not long after Mary Ellen died?"

"Are you suggesting the two are linked?" Zayne asked.

"Truth be told, I never considered the idea. Unfortunately, we can't question Mary Ellen," Hamilton said.

"True," Zayne agreed, "but I know just the person we can consult. In fact, that's actually the real reason I sought the two of you out. Mr. Theodore Wilder is waiting to speak with us in the library." He sent Eliza a wink. "I thought it prudent to have him remain there, seeing as how he's a private investigator and might have reacted rashly if he'd stepped into the garden and found you browbeating my brother."

Hamilton laughed as Eliza sent Zayne a scowl and couldn't help but admire her restraint when she didn't dignify Zayne's remark with a reply but, instead, turned back to him. "Why is a private investigator here?"

Hamilton stood and offered Eliza his arm, steering her in the direction of the house before he answered. "Zayne and I felt, given the results of last night, that our situation called for a professional."

He slowed to a stop when a tug on his arm made him realize Eliza was no longer moving.

"I can't afford to pay for a professional," she said.

"I'm more than able to cover the cost, and before you get all indignant again, you must realize there is a common thread between our situations, so it won't be much extra effort for Mr. Wilder to investigate Lord Southmoor as he goes about investigating Mr. Daniels."

She eyed him for a moment, nodded, and then allowed him to escort her into the house. He came to a stop when they reached the library door and Zayne stepped in front of him, a sneaky grin on his face.

"I'd like to go in first because I want to see Eliza's reaction to Mr. Wilder," Zayne said before he strode through the door.

"What do you think he meant by that?" Eliza asked.

"I have no idea," Hamilton said, stepping into the room with Eliza trailing behind him. He swallowed a groan when he got his first good look at Mr. Theodore Wilder. He pushed away the sudden desire he had to drag Eliza immediately back the way they'd come, because . . . Mr. Theodore Wilder stood well over six feet tall and was possessed of a face that could only be described as too handsome for his own good.

Eliza took that moment to stagger against him, but she didn't appear to notice as her eyes widened and stayed firmly directed at Mr. Wilder.

Hamilton would have never taken her for a woman who went for the blond Adonis type, but apparently she did.

"Happens every time," Zayne remarked pleasantly.

"What happens every time?" Hamilton bit out.

"You must be Mr. Hamilton Beckett," Theodore exclaimed as he strode across the room and took hold of Hamilton's hand, giving it a firm shake before he turned his head and his attention to Eliza and smiled a wicked smile. Hamilton found himself a bit perplexed as to why Zayne would associate with a man who was obviously arrogant and unpleasant. He tightened his grip, which had the unfortunate result of causing the all-too-handsome Mr. Wilder to wince.

His mood immediately improved until Mr. Wilder opened his mouth.

"You must be Lady Eliza Sumner," Mr. Wilder said with another smile that showed off his perfect teeth.

"She prefers Miss Sumner," Hamilton growled, darting a quick glance to Eliza to see if she'd heard his possessive tone of voice. Much to his dismay, Eliza did not appear as if she'd even noticed the fact that he'd spoken. Her eyes were still focused on Mr. Wilder's face, and she was now sporting a somewhat dazed expression.

He tightened his grip on Mr. Wilder's hand and then blinked when the man let out a grunt, reached out with his other hand, pried Hamilton's hand away, and then had the nerve to send him a knowing grin before he turned said grin on Eliza, which caused her eyes to widen.

"I understand you've suffered a bit of misfortune lately, Miss Sumner," Theodore said in a voice that, in Hamilton's opinion, was entirely too deep and raspy.

"Please, call me Eliza, and yes, I'm afraid I have suffered a great deal of misfortune lately."

Hamilton's mouth dropped open before he had the presence of mind to snap it shut. She was already giving this Theodore gentleman permission to use her first name? He'd only just been given permission, and he'd gotten the exasperating woman sprung from jail.

"You must call me Theodore."

Over his dead body, Hamilton thought, moving slightly to the left to force Theodore to take a step away from Eliza. He looked up to find his brother grinning back at him. He had the oddest desire to smack his brother over the head with any object close at hand.

"Do you think you'll be able to help me?" Eliza asked.

"It shouldn't be difficult to track down Lord Southmoor. It certainly doesn't sound as if he's trying to keep a low profile," Theodore said. "All I need to do is discover his social schedule, and I'll keep track of him by following him to society events."

"You can do that?" Eliza asked.

"Theodore's family is very well connected, Eliza," Zayne said. "His father is a well-known figure in the financial district, and his grandfather is . . . how can I describe the gentleman?"

"My grandfather is also a genius with finance and built up the business before my father took over, but his past is shrouded in mystery, and no one has ever had the nerve to actually ask him where he first made his money," Theodore said, his eyes twinkling. "I've always believed he acquired his first fortune through nefarious means."

"How fascinating," Eliza breathed, causing Hamilton to suddenly have the mad desire to make up a disreputable story of his own to tell her.

Nothing came to mind.

"But enough about my family," Theodore continued. "We have more important matters to discuss, and although Zayne has explained to me the pertinent details regarding the situation, I do have more questions."

Hamilton's opinion of the man reluctantly improved as Theodore escorted Eliza to a seat and sat opposite her, asking her question after question. He took notes and poked and prodded until he finally laid down his pad and nodded.

"That should give me a good start," he proclaimed.

"What do you intend to do first?" Eliza asked.

"I'm afraid I can't discuss my plans with you."

"Excuse me?"

"I hope you won't take offense, Eliza, but all too often people who hire me decide to involve themselves in the case, which results in mayhem and disaster. You wouldn't care for mayhem, would you?" Theodore asked.

"Well, no, but . . ." Eliza began.

"And because you're a woman, I can hardly believe you would actually be an asset to my investigation."

Hamilton couldn't hold back a smile as he saw the storm clouds gather in Eliza's eyes. Although he'd been impressed with the man's professionalism, he couldn't help but enjoy the fact that Eliza had apparently discontinued admiring the gentleman and now appeared as if she wanted to box his ears.

"May I inquire if you've discouraged Hamilton and Zayne from concerning themselves with your investigation?" Eliza asked in a slightly dangerous voice.

"Ahh . . . I have not," Theodore muttered.

Eliza arched a perfectly shaped brow.

"They're men," Theodore continued, as if that wrapped up the matter nicely. "They won't be a distraction, whereas I can't say the same about you." He sent Eliza a charming smile. "Surely you must understand that, as you are such an uncommonly beautiful woman, you would cause me to become diverted from my investigation the longer I spent time in your delightful company."

Hamilton's hand clenched into a fist over Theodore's blatant flattery, but before he had an opportunity to actually pummel the man, Eliza gave a very unladylike snort.

"Don't tell me those types of flowery comments work for you."

Theodore blinked. "Beg pardon?"

"As you should," Eliza said. "If Zayne and Hamilton are to be given access to your investigation, I must insist you allow me the same courtesy."

"You're a woman. This is hardly a matter for someone of a delicate nature."

Eliza narrowed her eyes as Hamilton's shoulders began to

shake with suppressed laughter. He almost felt sorry for the man, but one glance at Theodore's too-handsome face had all thoughts of compassion disappearing in a split second.

"My being a woman has nothing to do with the situation."

"It has everything to do with it," Theodore retorted.

"Let me put it as simply as possible, Mr. Wilder, so that your manly brain will be able to understand my poor little female thoughts. If you refuse to include me, I will continue my own investigation, and I will refuse to share with you any information I might garner," Eliza said.

"You could jeopardize the entire case," Theodore sputtered.

"I am not so inept I would jeopardize your case," Eliza returned with a lift of her chin.

"Oh? You don't consider landing yourself in jail inept?" Theodore asked.

"You told him that?" Eliza demanded, shooting Zayne a glare.

Zayne smiled weakly and apparently decided it was in his best interest to remain silent.

"May I suggest you save your arguments and simply trust me?" Theodore asked.

"I don't trust easily," Eliza said.

"I'm a professional and a gentleman. There is absolutely no reason for your lack of trust."

"As Mr. Hayes, alias Lord Southmoor, claimed to be a professional, yet stole my money, you can hardly blame me for my distrust. And," Eliza continued before Theodore could interrupt, "my ex-fiancé was considered an esteemed gentleman, yet he abandoned me without even the courtesy of an explanation the moment he learned my fortune had gone missing. Surely you can understand how your argument holds little weight with me."

"Well said," Hamilton exclaimed, earning a smile from Eliza and a scowl from Theodore.

Theodore studied Eliza for a moment as if she were some

strange creature who had somehow managed to fall into his midst. He released a sigh. "Very well, I'll keep you informed of my progress, but you must promise to stay out of the actual investigation."

"Are Zayne and Hamilton staying out of the actual investigation?"

"Eliza," Hamilton said, taking pity on Theodore, "Zayne and I both have a business to run. It's one of the reasons we decided to bring in outside help. That, and the fact that our foray into sleuthing did not turn out very well."

"But how am I to occupy my time? I've been let go from my position, you won't allow me to become a nanny to your children, and I have no funds at my disposal," Eliza said.

"I have never failed an investigation," Theodore stated, his tone affronted. "There is absolutely no reason to believe you will not soon be in repossession of your fortune."

"You are certain of that?"

"Did you miss the part where I said I've never failed?"

Eliza looked at him for a long moment before turning to Hamilton. "Since it would appear I'm to be at loose ends for the foreseeable future and Mr. Wilder believes he'll recover my fortune, would you truly consider lending me some money?"

"Of course. I already extended you that offer."

"Wonderful," she exclaimed, "because after all this time in male company, I feel the distinct urge for an enjoyable day of shopping with no gentlemen in attendance."

11

*E*liza placed Ben on his bed and watched him sleep for a moment, marveling over the fact that, in the two weeks since she'd first stepped foot into the Beckett house, she'd somehow managed to become firmly entrenched in their lives. She bent over and brushed a quick kiss on his forehead before straightening and walking out of the room. She made her way downstairs, snagged a coat from a peg by the back door, and threw it on as she slipped out into the garden.

"There you are," she called before striding over to where Piper sat playing with her doll underneath a tree.

Piper looked up. "Is Ben sleeping?"

"He is."

"Are you mad at him because he bit Miss Dragon?"

"Her name was Miss Dreyfus, and no, I'm not mad at Ben. I'm the one who hired the woman, and any and all blame for what happened today lies with me." Eliza took a seat next to

Piper and spread out her skirts to allow Charlie a more comfortable place to rest. She absently scratched his head and smiled when the dog rolled over on his back and presented her with his stomach. She stroked his soft fur and allowed herself a moment to reflect on the events of the past few weeks.

Hamilton had remained steadfast in his refusal to allow her to assume the position of nanny, but he'd finally relented and agreed she could at least take over the task of interviewing potential candidates. She never dreamed it would be so difficult. Every single woman the employment agency sent over seemed to have alarming deficiencies. None of them appeared to possess much compassion, or competency for that matter, and as Eliza dismissed candidate after candidate, she'd found herself confused regarding Gloria's amusement with the situation. When she'd dismissed candidate number thirty, Gloria had actually laughed out loud, sent Eliza a grin, and marched out of the room.

It had been most peculiar.

Because Piper and Ben were without a proper nanny and Eliza was having no luck obtaining one, she'd stepped in and spent almost every minute of the day with them, except for the trying times she spent interviewing more candidates.

To her dismay, she'd fallen head over heels in love with the children, something she'd sworn to herself she wouldn't let happen, considering her time in America was limited. In an attempt to create some type of distance, she'd finally extended an offer of employment to Miss Dreyfus, the only woman who appeared somewhat capable. The woman had arrived for work bright and early that morning.

Disaster soon followed.

"Are you mad at Charlie?" Piper asked, pulling Eliza from her thoughts.

"Of course not, Charlie was only trying to protect Ben," Eliza said, smiling when Charlie rolled to his stomach and plopped his head in her lap. "Miss Dreyfus shouldn't have slapped your brother or kicked Charlie."

"Ben shouldn't have bitten her."

"You're right, but Ben is only a baby and Miss Dreyfus is an adult. Seeing that she is a nanny by choice, I would have thought she'd have been capable of calmly pointing out the error of Ben's ways instead of completely overreacting."

"She seemed nice at first," Piper said. "I don't understand why Ben didn't like her."

Eliza was fairly certain she understood exactly why Ben hadn't taken a liking to the new nanny. He'd formed an immediate attachment to Eliza, and apparently seemed to fear he was going to lose all of his time with her when another woman entered the picture. She'd been hopeful he'd give Miss Dreyfus a chance, but that hadn't happened. Tears sprang to her eyes when the thought came to her that Ben was going to be devastated when she went back to England.

"Are you going to start crying?" Piper asked.

"I'm not crying."

Piper arched a brow in a manner far too old for her age.

"Oh, very well, I might have been about to cry."

"Why?"

"I was thinking how sad I'll be when I go home."

"Won't you be happy to see your family?"

"I don't really have a family," Eliza admitted.

"You should stay here," Piper proclaimed as she ripped the dress off her doll and stuffed her into another outfit.

"I can't do that."

"Can't do what?" Hamilton asked, causing a trace of something downright disturbing to run over Eliza as she turned her head and watched him come to a stop right before her.

"What are you doing here, Daddy?" Piper squealed before

she abandoned her doll and rushed to Hamilton's side, giggling in delight when he swept her up into his arms.

"I thought I'd come home to see how my girls are doing."

It almost seemed to Eliza as if Hamilton was including her as one of "my girls."

"Where's Ben?" Hamilton asked as he set Piper down.

"He's taking a nap," Piper replied.

"Isn't it late for his nap?" Hamilton asked.

"He had a traumatic morning and didn't settle down until an hour ago," Eliza explained.

"He bit Miss Dragon," Piper said. "She left in a huff."

A huff was putting it mildly.

"Miss Dragon?" Hamilton questioned.

"That's not her real name, Daddy, but after she slapped Ben and kicked Charlie, I renamed her."

"She slapped Ben?" Hamilton asked.

"Right after he bit her."

"It's my fault," Eliza said as Charlie rolled onto his back and began to whine. She found she couldn't meet Hamilton's gaze, so she gave her attention to the dog, causing Charlie to wiggle in sheer bliss. "It was inexcusable of me to allow a woman of such uneven temperament into your house."

"Miss Eliza set her straight in the end," Piper said, addressing Eliza with the more informal name they'd agreed upon. Ben had wanted to call her "Mama," but Eliza had remained firm even when Ben put up a good fight.

"I know I'll most likely regret asking this, but how did she set her straight?" Hamilton asked.

"See, once the screaming started, Charlie raced into the room and jumped on Miss Dragon, barking and snarling, and that's when Miss Dragon kicked him and then Miss Eliza ran into the room and . . ." Piper paused and looked at Eliza. "Is it all right if I tell him?"

"You might as well," Eliza said glumly, lifting her head. "He'll find out eventually."

"It sounds dire," Hamilton said with a smile.

"It is," Eliza admitted.

"She smacked her," Piper exclaimed.

"Miss Dragon, er, Dreyfus smacked Miss Eliza?" Hamilton asked.

"No, Daddy. Miss Eliza smacked Miss Dragon, and I think she pulled her hair, because it looked quite a mess after they were finished."

"I only pulled her hair because she went for mine," Eliza hurried to clarify.

Hamilton laughed, causing Eliza to frown. "It's not funny," she muttered.

"Of course not," Hamilton agreed, his smile fading, but his eyes still twinkling entirely too attractively down at her. She dropped her head and settled her attention back on Charlie, her mind searching for just the right words to explain.

"I'm not normally a violent person, but when I discovered that . . . that . . . that woman," Eliza sputtered, her temper flaring, "had touched my precious Ben, well, all I can say is that I lost complete control."

Eliza forced herself to meet Hamilton's gaze, and what she discovered there forced all the breath from her body even as her pulse began to race. He was watching her with what appeared to be tenderness in his eyes, as if something she'd said touched his very soul. Before she could even blink, the moment was broken when Gloria stomped her way through the garden and stopped beside Hamilton, clutching a piece of paper in her hand.

"We've been officially fired," Gloria stated.

"Fired?" Hamilton asked.

"Yes, dear, fired. It seems that the employment agency"—she looked at the paper—"after careful consideration has decided they can no longer supply us with another nanny. We are"— she consulted the paper again—"'unsuitable' and have 'unruly' children."

"What?" Eliza demanded, jumping to her feet and inadvertently dumping Charlie out of her lap in the process.

"Sorry, Charlie," she said before turning back to Gloria. "The children are not unruly. That agency provided us with an unqualified nanny who was ill equipped to deal with a precocious boy." She turned and began to stride toward the house.

"Where are you going?" Hamilton called.

Eliza stopped and spun on her heel. "I'm going to find that employment agency and demand they issue an apology at once." She sent Hamilton and Gloria a nod and set her sights on the house.

"Eliza, you might want to reconsider," Gloria yelled, causing Eliza to stop in her tracks and turn around.

"I will not. They have insulted Piper and Ben most grievously, and poor Piper didn't even do anything."

"Yes, but the letter also states if you're seen anywhere in the vicinity of their office, they'll have you arrested," Gloria said.

"On what charge?"

Gloria peered at the paper and then lifted her head. "Assault."

"That's preposterous," Eliza snapped. "Did they mention anything regarding Miss Dragon?"

"Dreyfus," Hamilton corrected.

"Same thing," Eliza muttered with a wave of her hand before moving back to peer at the letter over Gloria's shoulder. "She's on her way to the country to recover from her ordeal?"

Gloria nodded. "Did you get to the part where it says she's considering entering a convent?"

"As if that woman has the temperament required to become a nun," Eliza scoffed. "Instead of traveling to the country to settle her obviously high-strung nerves, she should be residing in jail, contemplating her lack of compassion. She slapped Ben."

"You rose to his defense quite admirably," Hamilton replied.

"She kicked poor Charlie," Eliza continued, ignoring Hamilton's statement.

"He appears fine," Hamilton said, gesturing to the now-snoozing Charlie.

"Charlie was whimpering right after she kicked him," Eliza said.

"Eliza, Charlie's fine, Ben's fine, and Miss Dreyfus is on her way to a convent," Hamilton said. "I think what you and the children need is a good distraction. I'm going to ask Cook to prepare us a picnic lunch, and we'll take it to Central Park."

"You want to go on a picnic?" Eliza questioned, her temper cooling instantly.

"I love picnics," Piper exclaimed, "almost as much as I love shopping."

"We're not going shopping," Hamilton said firmly. "You have dragged Miss Eliza and Grandmother all over the city these past two weeks, and I'm certain there are no shops left that you haven't visited."

Eliza smiled. What Hamilton said was indeed the truth. After he had pressed on her a more than generous loan, she'd taken to the streets of New York with Gloria and Piper and had been pleasantly surprised regarding the quality of the shops available in New York. It had become a favorite pastime for them, but as her wardrobe was sufficiently restocked, she preferred the idea of a picnic over shopping.

"Piper, your father's right. I believe we've had our fill of shopping for the moment," she said.

"A girl can never have her fill of shopping," Piper proclaimed.

Eliza grinned. "True, but Ben doesn't enjoy shopping."

"He liked it when he went with us the other day," Piper argued.

"Only because we bribed him with ice cream and extended trips on the steam elevator."

"I guess a picnic would be fun," Piper said, "but a ride on the El would be even better, and Ben loves the El."

Eliza suppressed a shudder. Although she found the city of New York fascinating, the El was not her favorite mode of travel. It was dirty and, to be honest, a little frightening as it rattled around the elevated track, but she would never admit that to Piper.

"We can ride the El another day," Eliza said, "and we can return to that department store with the steam elevators. Ben would like that, even though I will admit I do wonder what would happen if it ran out of steam."

"I bet it would fall right back down to the ground," Piper said, looking as if she would love nothing more than to plummet rapidly in a steam elevator.

"Yes, well, thankfully we don't need to worry about that today," Eliza muttered. "If everyone's in agreement regarding the picnic, I'll run up and fetch Ben."

"I'd offer to get him for you, dear," Gloria said, "but I know he prefers you, even though I am his grandmother."

"I'm sure that's not true," Eliza said.

"It doesn't upset me, Eliza. I'm quite delighted by the fact that Ben's finally opening up to someone," Gloria said before one of those annoying gleams entered her eyes and she batted innocent lashes in Eliza's direction. "Now that I think about it, though, the poor child did suffer quite the traumatic event today and probably needs his sleep, so I'll stay here and watch over him while all of you go on the picnic."

"Grandmother, we can't go without Ben," Piper exclaimed. "He wouldn't like that at all."

Gloria tilted her head. "You're right, Piper. He would certainly miss you. You can stay here with me, and your father and Eliza can go on the picnic."

It appeared as if Gloria was still intent on a bit of scheming. Eliza had known Gloria was up to something two weeks before when she'd insisted, completely out of the blue, on a shopping expedition, and the explanation for that little scheme came to Eliza a few days later when she'd realized how attached she'd become to Piper and Ben, which Gloria must have known would happen all along. The woman was tricky though, and over the past week had lulled Eliza into a false sense of security when no dastardly plots came to light, but now it was clear Gloria was ready to put another diabolical plan into action.

Eliza didn't know whether to be complimented or insulted.

She was spared a response when Hamilton released a snort.

"Mother, everyone's coming," he said. "Piper, go get your coat. Mother, go ask for a lunch." He stepped forward and offered Eliza his arm. "Do you mind if I come with you to fetch Ben?"

"Not at all," Eliza muttered, ignoring Gloria's dramatic sigh. She placed her arm on Hamilton's and allowed him to steer her toward the house.

"Your mother's up to something," she said as they walked up the steps.

"My mother's always up to something," he said. "You'll have to be ever vigilant around her now. She's beginning to abandon subtlety, which is never a good sign, and I fear, even though she knows perfectly well I'm not looking to form an attachment with anyone, she's set her sights on you as suitable candidate to become a mother to Piper and Ben."

Eliza's steps faltered and she forced a smile as he steadied her. Warring emotions roiled inside her, but she refused to allow Hamilton to see how his words unsettled her. Even though she was determined to avoid becoming attached to the gentleman, she was honest enough with herself to realize she was not quite being successful in that regard, and she'd thought, given the fact that he was continuously watching her with something warm in his eyes, that he felt the same way.

Apparently, she'd been mistaken.

12

*E*liza was thankful for the distraction as she tried to remove the last remnants of their picnic lunch from Ben's face while he squirmed on her lap,.

Hamilton obviously did not want to form an attachment with her, and even though she was of a like mind, given the fact that she was still determined to return to England, his words rankled more than she cared to admit.

She gave Ben one last swipe of the cloth and kissed his nose, her heart swelling when he kissed her right back, leaving a trace of slobber on her cheek. He grinned at her and scampered away, running as fast as his little legs could carry him to where Piper stood tossing a ball into the air. Her mood couldn't help but improve.

"He adores you," Gloria remarked as she chose another piece of chicken and took a dainty bite.

"The feeling is mutual," Eliza admitted before she frowned.

"Did it look to you like he has a bruise on his cheek where that woman struck him?"

"Ben's fine," Hamilton said, surprising Eliza from behind as he lowered his lanky frame next to her. She scooted away as casually as she could and ignored Gloria's curious look.

"We can't be certain he's fine," Eliza said. "He could very well be suffering an injury to his brain. Miss Dreyfus was somewhat hefty."

Hamilton gestured to where Ben was now shrieking in delight as Piper tickled him on the ground. "Does that look like a boy suffering from anything other than the giggles?"

"He was fussy when he got up from his nap," Eliza argued.

"I'm fussy when I get up from a nap," Hamilton said, leaning closer to her, which had a prickle of something annoying rolling down her spine. "You seem out of sorts, Eliza. Is something the matter?"

She was spared a response when a voice rang out in the distance.

"Any food left for us?"

"Ah, look, it's Zayne and . . . is that a young lady at his side?" Gloria asked.

Eliza swallowed a laugh at the telltale excitement in Gloria's tone. She pretended not to notice Hamilton's extended hand, struggled to her feet on her own, and noted in delight that Zayne was indeed with a young lady who just happened to be Agatha. She rushed forward. "Agatha," she exclaimed, giving her a hug. "How did you manage to escape your house? I thought your father confined you to your room."

Agatha smiled. "Mother convinced him I was looking peaked so I was allowed to visit the orphanage."

"I hate to be the one to point this out, dear," Gloria began, brushing the dirt from her skirt as she joined them, "but this isn't the orphanage."

"I know," Agatha said. "I've already been there, stopped by the church to say a few extra prayers, and since it didn't take up as much time as I thought, I decided to stop and check on Eliza. That was when I ran into Zayne at your house. It was a stroke of luck he'd just returned home and learned of the fact that all of you were having a picnic in the park."

Gloria tilted her head. "May I assume you're Miss Watson?"

"Mrs. Beckett, we've met before. Numerous times," Agatha said.

"We have?"

Agatha rolled her eyes. "It's fortunate I don't suffer tender feelings because it's become very clear to me that I've made little to no impression on your family."

"I did apologize for my lack of observation," Zayne pointed out.

"Yes, you did, and I very graciously forgave you," Agatha said.

"Have you been acquainted with Zayne long, Miss Watson?" Gloria asked, her expression so calculating that Eliza had to turn her head and pretend to cough when a laugh caught her by surprise.

"It would seem I've been acquainted with him longer than he's been acquainted with me," Agatha grouched. "Do you know he actually thought I was only just out of the schoolroom until a few weeks ago?"

"Again, I did apologize for that," Zayne muttered.

"How very curious," Gloria said, swinging her attention from Agatha to Zayne and then back to Agatha again. She stepped forward, took Agatha by the arm, and hustled her toward the blanket. "You must tell me all about it, my dear."

By the time Eliza took her seat, Agatha was speaking rapidly, explaining to Gloria what her latest article was about, and Eliza was hardly surprised to learn it concerned none other than ladies of the night.

". . . and I'm hopeful the paper will encourage me to pursue the matter further," Agatha said.

"I'm afraid I must have missed something," Gloria said. "Am I to understand you're a writer?"

"It's a recent occupation," Agatha said.

Eliza couldn't help but notice the way Agatha's gaze kept drifting to the food spread out around them. She leaned forward to pick up a plate to offer Agatha a meal, but stopped when Hamilton beat her to it. He piled chicken and potatoes on it and reached over Eliza to hand the plate to Agatha.

"You look hungry," he said with a charming smile as Agatha beamed back at him and settled the plate on her lap.

"I'm starving," Agatha proclaimed. "I've been refusing food for the past day, trying to force my father to see reason."

"So you stopped eating?" Eliza asked, watching in amazement as Agatha devoured an entire leg of chicken in less than a minute.

"I thought it was a good idea at the time, seeing as how my father is actually a nice man under all that bluster and wouldn't care to see his daughter go hungry. Unfortunately, I didn't realize he left on a business trip, so my attempt at forcing his hand was all for naught." She stabbed her fork into a potato and shoved it into her mouth.

"Any word yet concerning that first article you sent the paper?" Eliza asked.

Agatha chewed, swallowed, and then nodded. "The *New York Tribune* has only just accepted the piece on the clothing mills, and they want me to provide them with additional stories."

"It's quite the feat to write for that particular newspaper," Gloria said with a sly glance in Zayne's direction, which, Eliza saw, he blatantly ignored. "Are you going to be published under your name or have you assumed a pen name?"

"I was going to write under the name Polly Ponders, but the paper thought that name was a bit too frivolous for such a serious article," Agatha said before she grinned, took another bite of chicken, and then promptly choked on it.

Before Eliza had a second to react, Hamilton was by Agatha's side, pounding her on the back repeatedly until Agatha could finally breathe.

A tickle of something warm took up residence in Eliza's veins. She had the unusual thought that it was not so preposterous, the fact that she'd become attached to the man, because, well, he was constantly assuming the role of knight in shining armor. She forced the thought to the back of her mind, realized Agatha probably would appreciate a drink, and busied herself with pouring out a glass of tea, which Agatha accepted with a nod, her eyes watering and her face bright red.

"Thank you," Agatha said in a raspy voice as she gulped it down and then cleared her throat. "As I was saying, the editors didn't like Polly Ponders." She released a dramatic sigh. "You're now in the presence of Mr. Alfred Wallenstate."

"You don't look much like an Alfred," Zayne said, causing everyone to laugh.

Eliza's laughter died abruptly when Hamilton dropped down by her side and, for some unknown reason, began to play with the fabric of her skirt that was billowed out around her even as he continued bantering with his brother. She shot a look to Gloria and groaned. Of course the woman would have noticed her son's actions. She scrambled to her feet, made a circle around the blanket, and dropped back down on the other side of Agatha, far from Hamilton's reach.

"Didn't like where you were sitting?" Agatha muttered.

"I thought I'd get closer to you so we could chat," Eliza said. "So, is that why you came to find me, to tell me your good news regarding the paper?"

"Good grief, I completely forgot the real reason I came to see you," Agatha said, her eyes gleaming with excitement. "You'll never guess what I discovered. . . . Lord Southmoor is to attend the theater tomorrow."

"Are you certain?" Eliza asked as possibilities danced through her mind.

Agatha nodded. "Mother divulged that juicy little morsel to me this morning. She's already procured tickets for herself and Father because she's determined to become known to Lord Southmoor. I haven't bothered to explain to her that the man's a fraud."

"Why haven't you told her?" Eliza asked.

"It would defeat our purpose, wouldn't it? I mean, honestly, if she knew we were investigating him, she would hardly go out of her way to tell me when he'll be absent from his home. She's quite adamant in her determination to keep me out of jail."

"Don't tell me you're divulging this information to Eliza so the two of you can contemplate breaking into the man's house again," Zayne said.

"I don't see where it's any business of yours what Eliza and I do," Agatha returned.

"I'm making it my business because I have no desire to bail you out of jail again."

Eliza spent the next few minutes watching Zayne and Agatha exchange insults before she finally decided to step in, mostly because Agatha had taken to sputtering and was waving her spoon madly in the air. Since said spoon still had potatoes attached to it, Eliza was being splattered with food. She touched Agatha's arm to get her attention.

"Although it's an incredibly tempting idea to try our hand at Bartholomew's house again, Hamilton and Zayne have hired a professional to handle the matter."

"Where's the fun in that?" Agatha scoffed as she dropped the spoon.

"This is hardly an amusing subject," Zayne scoffed right back, earning another glare from Agatha in the process.

"Mr. Wilder comes highly recommended," Hamilton said.

"Mr. Wilder?" Agatha gasped. "Mr. Theodore Wilder?" Zayne nodded.

"Oh . . . he is divine," Agatha breathed.

"What does that have to do with anything?" Zayne questioned, his voice ringing with indignation.

"Nothing at all," Agatha retorted, "I was simply making an observation."

"Yes, well, Mr. Wilder has the matter well in hand, so there will be no need for you or Eliza to concern yourselves with this," Zayne said.

"We should pen Mr. Wilder a note," Agatha exclaimed. "I will accept the task."

"There is no need to pen Mr. Wilder a note," Zayne snapped.

"Don't you think he'll find it interesting to learn Lord Southmoor is to be absent from his home tomorrow night?" Agatha asked.

"Oh, he'll find it interesting, but there's no need to pen a note as the gentleman is currently riding this way."

Everyone turned to look where Zayne was staring and sure enough, Theodore was galloping toward them, a grin on his handsome face.

"Good heavens," Gloria exclaimed as she fanned her cheeks with a napkin, "he is divine, isn't he?"

"Mother," Hamilton said, "what would Father think if he could hear you now?"

Gloria leaned forward, ignoring her son's remark. "I wonder how he knew where to find us?"

"I left word back at the house," Zayne admitted. "I was to meet him there, but when Miss Watson showed up, I thought it best to escort her here."

"I told you I was perfectly capable of traveling to Central Park on my own. I do it all the time," Agatha said.

"Which is a frightening thought to be sure," Zayne replied before he turned from a once-again sputtering Agatha to greet his friend.

"Theodore, I see you found us," Zayne called.

Theodore nodded, swung out of his saddle, and began striding toward them, his blatant male swagger causing Agatha and Gloria to sigh loudly. Eliza refrained from doing the very same thing, as she was not overly fond of Mr. Wilder's personality.

"This is a lovely day for a picnic," Theodore exclaimed as he smiled down at Agatha.

Eliza resisted the urge to roll her eyes, even when Agatha began batting her lashes.

"Theodore, are you acquainted with Miss Watson?" Hamilton asked.

"I have not been given that pleasure," Theodore said as he leaned over and took Agatha's hand in his, bringing it to his lips.

"Miss Watson, this is my friend Mr. Theodore Wilder," Zayne said, although the introduction came out somewhat begrudgingly.

"Delighted to make your acquaintance, Miss Watson," Theodore said as he released Agatha's hand and turned his attention to Gloria. "You must be Zayne's sister."

Gloria beamed while Zayne scowled. "She's my mother, Mrs. Gloria Beckett."

"Mrs. Beckett," Theodore replied, moving to kiss her hand.

Eliza bit back a snort as both Agatha and Gloria blushed. She felt a hand on her shoulder and looked around to discover Piper standing behind her, watching Theodore with a rather fierce expression on her face.

"Ah, Piper," Hamilton said. "You're just in time to meet Mr. Wilder."

Theodore let go of Gloria's hand and smiled at Piper. "Miss Beckett, aren't you a little beauty in the making," he said, his smile dimming when Piper glared back at him even as she dipped into a small curtsy.

"Are you here to see Miss Sumner?" Piper demanded.

"Ahh, I am, but I'm also here to speak with your father and uncle," Theodore said, looking a bit bemused seemingly because of Piper's animosity toward him.

Piper narrowed her eyes, nodded once, and then spun on her heel and stalked away.

"Bet that doesn't happen often," Zayne muttered.

"You'd be surprised," Theodore admitted.

"Mr. Wilder," Agatha said, "perhaps you would allow me to interview you in the near future. I'm certain there are many readers who would be thrilled to learn more about you and the life of a private investigator."

"Interview me?" Theodore asked.

"Agatha has recently obtained a job as a journalist for the *New York Tribune*," Eliza said, holding her breath in anticipation of Theodore's response to that information.

"That's hardly an appropriate choice of employment for a young lady."

Agatha's mouth dropped open. "I beg your pardon?"

"Do you still have a father?" Theodore asked.

"I do."

"And he's given you his permission to pursue such a career?"

"I wouldn't go so far as to say that," Agatha muttered.

"Then may I suggest you seek his counsel before entering into such a scandalous occupation? Gentlemen are much more adept at understanding the complexities of the world, and I would not wish to see you ruin your future by dashing into a position which is not at all suitable for a delicate and refined lady."

"Here it comes," Zayne exclaimed.

Agatha rose to her feet, her face an interesting shade of purple. "You are not divine in the least."

"Excuse me?" Theodore asked.

Agatha stalked her way around the blanket until she was within a foot of Theodore. She placed fisted hands on her hips. "This is 1880, and women no longer have to abide by the dictates of men."

"You can't even vote," Theodore said.

Gloria began to sputter, and Eliza watched in amazement as she pushed up from the blanket, crossed her arms over her chest, and began tapping her foot against the grass. "Am I to assume, Mr. Wilder, that you don't support the women's suffrage movement?"

"I think it's a frivolous movement that has no hope of succeeding," he returned.

"To think I was actually musing on an interesting idea just now to put you into direct contact with my darling Arabella," Gloria said.

"I think I should go check on Ben," Eliza muttered before she jumped to her feet and hurried away, hoping no one would notice the fact that her shoulders were shaking with laughter. She set her sights on the spot where Piper and Ben were chasing what appeared to be bugs and made her way over to them.

"I got a beetle," Ben said as he scampered to her side and held out his hand.

"Very nice," she said with a smile.

"I'm going to give it to Piper to make up for Herman," he said before he barreled away from her to join his sister. She watched them for another minute and then turned, her amusement now firmly in check, but had to bite back a grin when she returned to the picnic site, because Agatha and Gloria were apparently still put out with Theodore, both scowling in his direction. She almost felt sorry for him, but . . . no, he deserved to be taken down a peg or two.

". . . and all of this is completely beside the point," Theodore was saying. "I'm here to discuss the investigation."

"Well, go on then, what progress have you made?" Agatha asked.

Theodore sent Agatha a less than pleasant smile, but refrained from responding as he gestured them back toward the blanket and waited as everyone took a seat before he sat down on a mound of dirt, far away from the picnic blanket.

"Where was I?" Theodore asked.

"I don't think you'd gotten anywhere," Zayne replied dryly. "Why don't you begin by telling us what you've discovered so far?"

Theodore blew out a breath. "Well, the sad fact is, I haven't discovered much. Lord Southmoor's been sticking close to home because he's concerned about thieves, most likely due to the fact that someone broke into his office and left a rather telling mess." Theodore paused and sent Agatha and Eliza a pointed look. "So, because of that, I haven't had an opportunity to introduce myself to him or search his house."

"He'll be at the New York Theater tomorrow night," Agatha said.

Theodore frowned. "How did you come by that information? I'm having him watched around the clock and no word of his attending the theater has reached my ears."

"I'm a journalist."

"Her mother."

Agatha and Zayne had spoken at the same time, and it was clear Agatha was less than pleased with Zayne's response because she stuck her tongue out at him.

"You're sure your information is reliable?" Theodore asked.

"Of course it is," Agatha said with a sniff. "My mother's a master at ferreting out social tidbits."

"Has your mother spoken about Mr. Eugene Daniels?" Theodore asked.

"I can't remember her ever speaking about him, but may I assume Mr. Beckett was right and this Eugene fellow is involved?" Agatha asked.

"Perhaps," Theodore replied. "It's unfortunate your mother hasn't mentioned him, as I've been encountering difficulties tracking the man down."

"Eugene's left town?" Hamilton asked.

"I don't know, but if he's still in New York, he's gone to ground."

"Maybe he's decided to move on," Zayne suggested.

"Why would he do that?" Hamilton asked. "He's been building up a substantial business with all those clients he stole from us."

"Maybe he realized we were on to him and decided to cut and run," Zayne said.

"We've been on to him from almost the beginning," Hamilton argued. "Our only problem is that we haven't been able to discover how he obtained access to our bids."

"Isn't that against the law?" Agatha asked.

"If he obtained the amounts we were bidding through illegal means, yes, but we've not been able to gather any proof as to how he's managed to do it," Hamilton said.

"Does he underbid jobs from other businesses or only your business?" Agatha pressed.

Hamilton frowned. "I've never looked into that aspect of the situation."

"Perhaps you should," she suggested. "What if this Mr. Daniels holds a personal grudge against your family?"

"Agatha has a good point," Zayne said. "Which brings me back to Eliza's question from a few weeks ago regarding the timing of Mary Ellen's death and the beginning of our trouble with Eugene. What if Mary Ellen was acquainted with Eugene, and for some reason, was feeding him information regarding our company?"

"I would hope she didn't hate me that much," Hamilton muttered. "Besides, Mary Ellen enjoyed the life my wealth afforded her. I can't believe she'd have done anything to disrupt her income."

Theodore cleared his throat. "It still warrants further investigation, and to tell you the truth, I was planning on looking into the connection between your deceased wife and Mr. Daniels, but I readily admit I've been spending my time trying to trail Lord Southmoor and simply locate Mr. Daniels." Theodore released a breath. "Since I have not been successful with any of my attempts, I might just have to make a late-night stop at Lord Southmoor's home tomorrow night and hope I discover something that may show us a connection to the two men, or better yet, Miss Sumner's lost fortune."

"Do you need any help?" Agatha asked.

"Did you not hear the part where I explained Lord Southmoor's suspicions have been raised because he believes thieves might have broken into his house?" Theodore asked.

"My hearing is excellent," she returned.

"Wonderful, but as I know for a fact that you and Miss Sumner are responsible for causing the suspicion in the first place, I will have to refuse your kind offer of assistance."

"Zayne and Hamilton broke into the house too," Agatha grouched.

"And then they hired me because they were intelligent enough to realize they were in over their heads."

Eliza held her breath and waited, knowing without a shadow of a doubt an explosion was imminent.

She did not have long to wait.

13

"That was quite enjoyable," Gloria said as she held the door open for Eliza, who was carrying a drowsy Ben in her arms. Eliza rolled her eyes and stepped over the threshold, pausing to wait for Agatha, who breezed into the house with Piper trailing a step behind.

"Theodore Wilder is a menace to all women," Agatha declared.

"He sure did leave in a hurry," Piper said.

"I would have left in a hurry too if Miss Watson had been shrieking at me in that manner," Zayne said as he walked through the door.

"I wasn't shrieking," Agatha muttered.

"Tell that to my ears," Zayne returned.

"I didn't like Mr. Wilder," Piper proclaimed.

Eliza shifted Ben in her arms. "He's not so bad, Piper, if you overlook his tendency to be condescending."

"And narrow-minded and chauvinistic," Agatha finished for her.

"I think a nice cup of tea is in order before we continue our discussion of Mr. Wilder and his many faults," Gloria said. "May I suggest we make ourselves comfortable in the parlor?"

"I'm going to put Ben down for a nap," Eliza said, taking a step forward only to come to a stop when Hamilton placed his hand on her arm.

"I'll take him," he said.

"I've got him."

Hamilton frowned. "May I ask what I've done to upset you, Eliza? You've been cold to me all day."

Since Eliza had no intention of telling Hamilton he'd hurt her feelings by warning her about Gloria's matchmaking efforts, she settled for sending him a shrug and then busied herself with handing Ben over to him.

"I did do something to upset you," Hamilton said as he settled Ben against his shoulder.

"It's nothing," she mumbled. "I'm just a bit out of sorts today. It's not my normal tendency to become involved in a bout of brawling with a deranged nanny."

"Why do I get the feeling you're not being completely truthful with me?" he asked.

"I have no idea," Eliza said, turning on her heel and looking back over her shoulder at him. "I really should go and join Agatha." She set her sights on the library, feeling Hamilton's gaze on her back with every step she took.

Honestly, what did the man expect? He'd made his feelings, or lack thereof, perfectly clear. She needed to keep a distance between them, but that was a bit difficult to do when the man seemed to appear at her side every other minute. She strode into the library, smiling when she discovered Gloria and Agatha still continuing their discussion of Theodore. She hurried to join them on the settee.

". . . and to think I actually considered the man a good match for Arabella," Gloria was saying. "Why, Arabella would never forgive me if I put her into contact with such an old-fashioned and less than progressive gentleman, although they would make an incredibly pretty pair."

Eliza noticed the now-familiar speculation residing in Gloria's eyes. She exchanged a grin with Agatha and returned her attention to Gloria. "Am I to assume Arabella is an attractive lady?"

"Attractive doesn't begin to describe her," Zayne said, stepping around a tea service and handing Eliza a cup of tea. "Arabella has been blessed, or cursed, as she claims, with incredible beauty, but her disposition is hardly one of complacency. She'd eat Theodore up and spit him out within minutes."

A tingle took that moment to sweep down Eliza's spine, but she refused to look up and acknowledge Hamilton's presence, knowing if she caught his gaze the man would probably see that as an invitation to join her and . . .

"Eliza, don't you agree?"

Eliza blinked and discovered Agatha smiling back at her. "Agree?"

"That you should come and visit me tomorrow, seeing as how my parents won't be at home and I'll be left all alone."

"And to think you had the nerve to call poor Theodore a menace," Zayne muttered.

Eliza snorted into her tea when Agatha tilted her chin and narrowed her eyes. "What could you possibly be implying?"

Eliza's snort turned into a hiccup when Zayne narrowed his eyes right back. "Do you honestly think anyone in this room doesn't know the real reason you want Eliza to keep you company tomorrow night? You're intent on a bit of subterfuge."

"That's ridiculous," Agatha said with an innocent batting of her lashes.

"Is it?" Zayne returned. "Perhaps we should employ a nanny tomorrow night to keep an eye on you."

"Nannies are bad, and you shouldn't tease Miss Agatha like that, Uncle Zayne," Piper said.

Zayne blinked. "Why are nannies bad?"

"Eliza and our former nanny got into an altercation today over the fact that the woman got violent with Ben," Gloria explained.

"Miss Eliza pulled her hair," Piper said.

"Yes, thank you for bringing that up again, Piper," Eliza said before noticing that Agatha was beaming back at her.

"This is marvelous," Agatha exclaimed, "and I must state here and now that I'm going to have to take a bit of credit for your improved circumstances."

"How in the world do you reason out that getting into a brawl with the nanny is an improvement in my circumstances?" Eliza asked.

"Well, you've clearly formed lovely attachments to Ben and Piper, which I would have to assume has improved your life. Only think, if I hadn't interceded on your behalf, sending up a special prayer to God to assist you with your situation, well, poor little Ben wouldn't have had a champion to rescue him from the clutches of a deranged nanny."

"I'm the one who hired the woman in the first place."

"Hmm . . . true, but no matter, it's all still a part of a bigger plan for you."

Eliza released a sigh. "Agatha, I'm perfectly willing to accept the possibility of God's provision, but your reasoning is a bit odd in this particular instance. My life is still unsettled, I have yet to be reunited with my fortune, and I'm now missing a chunk of hair from my spat with the nanny. I don't believe God is currently guiding my path."

"Of course He's guiding your path, child," Gloria said. "You might not realize it yet, but all of these trials you've experienced are happening to you for a reason. You simply need to wait to see what the outcome will be."

Eliza chanced a glance to Hamilton and found him watching her from his position by the fireplace. He sent her a smile and then turned to Gloria. "It's clear this isn't a conversation Eliza's comfortable with, Mother. May I suggest we change the subject?"

Gloria looked as if she wanted to argue the point, but finally nodded and smiled at Eliza. "Forgive me, dear. I did not mean to upset you. I sometimes forget that not everyone believes as I do."

Eliza leaned forward. "Mrs. Beckett, I didn't take offense at either your or Agatha's words. It's apparent the two of you are women of strong faith, but at the moment, my journey is not as clear. I willingly admit I harbor anger toward God for allowing my life to take such a turn, but I do hope you and Agatha are right and that there is a plan for me. It's a lovely thought, but one I can't embrace wholeheartedly at this particular time."

Agatha reached out and patted Eliza on the knee. "Fair enough. I, for one, will not say another word about the matter." She grinned. "So, did you want to come over tomorrow? I know my sisters would love to see you."

"I'm not certain your parents would approve of having me in the house," Eliza said slowly.

"Excellent point," Zayne exclaimed as he got up from his chair. "That settles the matter nicely."

Agatha raised her chin. "I'll have you know, my mother would not be opposed at all to having Eliza visit. Grace and Lily have been bereft without her, and Mother has come to believe that she may have been a bit hasty in agreeing with Eliza's dismissal." Agatha turned to Eliza. "My sisters claim their new governess is hardly proficient at anything, and I understand she flatly refuses to read any books with pirates in them."

"Lily and Grace can't be too happy about that," Eliza said.

"That's why you must agree to come over tomorrow," Agatha

said. "We'll pull out the pirate books and have a lovely evening with the girls."

Before Eliza could respond, Gloria made a *tsk*ing sound, drawing everyone's attention. "Surely you don't think we believe that piece of nonsense. Your sisters, Miss Watson, will be in bed by nine at the latest, and that leaves all sorts of time for the two of you to get into mischief."

She ignored Agatha's huff and continued. "I already have a solution."

"This should be good," Eliza muttered.

Gloria sent her a stern look, took a deep breath, and smiled. "I do believe I might have forgotten to mention this, but we've been invited to the Murdocks' for a night of dinner and dancing, and I've taken it upon myself to accept their invitation."

"Excuse me?" Eliza sputtered.

"We're going to a ball tomorrow night."

"A ball?" Eliza repeated weakly.

"Yes, dear, and do not attempt to convince me you'll be uncomfortable, as I know full well you attended many balls back in England."

"Yes, but I was not attempting to go unnoticed at the time, which, if you've forgotten, I am attempting to do at the moment, and I hardly see how I can remain inconspicuous if I show up at a ball. Besides, I have nothing suitable to wear."

"I took the liberty of ordering you a stunning gown from B. Altman's," Gloria said.

Eliza opened and closed her mouth, but couldn't think of a single reply to that. She exchanged glances with Agatha and then turned back to Gloria. "What of Agatha? I can't simply leave her by herself. You know perfectly well she'll—"

"I suggest you don't finish that sentence," Agatha grouched.

"She'll come with us," Gloria declared. "The more the merrier,

I always say. We'll make it a party of . . . let's see. Me, Eliza, Miss Watson, Hamilton, and Zayne—five."

"I don't remember responding to an invitation to the Murdocks'," Hamilton said.

"I replied for you," Gloria said with an airy wave of her hand.

"I didn't receive an invitation to the ball," Agatha said. "It wouldn't be proper for me to simply show up there."

"I'll secure you an invitation, dear," Gloria said. "I'm good friends with Mrs. Murdock, and I know she'll be only too happy to include you in the festivities."

"I'm not certain my father is willing to allow me my freedom just yet," Agatha said. "He was most distraught that I landed myself in jail. In fact, I overheard him speaking with Mother, and he's contemplating sending me off to stay with my aunt Mildred." She grinned at Eliza. "You saw Aunt Mildred's gown. Her personality is much like the garment you wore."

Eliza returned the grin.

"Your father won't balk in the least if I send him and your mother a personal note," Gloria said. "The Murdocks are a well-known society family, and with three eligible sons, your parents will be only too happy to allow you to go with us." She stood up and made her way to the door, looking over her shoulder. "I'll go and pen a note to your parents now, Miss Watson. You may take it with you when you leave."

Eliza noticed Agatha sneaking a look at Zayne before she raised her head and smiled at Gloria. "May I suggest you send a note with a servant instead of sending it home with me? Our efforts might be for naught if my father discovers I've been anywhere but the orphanage today."

"Good point," Gloria said. "I'll send Matthews with it and instruct him to wait for a reply." She nodded once and then strode from the room.

Eliza leaned closer to Agatha and lowered her voice. "Why

did you agree to go to the ball when only a few minutes ago you were determined to spend the evening with me?"

Agatha turned an interesting shade of pink. "I've always wanted to go to one of the Murdocks' balls. I hear they're very entertaining."

Eliza lowered her voice to a mere whisper. "You haven't completely put your infatuation aside, have you?"

"Don't be silly."

"What are you two talking about now?" Zayne asked. "You're not trying to figure out a way to sneak from the ball and continue with your investigation, are you?"

"They were talking about inflabulations," Piper said.

"Good heavens, Piper, I forgot you were here," Agatha said, her color deepening to a lovely shade of purple.

"What are inflabulations?" Zayne asked.

In order to rescue Agatha from an incredibly mortifying situation, Eliza decided it was time to change the subject. "You know, since Agatha has agreed to attend the ball, there really isn't any need for me to go. It's not as if anyone needs to be concerned I'll try to sneak out of the house."

Apparently, that had been a concern, as Eliza found herself the next day sitting in a chair while Mabel worked on her hair. "I hope your face doesn't freeze like that," Piper said as she skipped into the room.

Eliza narrowed her eyes at the child, who had been instrumental in convincing Hamilton of the fact that Eliza should not be left alone in the house while everyone else attended the ball.

"Aren't you supposed to be playing with Ben?"

"He's fine. Miss Jamison is playing war with him."

"Do you think he likes Miss Jamison?" Eliza asked.

"Yes, because she's a cook, not a nanny," Piper replied.

"That makes sense in a Ben kind of way."

"I told Grandmother she should ask Miss Jamison to be our nanny after you leave," Piper said, leaning closer to Eliza as she lowered her voice. "She's not very good at cooking."

Eliza exchanged a smile with Mabel before returning her attention to Piper. "It would hurt Miss Jamison's feelings if she heard you say that."

"She's the one who told me she's a horrible cook. She only took on this assistant cook job because her aunt is a head cook and talked her into it."

The way people opened up around Piper really was amazing. They obviously overlooked the fact that, even though she was only five, she was incredibly intelligent.

"Why did you say Miss Jamison could be Ben's nanny after I left?" Eliza asked.

Piper rolled her eyes as she plopped down on a nearby chair. "He won't like her if he thinks she's his nanny while you're still here." Piper apparently believed that settled the matter because she switched topics and began launching questions at Eliza on topics ranging from the latest fashions to whether or not Eliza had ever been fortunate enough to ride a tricycle.

Time flew, and before Eliza realized it, Mabel was assisting her into her corset and bustle with Piper flitting around her, trying to help.

"Why do ladies wear these bustles?" Piper asked as she eyed the contraption tied to Eliza's back. "It looks like you have two behinds."

"Exactly the effect I was hoping for," Eliza said as she lifted her arms to allow Mabel to slip the gown carefully over her head. Mabel tugged the gown into place and buttoned up the back.

"You look a sight," Mabel proclaimed.

"Thank you, Mabel," Eliza replied, turning her head as she heard the door open.

"Oh, wonderful, you're ready," Gloria said, bustling into the room and beaming at Eliza. "You will be the most beautiful woman in attendance tonight. That blue really brings out the color of your eyes."

"I was hoping to remain inconspicuous."

"No chance of that, my dear," Gloria replied as she surveyed Eliza. "That gown fits to perfection, and Mabel has outdone herself with your hair. You are enchanting."

Before Eliza had an opportunity to glance at her reflection, Gloria took her by the arm and maneuvered her out of the room and down the stairs. She was so intent on watching her every step that she wasn't aware Hamilton was waiting for her until Gloria came to a sudden stop and Eliza noticed a pair of men's shoes only a few feet away. She raised her gaze and felt all the breath leave her in a split second.

Hamilton was the most handsome gentleman she'd ever laid eyes on, but that wasn't what caused all the air to leave her lungs. No, it was the look in his eyes—a look that was admiring, warm, and held a hint of something Eliza didn't quite understand.

It certainly wasn't a look of disinterest.

She felt the strangest urge to flee back to her room.

14

*H*amilton was unable to move.

The sight of the gorgeous creature who was obviously Eliza, but not the Eliza he was accustomed to seeing, made even the simple act of breathing impossible.

The woman who was more often than not streaked with smudges from Ben's grubby little hands was nowhere to be found, and in her place stood a woman who was elegance personified.

Eliza's glorious red hair was swept off her face and pulled to the top of her head with gleaming ringlets cascading around her shoulders and framing her delicate features. Her eyes sparkled, and there was a delightful flush to her creamy skin. His gaze traveled along the soft, exposed expanse of her shoulders, and he wanted nothing more than to reach out and touch the softness, if only to ascertain she was real.

It came to him then that the woman standing beside his mother was someone he knew relatively little about.

The thought took him aback.

He'd been trying, unsuccessfully of course, to maintain a bit of distance from Eliza, as she'd been more than vocal regarding her intention to return to England. Unfortunately, the woman drew him in a manner he couldn't ignore. He'd been driving himself mad trying to figure out what he'd done to annoy her, because annoy her, he most certainly had. She'd been a bit cool with him over the past two days, but she wouldn't explain the reason behind the coolness. He'd assumed she was trying to maintain distance from him as well, but at times, he was quite sure he'd detected a small trace of hurt in her eyes.

A loud cough from his mother had him blinking back to awareness. He stepped forward, but was thwarted from extending Eliza his hand when his brother brushed past him and beat him to it.

"You look absolutely lovely, Eliza," Zayne said, taking her hand and bringing it to his lips. He dropped it and turned to his mother. "As do you, Mother."

"Charming as ever," Gloria said before arching a brow at Hamilton.

He cleared his throat. "The two of you make a pretty picture."

Gloria's brow arched higher.

Now that was less than eloquent. He tried again, this time directing his comments to Eliza. "Your appearance is very regal this evening, Eliza," he said, attempting not to wince when he heard the words come out of his mouth. What was wrong with him? He was normally perfectly capable of turning out a pretty phase when the occasion called for it.

Eliza's brow now matched his mother's, and there was a distinct touch of annoyance in her gaze.

"Lovely?" he offered.

"I already used that word," Zayne said.

"Different," Hamilton proclaimed. "You look different."

Gloria rolled her eyes, handed Eliza over to Zayne, and sniffed when Hamilton offered her his arm, walking out of the house on her own rather than accepting his assistance.

He found himself trailing after everyone down the hallway, gritting his teeth when Eliza's laughter trailed back to him.

Apparently, she wasn't annoyed with Zayne.

". . . have the tongues wagging tonight," Zayne finished saying.

Hamilton ran into the back of his brother as Eliza suddenly stopped in her tracks and turned a glare on him. He blinked. Why was she glaring at him? He hadn't said a word.

"Why will there be tongues wagging?" she demanded.

He looked at his brother. "Yes, Zayne, why will there be tongues wagging?"

"New York isn't accustomed to receiving English aristocrats on a regular basis," Zayne replied.

Hamilton shot a glance to his mother and found her muttering furiously under her breath even as she glared at Zayne. She drew in a deep breath, blew it out, and then directed a somewhat weak smile at Eliza, who was standing there with her mouth hanging open.

Hamilton held his breath, knowing disaster was imminent.

"How, may I ask, would anyone know I'm a member of the aristocracy?" Eliza asked in a voice Hamilton had never heard before. It was somewhat haughty and had a nasal tone to it that gave credence to the fact that Eliza was, indeed, an aristocrat.

He didn't particularly like that voice.

Gloria moved to Eliza's side and patted her arm. "Now, there's no need for alarm, dear, but you see, I thought it would be in your best interest if everyone knew exactly who you truly are, so . . . I let Mrs. Murdock know she'd be entertaining Lady Eliza Sumner."

Eliza squared her shoulders, and Hamilton thought she was

going to start yelling, but instead, she lifted her nose, turned on her heel, and began walking back down the hallway.

"I'm not going," she said over her shoulder.

"Go after her," Gloria hissed under her breath.

"Not on your life," Hamilton hissed right back. "I'm not the one who let the cat out of the bag."

Gloria released a dramatic sigh and stomped after Eliza. Hamilton found himself walking behind her, not really certain why, but unable to help himself.

"You're overreacting," Gloria said.

Eliza turned. "I didn't agree to attend this ball as Lady Eliza."

"But, my dear, that's who you are, and it's ridiculous for you to continue hiding from that fact."

Eliza shook her head, causing a riot of curls to tumble around her face, her appearance at distinct odds with her refusal to admit she was indeed *Lady* Eliza Sumner and no simple *Miss*. "Not in this country. You know perfectly well I'm trying to remain inconspicuous, and there's no possible way that will happen if I attend the ball as an aristocrat."

"It's not as if you could remain inconspicuous forever," Gloria argued. "You have a demeanor about you which screams the fact that you've led a life of privilege. Besides, talk was already swirling around town."

"I think I've just been insulted," Eliza said with a sniff before her eyes narrowed. "What talk?"

"Come now, Eliza, you've visited practically every store in New York with me. People were bound to notice," Gloria said.

"I wore a hat."

"Honestly, a woman as beautiful as you can hardly hide beneath a measly old hat. You have an inherent grace about you which draws attention."

"I'm sure I should thank you for your compliment, but I don't think I have it in me at the moment." She turned to Hamilton. "Did you know about this?"

"I swear I did not. If I'd known what my mother intended, I would have attempted to dissuade her."

"Traitor," Gloria muttered.

"Now Mr. Hayes is certain to discover I'm in town," Eliza said, her shoulders slumping, which caused Hamilton to move to her side and take her hand in his, ignoring the hiss she emitted.

"Eliza, Theodore is working diligently on the case, and I have to assume it will not be long until he is able to bring Mr. Hayes to justice," Hamilton said.

"What if he flees to escape prosecution?"

"From what we've learned of the man thus far, he's hardly likely to abandon his newfound status without a fight," Hamilton said.

"Are we willing to chance that?" Eliza shot back.

Gloria heaved a sigh. "It's not as if we have any choice in the matter now, dear. I'm certain Mrs. Murdock has already informed her many guests of your expected arrival."

"So what you're suggesting is that I really have no option other than to attend the ball," Eliza grouched.

"I'm afraid so," Gloria muttered, although she looked anything but contrite.

Hamilton offered Eliza his arm and then was forced to exert a touch of pressure to prod her back down the hallway and out the door. He helped her into the carriage and turned to his mother, not surprised in the least when his mother took the seat opposite Eliza and demanded Zayne sit next to her. This left him no choice but to sit by Eliza, his lips twitching when she began inching away from him.

She seemed to make a habit of doing that.

An uneasy silence filled the carriage as Eliza spent the ride glaring at his mother, then him, then Zayne, and then back at his mother, all the while repeatedly smoothing her gown down.

A trace of disgust washed over him.

She was nervous, and he'd neglected to do anything to calm her nerves. He cleared his throat, drawing her attention away from Zayne, who was the current victim of one of her glares. He caught Zayne's relieved smile, sent him a brief nod, and turned back to Eliza.

"You mustn't worry about the ball, Eliza," he began. "You're certain to receive a warm welcome there."

Eliza's hands stilled. "I'm not nervous, Hamilton, I'm annoyed; there's a difference. I was presented at court when I made my debut, and honestly, after surviving that, a ball doesn't faze me in the least."

"You were presented to the queen?" Hamilton asked.

"Queen Victoria was very gracious, if a bit intimidating. After you've been presented to a queen, everything that comes after pales in comparison."

Who was this woman?

Hamilton forced a smile before he turned to look out the window. He didn't notice all the sights rumbling by him as he sat lost in thought, wondering why the knowledge Eliza had obviously lived an indulgent life rankled.

Why hadn't she mentioned she'd met Queen Victoria?

What else had she neglected to mention?

Mary Ellen had been a master at concealing things. Did the two women share something in common?

That thought had doubt niggling through him. He'd sworn he would never become involved with a woman who had secrets, and yet, here he was, unable to help himself in regard to Eliza.

"Ah, we've arrived at the Watsons'," Zayne declared. "Shall I go fetch Agatha?"

"We'll both go," Gloria said. "By the enthusiastic response I received from Mrs. Watson, I'm afraid the woman is still hopeful of a match with either you or Hamilton; I don't believe she cares which one."

"That's a bit insulting," Zayne remarked.

"If you're fortunate to have daughters of your own someday, dear, you'll come to understand Mrs. Watson's reasoning. You know how I fret about Arabella's future, and poor Mrs. Watson has three daughters to see settled. It's no wonder she's desperate. The eldest Miss Watson is not getting any younger."

"Don't let Agatha hear you say that," Zayne muttered as he offered his mother a hand and helped her out of the carriage.

Hamilton turned his head and found Eliza watching him. He tried for a smile, but realized he'd failed miserably when she rolled her eyes.

"Judging from your expression, I would have to assume something I said bothered you," she said.

"You never told me you were presented to the queen."

"I didn't know it was a matter of great importance."

"What else have you neglected to tell me?"

"How in the world do you expect me to answer that?" she asked.

"You have withheld pertinent information from me regarding your life."

"Being presented to the queen when I was all of sixteen years old was not overly pertinent," Eliza said. "Every young lady who has a social standing in society is presented at court."

"I had no way of knowing that."

"You could have simply asked instead of behaving in such a boorish manner."

"I'm hardly boorish."

"Brooding, then."

"Am I interrupting?" Agatha questioned as the door to the carriage opened and she struggled in, the extensive bustle attached to her dress almost knocking Hamilton from his seat as she turned and plopped down on the other side.

"We should have brought a larger carriage," Zayne said as he steadied Agatha, who was listing to the side, and then turned to help his mother into her seat, eyeing the remaining space skeptically.

"Here, sit between us," Gloria instructed. "We'll use you for extra support."

Zayne heaved a sigh and maneuvered his large frame between the two ladies.

"Comfy?" Hamilton asked.

Zayne raised a brow, but refrained from replying when the carriage lurched forward and Agatha fell into his lap.

Hamilton grinned and watched his brother push Agatha back into a sitting position, but his grin disappeared when Agatha opened her mouth.

"Was someone saying something about brooding?"

"Who's brooding?" Gloria inquired.

"If I were to hazard a guess, I would say your son," Agatha said.

"Hamilton?"

"Of course," Agatha replied. "Zayne doesn't have the propensity to brood." She turned her attention to Eliza. "I did warn you about this when we first became acquainted. I distinctly recall mentioning Hamilton's brooding nature."

"Why were the two of you discussing my brooding nature?" Hamilton asked, curious in spite of himself.

"Never mind that," Agatha said quickly when Eliza began sputtering. "I believe we were discussing why you're brooding at the moment." She frowned at Eliza. "Did you do something to him?"

"From what I can discern, Hamilton is brooding because I neglected to mention to him the fact that I was presented to the queen, but honestly, I don't understand why he got all huffy about that. If anyone has a right to be huffy at the moment, it's me."

"Because . . . ?" Agatha asked.

"It's my fault," Gloria said, speaking up. "I revealed Eliza's true identity to Mrs. Murdock."

Hamilton bit back a groan when Agatha sucked in a sharp breath. "Good heavens, Mrs. Beckett, do you think that was wise? You know how Mrs. Murdock loves to gossip."

"That was exactly the point I was trying to make," Eliza said. "Well, not about the gossiping business, seeing as how I've never met Mrs. Murdock before, but I'm concerned that after tonight, everyone will know who I am, including Bartholomew Hayes."

Agatha looked out the window and then back to Eliza. "Well, it's too late to do anything about it now. We're here."

The carriage rolled to a stop and Hamilton got out first, helping his mother, Agatha, and then Eliza down before exchanging a telling glance with Zayne.

"You think she'll be all right?" Zayne whispered with a nod in Eliza's direction.

Hamilton looked to Eliza, who was tilting her chin in that unfamiliar haughty manner. "I think Eliza is more than accustomed to this type of setting."

"And that bothers you," Zayne said.

Hamilton ignored the remark and moved to Eliza's side, surprised when she accepted his arm. He nudged her up the walk, until they came to a stop at the end of a very long line of guests waiting to make their entrance.

"I'll be right back," Gloria said before she strode away, dodging the guests and soon disappearing from view.

"Where do you suppose she's going?" Zayne asked.

"Knowing Mother, she probably told Mrs. Murdock to make some big presentation of Eliza. Hopefully, she's come to her senses and is on her way to correct that little situation," Hamilton said dryly. He squeezed Eliza's arm. "Are you certain you're not nervous?"

"I may be a little nervous," she admitted. "At least I knew everyone in England."

"Do you have many friends in England?" Zayne asked.

"I used to, before I lost my fortune," she said.

"Those people were never your friends," Agatha said softly. "Friends are those who stick with you in good times and bad."

"Truer words have never been spoken," Eliza returned. "I'm curious as to how they'll react when I return with my fortune restored, especially Lawrence."

"Lawrence was your fiancé, right?" Agatha asked.

Eliza nodded.

"If you ask me, you were fortunate to lose your wealth," Agatha said. "If you hadn't lost all your money, you would have married a man of questionable integrity."

"You're right, but I must confess I've enjoyed thinking up all sorts of nasty schemes to seek retribution from him once I secure my fortune and return home," Eliza said before she looked up at Hamilton. "Do you think that makes me a bad person?"

Hamilton studied her for a moment as his mind flashed to an image of her playing with his children. "I must admit I never considered you to be a woman who would harbor thoughts of revenge."

"I'm not certain the thoughts I'm harboring are exactly revenge," Eliza said slowly. "They're more . . ."

Before Eliza could finish, Gloria marched up to them, a beaming woman by her side.

Hamilton watched in amazement as right before his eyes, Eliza changed into a smiling, gracious aristocrat.

"Lady Eliza Sumner, may I present to you our hostess, Mrs.

Murdock," Gloria said. "Mrs. Murdock, this is Lady Eliza Sumner."

"My dear Lady Eliza," Mrs. Murdock gushed, "I have been anxiously awaiting your arrival. I must tell you, I adore all things English."

"You're too kind," Eliza replied, her tone causing Hamilton's teeth to click together. She sounded as if she'd turned more English, more proper, and didn't sound anything like the Eliza he thought he knew.

His temper began to simmer when Eliza took Mrs. Murdock's arm and strolled with the lady back up the walk, his mother on her other side, apparently forgetting all about him.

"She really is an aristocrat, isn't she?" Agatha asked as she took Hamilton by the arm and propelled him forward, Zayne trailing in their wake.

Hamilton forced a smile as they moved through the receiving line, his thoughts so distracted that he wasn't able to fully appreciate the lavishness of the decorations. Mrs. Murdock had apparently taken the fall season to heart; sputtering pumpkins filled the house, while garlands of festive red and yellow leaves draped across the ceiling. He was relieved when Agatha and Zayne went in search of some drinks, leaving him to slouch against a wall. His mood became more dismal by the second as he watched Eliza twirl around the dance floor in the arms of some nameless gentleman.

It certainly hadn't taken much time at all for the hounds to come sniffing around.

"Eliza seems to be adapting well," Zayne remarked, handing Hamilton a glass of champagne before moving to take up wall space right beside him, an annoying grin on his face. "Just a word of advice, Hamilton. You might try to soften your expression a bit. You're scaring the ladies."

"I'm not scaring any ladies."

"Oh?" Zayne questioned as he nodded toward a group of young ladies who were definitely giving them a wide berth as they moved quickly out of range.

Hamilton pasted a smile on his face. "There, satisfied?"

"You look deranged."

"Go away."

"Not until you tell me what's wrong. Is it Eliza?"

"No."

"Why do you keep throwing her nasty looks, then?"

"I'm not throwing her nasty looks."

Zayne rolled his eyes.

"Besides, it's not as if she'd even notice," Hamilton muttered when he saw she'd moved on to another dance partner. He released a sigh. "I don't know her at all. From what I can tell, it seems as if she enjoys being frivolous."

"Is it a crime now to enjoy a bit of frivolity?" Zayne asked.

"Mary Ellen was frivolous."

"You're comparing Eliza to Mary Ellen?"

"I cannot overlook the similarities," Hamilton said. "It became crystal clear to me this evening that there is too much regarding Eliza I just don't know."

"Of course there is. You only recently met her. There's hardly been enough time to learn everything about her, but that's what makes life interesting."

"I don't want an interesting life. I want a stable life. I need a stable life and a stable companion who will provide a stable home for my children."

Zayne's mouth dropped open. "You're considering marriage again."

"I *was* considering marriage," Hamilton corrected. "I have since come to my senses."

"What are you talking about? Eliza's wonderful."

"She was presented to the queen," Hamilton said.

"What does that have to do with anything?"

"She has high expectations of life. I could not fill those expectations. I've never been presented to the queen," Hamilton said.

"Because we live in America and don't have a queen."

Hamilton's lips twitched. "You think I'm being ridiculous."

"I think you're lying to yourself," Zayne corrected. "You're inventing reasons to push Eliza away. You're trying to use Eliza's privileged upbringing as a reason to discontinue your relationship with her."

"We don't have a relationship."

"You just admitted you were considering marriage."

"That was before I came to the realization that a woman bent on revenge would hardly have any room in her heart for other emotions such as love," Hamilton said.

"Eliza didn't actually say she was bent on revenge," Zayne said. "If you ask me, I think she was simply speaking out of hurt. Besides, you're intent on revenge in regard to Eugene Daniels. Does that mean you have no room for love?"

"That's different. I'm a man."

"Now you sound like Theodore."

Hamilton grinned as he shifted his gaze away from his brother and settled it on Eliza, who was still on the dance floor, her partner beaming back at her as if he could not believe his good fortune.

"She's a remarkable woman, Hamilton. I would hate to see you lose her because your past has clouded your judgment. I have not broached this subject because I didn't believe you were ready to hear what I needed to say, but I think you need to hear it now. It is time you mended your differences with God. You need His help, and He'll show you the way," Zayne said before he clapped Hamilton on the shoulder and then sauntered away, leaving Hamilton to his thoughts.

Was Zayne right? Was he allowing his past to cloud his

judgment? He watched Eliza laugh with her dance partner and realized he was behaving like an idiot.

A feeling of remorse swept over him as he recalled his dismal behavior toward Eliza as they'd traveled to the ball. She must think he'd lost his mind, and truth be told, she wouldn't be far off the mark. He took a deep breath, sent up a quick prayer for guidance, and pushed himself away from the wall, determined to seek her out.

15

*E*liza accepted a glass of lemonade she did not particularly want from Mr. Jeffrey Murdock, Mrs. Murdock's seemingly eligible son, and suppressed a groan when half of the contents sloshed over her hand when Hamilton's sudden appearance by her side startled her. She sent him what she could only hope was a cool glance before wiping her hand with the handkerchief Mr. Murdock immediately extended to her, and turned her back on Hamilton, summoning up a smile for Mr. Murdock.

"Thank you for fetching me a drink, Mr. Murdock," she said. "It's quite warm in here."

"Perhaps you're overly warm because you haven't sat out a single dance," Hamilton said.

Eliza refused to acknowledge his remark and kept her gaze on Mr. Murdock. "I've been delighted over the charming welcome I've received tonight."

"As you are the most beautiful woman to ever grace a New York ball, you should expect nothing less," Mr. Murdock said.

Eliza resisted the urge to sigh. Although she'd been accustomed to people fawning over her back in England before the scandal, she now found it somewhat uncomfortable. She'd been showered with compliments from every single gentleman she'd danced with this evening, and truth be told, she found it rather embarrassing.

"You are too kind," she finally managed to say.

"Mr. Beckett," Mr. Murdock said, turning to address Hamilton, who was in the process of coughing quite loudly into his hand, "may I order you a drink?"

"No need, Mr. Murdock. I'm not particularly thirsty," Hamilton said.

"My mother has a wonderful tonic for chronic coughs," Mr. Murdock continued. "You should seek her out so she can fetch it for you."

"It was only a small tickle," he proclaimed.

"My sister made mention of the fact that she was hopeful of a dance with you," Mr. Murdock said, reaching out an arm and snagging a woman who'd been chatting with friends behind them. "Here she is now."

Eliza was suddenly faced with a woman dressed in the most peculiar outfit she'd ever seen. The gown was cut from yards and yards of billowing yellow fabric and trimmed with garish green ribbons, which did little to complement the woman's light complexion. Mr. Murdock's sister had, for some odd reason, scraped her white-blond hair back in a severe chignon, but after a brief moment of closer perusal, Eliza found herself surprised. The lady's features were delicate and unusual, and Eliza couldn't help but wonder why the lady would go to such an obvious effort to divert attention from her unique looks. Before she could contemplate the matter further, the lady blinked at everyone and then sent her brother a glare.

"Did you need something, Jeffrey?" the woman asked.

"Felicia, here is Mr. Beckett. You do still have open spots on your dance card, don't you?" Mr. Murdock asked.

Felicia's face turned bright red. "I do. Thank you for bringing that to everyone's attention," she said between clenched teeth.

Eliza immediately took pity on the woman. "I don't believe we have been introduced. I'm Lady Eliza Sumner and you must be Mr. Murdock's sister."

"Unfortunately," Felicia muttered before dipping a curtsy in Eliza's direction. "It's very nice to meet you, Lady Eliza. I'm Miss Felicia Murdock."

"Miss Murdock," Eliza returned, dipping into a curtsy of her own.

Hamilton stepped forward, smiled, and bent over Felicia's hand. "I would consider it a great honor if you would take a turn around the dance floor with me. I have not yet had the pleasure of a dance this evening."

Felicia turned an even darker shade of red, but accepted Hamilton's arm, allowing him to guide her away to the dance floor.

Although Eliza was still angry with Hamilton, seeing as he'd been scowling at her all evening, his kindness to Felicia had the beginnings of a smile tugging her lips.

"I must tell you, Felicia will be over the moon about dancing with Mr. Beckett. She and her friends spend hours talking about him and his brother," Mr. Murdock said.

Eliza's smile slid off her face. "Is Mr. Beckett much sought after?"

"Indeed, there's not an unmarried lady here who doesn't secretly hope to form an attachment with him, but enough about Mr. Beckett. I believe the next dance is about to begin, and you did promise it to me."

Eliza handed her glass to a passing servant and accepted Mr. Murdock's arm, walking with him to the dance floor. Hamilton and Felicia were already in place, and Eliza's eyes lingered on Hamilton while she waited for the music to begin. Although he was giving Felicia the proper amount of attention, Eliza was certain he was also keeping an eye on her. It was rather odd, this sudden change in temperament. Where was the sullen man from the beginning of the evening?

When the dance ended, Mr. Murdock attempted to steer her toward a large double door, which more than likely led to a terrace. As Eliza had no intention of spending a moment alone with the gentleman and possessed more than enough experience deflecting just such situations, she discreetly put pressure on his arm, forcing his direction to change. She breathed a silent sigh of relief when Hamilton stepped in front of them.

"I believe dinner is about to be served," Hamilton said, his eyes glinting somewhat dangerously at Mr. Murdock.

"Lady Eliza is to join my family at the main table," Mr. Murdock said, his eyes glinting right back at Hamilton.

"I know," Hamilton said with a smile. "My mother, brother, Miss Watson, and I are to join you. Your mother arranged it."

Eliza found her arms taken in strong grips, one by Hamilton and one by Mr. Murdock. She was marched rather clumsily into the room set up for dining and could only hope she would arrive in one piece, as both men seemed intent on hurrying her along. For what purpose, she had no idea, but her sense of humor kicked in and by the time they reached the table, she was grinning.

"Sit here," Mr. Murdock said as he dropped her arm and pulled out a chair.

"I think you'll be more comfortable here," Hamilton argued, spinning her into a seat right next to Gloria and sitting down in the empty chair beside her.

What was wrong with the man? He was very nearly being rude to poor Mr. Murdock, who, Eliza noticed, was glaring openly at Hamilton but quickly recovered his amiable demeanor when Agatha sidled up to the table.

"Is there room for me?" Agatha asked.

"Of course," Mr. Murdock said. "I would love nothing more than to share your company over dinner."

Eliza watched Agatha send Mr. Murdock a pretty smile that prompted Zayne to release a huff of annoyance on the other side of Gloria.

"Have you been having fun, Eliza?" Gloria asked.

"She's danced every dance," Hamilton said before Eliza could respond.

"How wonderful," Gloria exclaimed. "See, I told you there was no reason for your earlier distress."

"You were distressed?" Mr. Murdock inquired as he leaned forward over Agatha.

"It was only a little case of nerves," Eliza returned, her eyes widening when Hamilton absently traced a finger down her arm.

The action was not lost on Mr. Murdock. He sat back in his seat and turned his head to address the guest on his left.

"What are you doing?" Eliza hissed. "If you're not careful, everyone will believe there's soon to be an announcement."

"That would bother you?"

And just what did he mean by that? She took a deep breath and slowly released it. "You've obviously lost your mind."

Hamilton sent her a wicked smile and refused to say another word, although he did remove his finger from her skin.

The next ten minutes were spent greeting other guests, and all was going well until a loud gasp sounded from the other side of the table. Eliza looked up and could not quite stifle a groan. It was Mrs. Amherst, the woman Eliza had spoken with at the Watsons' dinner party.

A sense of déjà vu descended.

"Is that you, Miss Sumner?" Mrs. Amherst questioned.

"Why, Mrs. Amherst," Eliza replied with an attempt at a smile, "how lovely to see you again."

Mrs. Amherst arched a brow. "I must say you've improved your appearance remarkably, my dear. But tell me, is it becoming the fashion to include governesses in all society events?"

Eliza was spared a response when Mrs. Murdock leaned forward in her seat and gave a tittering laugh. "I'm afraid you've gotten Lady Eliza confused with someone else, Mrs. Amherst."

"*Lady Eliza?*" Mrs. Amherst questioned.

"I told you a member of the aristocracy was attending tonight," Mrs. Murdock said.

"Perhaps someone would be so kind as to explain to me why, when I met this woman a few weeks ago, she was a mere governess pressed into service because of some dire illness Miss Watson had developed." Mrs. Amherst's eyes suddenly narrowed as she set her sights on Agatha. "You seem to have made a remarkable recovery."

Agatha blinked and then smiled. "Yes, thank you for noticing, Mrs. Amherst. I do so appreciate your concern."

"Why is your governess portraying herself as a lady?"

Silence settled over the table.

Agatha straightened in her chair. "I'm afraid the tale is less than dramatic."

"Do tell," Mrs. Amherst encouraged.

Agatha sent Eliza a look that clearly stated she needed assistance. Eliza cleared her throat.

"Agatha and I are good friends," she began, her mind whirling with some sort of plausible explanation that wouldn't be an outright lie. Before she could come up with anything else, Agatha interrupted.

"That's right. Lady Eliza and I are good friends."

"I'm afraid that doesn't explain why she was passing herself off as a governess," Mrs. Amherst said.

"Ahh, you see," Agatha began, "Lady Eliza didn't want anyone to know her true identity."

"Why would you want to disguise your identity?" Mrs. Amherst asked, turning to Eliza.

"Hmm . . ." Eliza said. "I didn't care to bring attention to myself?"

"Exactly right," Agatha said with a nod.

"And you and your parents were fine with her charade?" Mrs. Amherst asked, swirling her head back to look at Agatha.

"*I* was perfectly fine with it," Agatha replied.

"But how did the two of you become such fast friends?" Mrs. Amherst asked. "Was it through correspondence?"

"W-well . . ." Agatha stuttered.

"I have always believed corresponding with a person from another country improves one's education," Gloria said, smoothly insinuating herself into the conversation. "Why, I used to correspond regularly with a woman from France, and it helped my written French tremendously."

Mrs. Amherst ignored Gloria's statement, her eyes darting between Agatha and Eliza. "But, why did you, Lady Eliza, attend the Watsons' dinner party as a governess and yet you're attending this party as an aristocrat?"

Hamilton stopped Eliza from answering by placing a hand on her leg under the table. She almost jumped out of her seat at his forwardness, but when his hand tightened on her leg, she settled for sending him a frown and waited to hear what he was going to say.

"Lady Eliza was not supposed to attend that party, Mrs. Amherst, as you very well know, until Miss Watson became indisposed. From what I understand, there was no time for Lady Eliza to properly dress, so it was decided she would keep her identity secret and attend the dinner as the governess," Hamilton said.

"I find it difficult to believe Mr. Watson was agreeable to this plan," Mrs. Amherst said.

"Father has a wonderful sense of humor," Agatha said weakly.

"Does he?" Mrs. Amherst asked before she set her sights on Eliza. "I thought I heard you were currently staying with Mrs. Beckett."

Eliza took a sip of water, wondering how to explain that part of the story, but was spared a reply when Gloria threw herself back into the conversation.

"Lady Eliza is indeed staying with me," Gloria said. "Her mother and I, Lady, err . . ."

"Sefton," Eliza supplied under her breath.

"Lady Sefton and I were always meant to be good friends, but alas, our friendship never had time to fully develop because Lady Eliza's dear mother, ahh . . ."

"Alice," Eliza whispered.

"Dear mother Alice passed away," Gloria finished with a pleasant smile.

"You lost your mother?" Mrs. Murdock exclaimed. "How horrible for you. May I presume your father is still with us?"

"I'm afraid he died over a year ago."

"Good heavens, I can certainly see why you felt the need to travel to America. You needed a distraction," Mrs. Murdock said, sending a frown in Mrs. Amherst's direction.

Mrs. Amherst pretended not to notice the frown and leaned forward. "I distinctly remember you telling me you were not familiar with Lord and Lady Southmoor."

"I'm not overly familiar with them," Eliza said slowly.

"How very odd," Mrs. Amherst mused. "From the few conversations I've enjoyed with the countess, it appeared to me as if she knew every high society family in England, and I distinctly remember her mentioning a Lady Alice Sefton, as I believe I mentioned to you the last time we spoke."

"Did you?" Eliza asked.

"You don't remember the countess ever visiting with your mother?"

"She might have done so at some point in time, but as I said, I'm not overly familiar with the lady."

Thankfully, Mrs. Amherst was distracted from the conversation when another guest demanded her attention, and Eliza was free to breathe a sigh of relief.

"What an interesting ball," Agatha said.

"For a woman who claims a deep, abiding faith, you're remarkably proficient at spinning false tales," Eliza said, her voice a mere whisper.

Agatha rolled her eyes. "I didn't lie. I simply neglected to add details, and it was Gloria who led the conversation away from the correspondent part. Quite honestly, I don't believe God will think ill of me for being somewhat vague regarding your situation. I couldn't very well let you sit there and take the brunt of Mrs. Amherst's questions. We're friends, and friends look out for one another."

Warmth spread through Eliza at Agatha's words. It had been so long since she'd been able to claim a friend that she couldn't help the tears that suddenly welled in her eyes. She was grateful when Mr. Murdock stood and asked everyone to join in the blessing because it allowed her to drop her gaze and hide her emotions from the rest of the table.

A soft squeeze on her arm made her realize Hamilton was aware of her distress. His small act of reassurance caused the last of her annoyance with him to fade to nothing. She sent him a smile and then looked down at her plate before closing her eyes and focusing on the blessing Mr. Murdock was saying. She whispered a soft "amen" when he finished and lifted her head, relieved when Gloria began telling an amusing tale regarding Piper and Ben, which diverted attention away from her.

Dinner passed quickly and before Eliza knew it, servants were whisking the plates off the table and Mrs. Murdock was encouraging everyone to return to the ballroom. She found her arm taken in Hamilton's firm grip as he lifted her from her seat and maneuvered her past countless gentlemen with whom she'd agreed to dance. Apparently Hamilton wasn't going to allow her the opportunity to see her promises through to fruition. He brought them to a halt on the farthest recesses of the dance floor and grinned down at her.

"You do realize this dance is promised to someone else," Eliza said even as she felt a traitorous tremor run over her when he pulled her into his arms. "You're not even on my dance card."

"That's why I've been forced to take such drastic measures."

"You're insane."

"Perhaps," he agreed cheerfully before twirling her around as the music began.

"Why are you being so nice to me?" she asked after she caught her breath.

He pulled her closer to him and caught her gaze, never missing a single step. "I must apologize for my earlier behavior. You did nothing to deserve it, and I'm trying to make it up to you."

"Is that what you're doing?"

"Is it working?" Hamilton countered.

Eliza thought it might very well be working, whatever it was he was attempting to do. Her pulse was pounding in her veins, and she felt rather light-headed at his nearness. She'd wondered more than once this evening how it would feel to dance with Hamilton, and now she knew.

It was lovely; there was no other way to describe it.

Their steps were perfectly matched, and she'd never had a partner who suited her better.

That had her stumbling.

"Are you all right?" Hamilton asked as he steadied her.

Before she could reply, the music came to an end, but instead of returning her to the group of gentlemen waiting on the edge of the dance floor, he sent her a slightly mischievous smile and pulled her beside him in the opposite direction and right through a door. She found herself standing on a charming patio as a brisk breeze hit her square in the face.

"Why did you bring me out here?" Eliza asked, unable to suppress a shiver as another gust of wind swept over her.

"I needed to speak with you, and I knew no one would be out here, seeing as how the night has turned a bit brisk," he said, shrugging out of his coat and placing it around her shoulders.

Wonderful warmth enveloped her, and she resisted the urge to sigh in delight. "What did you need to say?"

"I wanted to apologize properly for my earlier behavior. I was incredibly surly with you."

"There's no need to apologize again, Hamilton. I readily admit to fits of sullenness at times, and I certainly wasn't crushed by your behavior."

"Fits of sullenness?"

"It happens," Eliza admitted. "I'm afraid an uneven temperament comes with my red hair."

"You do have a temper," Hamilton mused.

"Yes, well, back to you," Eliza said with a roll of her eyes, "why were you in such a dismal mood?"

"I'm afraid I was allowing my past to once again get in the way of my future."

"I'm sorry?"

"I was comparing you with Mary Ellen." Hamilton reached out and took hold of Eliza's hand, causing her to draw in a sharp breath before he continued. "You must realize I've developed feelings for you."

"What kind of feelings?" Eliza asked warily.

"I've been considering our future."

Panic swept over Eliza. She wasn't prepared to discuss feelings or a future with him. "Hamilton, I don't think this is the proper time for this. Besides, you know I have to return to England."

"You don't *have* to do anything of the sort," Hamilton argued.

"What exactly are you suggesting?"

"I thought, given the fact that you get along so well with my children, you might consider the idea of becoming a mother to them."

Eliza blinked as her temper flared. It seemed as if he might be suggesting marriage to her, but only because he needed a mother for his children. Good heavens, it was Lawrence all over again. He'd wanted to marry her because of her fortune. Could she ever just encounter a man who wanted to become close to her because he was swept away by his feelings for her?

"May I assume you're attempting to propose to me?" she asked, resisting the urge to throttle the man on the spot.

"I suppose I'm making a bit of a mess of this, aren't I?" Hamilton asked, having the audacity to send her one of his charming smiles.

She tilted her chin. "A mess is putting it mildly."

Hamilton frowned. "Have I said something to upset you?"

"What could you possibly have said to upset me?" Eliza asked as she tapped her finger on her chin. "Oh yes, now I remember. You issued me a proposal of marriage, I think, based on the assumption I would be a suitable mother figure. I have no idea why that would upset me."

"Perhaps I was not very clear," Hamilton said. "You must realize I hold you in high esteem."

"Do you?"

"Of course, why else would I ask you to marry me?"

"See, that does seem to be an issue here. You did not actually ask me to marry you. You simply threw it into the conversation."

"That's a little harsh. Granted, I wasn't as eloquent as I intended, but . . ."

Eliza didn't hear the rest of Hamilton's words because the door to the patio burst open, and Agatha barreled through it, skidding to a halt when she caught sight of them.

"I do so hate to interrupt, but we have a bit of a situation," she said, panting as if she'd run a far distance. She moved to Eliza's side, took her by the arm, and began pulling her toward the door. "We have to get you out of here immediately."

16

liza tried to shake off Agatha's hand, but found she wasn't up for the task. Agatha had a death grip on her, and only Hamilton's stepping in front of them and blocking their path stopped Agatha in her tracks.

"What's happened?" Hamilton asked.

"I don't have time to explain," Agatha retorted. "In fact, what was I thinking? Eliza can't go back through the ballroom." She swiveled her head and looked around. "There, see that wall over there? You'll have to climb over it, and I'll have the carriage brought around to pick you up."

"I'm not scaling a wall dressed in a formal gown," Eliza sputtered.

"You can't go back through the house," Agatha said.

"Why?" Eliza asked.

"Because the lead actress at the New York Theater developed a stomach ailment and was unable to finish the play," Agatha said.

"How could that possibly affect me?" Eliza asked.

"The play was cut short," Agatha replied before pointing off in the distance. "There's a handy tree over there. You should be able to climb it and slip over the wall without too much damage to your gown."

"Agatha, you're not explaining very well," Hamilton said. "Calm down and tell us in explicit detail what's wrong."

"I already told you, the play was cut short, and because of that, Lord and Lady Southmoor are here."

"Mr. Hayes is here?" Eliza asked.

"It gets so confusing, this Lord Southmoor, Mr. Hayes business. Can't we just agree to call him Lord Southmoor to make things easier?" Agatha asked.

"Certainly not, the man's a fraud. His title is a clever bit of fiction," Eliza said.

"But you know who I'm talking about."

Eliza folded her arms over her chest.

"Fine, Mr. Hayes, then. I think he's here," Agatha said. "I can't be sure, though, because I've only seen Lady, umm, Mrs. Hayes, but I would have to assume Mr. Hayes is here if she's in attendance."

"You truly believe, because they're here, I should leap over that wall and slink away into the night?" Eliza asked as she slipped out of Hamilton's coat and lifted her chin. "I will not disappear as if I have done something wrong." She handed the coat to Hamilton.

"What do you intend to do?" Agatha asked slowly.

"I have no idea, but I won't give them the satisfaction of learning I've fled."

"They don't know you're here," Agatha pointed out.

"You think Mrs. Amherst will keep that to herself? Please, I bet she'll make a beeline for Sally the moment she becomes aware of her presence."

"Sally's really Mrs. Hayes, right?" Agatha questioned.

"Yes."

"I told you it was getting confusing," Agatha grouched.

Eliza squared her shoulders and moved around Hamilton to gain access to the door.

"Eliza, wait, you could be jeopardizing everything," Agatha said.

"I don't care. I won't run; they're the criminals, not I. Besides, it's not as if I'm going to go looking for them. I'm simply going to locate Mrs. Murdock and apologize for leaving her ball early."

"You're not intending on seeking out Bartholomew and Sally?" Hamilton asked.

"I don't think that would be prudent at the moment, as I'm quite certain I might be prompted to do them physical harm," Eliza said.

"Perhaps you really should consider going over the wall," Agatha suggested, a trace of panic in her voice.

Eliza pretended not to hear Agatha as she turned on her heel and marched determinedly to the door, ignoring the worried looks Hamilton and Agatha exchanged. She stalked into the house and paused on the edge of the dance floor when she noticed Gloria hurrying toward her, Zayne only a step behind. She craned her neck to look past them and a wave of relief swept through her. There was no sign of Bartholomew or Sally.

"Did you hear?" Gloria whispered, stopping by Eliza's side.

"I did."

"We must leave immediately," Gloria said.

"We must first speak with Mrs. Murdock," Eliza argued. "It would be beyond rude if we simply vanished from her ball."

"Good heavens, child, if there was ever a time to abandon good manners, this would be it."

"There you are," a voice exclaimed from behind them. "I've been searching everywhere for you."

Eliza turned to find Mrs. Amherst standing a few feet away, a wide smile on her face.

"I have the most delightful news," Mrs. Amherst continued. "Lady Southmoor is here, and I want to surprise her with you."

"Like a present?" Eliza muttered under her breath as a grin stole over her face at the thought of how Sally would react to being presented with her.

Mrs. Amherst's smile faltered. "I beg your pardon?"

"I'm sorry, Mrs. Amherst," Hamilton said as he stepped forward to take Eliza's arm, "but I'm afraid Lady Eliza won't be able to speak with Lady Southmoor at the moment. We're on our way home as my mother isn't feeling well."

"Your mother appears perfectly fine to me."

Gloria shot Hamilton an exasperated look before turning her attention to Mrs. Amherst. "I've developed a bit of a stomach upset."

"Oh?"

"It must have been the fish."

"We were not served fish."

"Perhaps it was the quail."

"Agatha," another voice called before Mrs. Amherst was able to retort.

"It's my mother," Agatha mumbled.

Eliza found she was rooted to the spot. Walking toward her was none other than Sally Hayes, spectacularly dressed in a gown of silk with delicate, obviously expensive, lace edging the sleeves and neckline. Sally was holding Mrs. Watson's arm, smiling and nodding regally at guests as she drew ever closer. Her smile faded and her steps faltered when she glanced at Eliza, and then she froze completely when recognition obviously set in.

"Lady Eliza," she gasped.

"Sally," Eliza replied coldly.

"My goodness," Mrs. Amherst exclaimed, "what an informal

manner you have of addressing the countess, Lady Eliza. I thought you said you were not intimately known to Lady Southmoor."

"We are not what anyone would consider close friends. In fact, I have not actually spoken with Sally since I left the schoolroom," Eliza bit out, feeling a small sliver of satisfaction when Sally flushed at the veiled reminder she'd once been Eliza's governess.

"What a surprise to find you in New York," Sally said, her voice unnaturally high.

"I'm certain it's quite a surprise, Sally," Eliza said, drawing out her name to draw more attention to the fact that she was deliberately baiting the woman. "Where is your delightful husband?"

Sally didn't respond as her hand moved nervously to her neck. Rage swept over Eliza when she recognized her mother's necklace encircling Sally's neck.

"What a pretty necklace," Eliza managed to get out. "Is it a family heirloom?"

"Not at all," Sally replied, her face blanching and her voice turning shrill. "Lord Southmoor bought it for me here in New York."

"Oh? How odd. I could swear I've seen that necklace worn about England. In fact, if memory serves me correctly, I last saw it on my eighteenth birthday ball. I believe it was worn along with a lovely white gown trimmed in periwinkle blue."

"I've never worn a white gown trimmed in periwinkle blue," Sally said, her face now an unusual shade of pink.

"Why does everyone keep calling Miss Sumner Lady Eliza?" Mrs. Watson suddenly asked.

"Oh, Mother," Agatha said quickly before anyone else could speak, "Lady Eliza has abandoned her desire to remain unnoticed. We don't have to address her anymore as Miss Sumner. Our little ruse has come out into the open."

"Ruse?" Mr. Watson questioned as he joined them. "What's this about a ruse and . . . what is *she* doing here?"

"Mr. Watson, there's no need to continue with your false outrage," Mrs. Amherst tittered. "We heard all about the charade, and I must tell you, sir, I was delighted to hear you have such a wicked sense of humor. It was brilliant to allow Lady Eliza to disguise herself as a governess, so very understanding of you to sympathize with her desire to remain inconspicuous."

"Inconspicuous?" Mr. Watson asked.

"Exactly, Father," Agatha said, speaking up before Mrs. Amherst could say another word. "Everyone found the tale of Eliza and her unorthodox entry into this country quite riveting."

"I see," Mr. Watson muttered, clearly not seeing at all.

"I must say you might have let a few chosen people know what was going on," Mrs. Amherst continued. "Lady Eliza is such a delightful woman, and I admit I'm a touch miffed you didn't allow a few of your closest friends to be made known to her."

Eliza didn't bother to watch Mr. Watson's reaction to what had to be a very confusing conversation, but kept her eyes on Sally, who was once again growing pale and appeared to be searching for a means of escape. Eliza sent her a smile.

"It's wonderful your daughter was able to form an attachment to Lady Eliza through correspondence, Mr. Watson," Mrs. Amherst said. "May I assume you were well known to her father?"

Eliza held her breath as Mr. Watson turned to his daughter and quirked a brow. Her gaze moved to Agatha, who was seemingly trying to send her father a silent message by batting her lashes rather rapidly. She switched her attention back to Mr. Watson, who, to her surprise, was apparently trying to hold back a laugh. Her surprise increased when Mr. Watson turned to Mrs. Amherst and smiled.

"Lady Eliza's father, Lord . . . er . . . ?"

"Sefton," Eliza supplied.

"Exactly, Lord Sefton and I enjoy each other's company tremendously whenever we have an opportunity to see each other."

"But he's dead," Mrs. Amherst said.

"*Did* enjoy each other's company," Mr. Watson corrected. "He was a most capital fellow until he died such a tragic death. Hunting accident, I believe."

"Illness," Eliza muttered under her breath.

"Yes, quite right, a very lingering illness."

"There's something peculiar going on here," Mrs. Amherst said.

"You have no idea," Eliza replied brightly.

As Mrs. Amherst gaped at Eliza, Sally drew a deep breath and took a step backward.

"It was lovely to see you again, Lady Eliza, but I really should take my leave. Lord Southmoor is most likely looking for me."

"I'm certain you have much to tell him, Sally, but please do promise to give him my warmest regards," Eliza said.

"Lady Eliza, I must insist you cease addressing the countess as Sally," Mrs. Amherst said. "Her name is Salice, and you really should show her a proper level of respect; I believe her position outranks yours."

"Yes, dear," Sally said, nodding her head as a smug smile crossed her face, "you really should not be so disrespectful. After all, I am a countess and you, well, you have that horrid family scandal staining your name. I've heard the rumors regarding your father, and I would so hate to have to disillusion your friends here in New York."

The ballroom turned red. Perhaps it was the remark regarding Eliza's father, or perhaps it was her mother's necklace winking at her from Sally's neck, or perhaps it was the very idea the woman was attempting to chastise her. Whatever the reason, a buzzing sound began ringing in Eliza's ears, and she stepped forward, snatching the necklace from around Sally's neck and causing the crowd around them to fall silent. She stood there for a moment, her mother's necklace clutched in her hand, shaking with rage.

"Lady Eliza," Mrs. Amherst snapped, "have you taken leave of your senses? Return that immediately to Lady Southmoor."

"Her name is Sally," Eliza hissed, "not Salice, not Lady Southmoor, but plain old Sally."

Sally drew herself up and attempted to look down her nose at Eliza. "My name is Salice Southmoor."

"Southmoor is your fictitious title, Sally, not your last name. If you were truly a member of the aristocracy, you would know that," Eliza raged. "This"—she held up the necklace—"belonged to my mother, and you will never wear it again."

"It's mine," Sally said.

"It's not. My mother's initials are engraved on the back, and my father also had it inscribed. Shall I read the inscription?"

Sally remained silent even as she glared back at Eliza.

"Very well, I'll tell you, as I have no need to read it. The inscription says, 'To my darling Alice. I will love you forever.'" Eliza thrust the necklace at Mrs. Watson. "You may verify that for me."

Mrs. Watson peered at the necklace and then nodded. "It reads exactly as she said."

"Your father sold that piece to sustain his style of living," Sally spat. "You're trying to cover up the fact that he was a wastrel by diverting attention to me, but it won't work. Everyone will soon realize you're unbalanced, and then you'll be forced to return home without a shred of dignity left to your name."

"My mental health has never been in question, Sally. I'm not the one who invented elaborate lies to explain incredible wealth and a title that doesn't exist. I find myself wondering if you've actually begun to believe the lies you've spread."

"I have not lied about anything."

"You were, at one time, my governess, and your husband was my father's man of affairs. As you have somehow convinced the city of New York that you're close to royalty, I would have to say you've become most adept at spreading tales."

Sally's mouth opened and closed, but no words came out. She moved toward Eliza, but faltered when Hamilton took a step forward.

"You will not get away with this," Sally spat.

"What are you going to do? Go after my fortune?" Eliza let a bitter laugh escape. "Oh yes, I forgot, you've already done that." She lowered her voice. "Heed me well, Sally. You're the one who will not get away with what you've done. I will not rest until I see you in jail."

"I'd like to see you try to bring me down," Sally snarled. "You have no proof."

"Maybe not," Eliza said with a shrug, "but know this, Sally. God works in very mysterious ways, and I've recently come to the conclusion He will set matters straight in the end, you mark my words."

Sally stared at Eliza, her chest heaving and her breath ragged. She spun around and raced through the crowd.

Hamilton grabbed hold of Eliza's hand as she made to follow.

"Let her go, Eliza."

"She's going to tell Mr. Hayes."

"If Mr. Hayes is also Lord Southmoor, he's not here," Mrs. Watson said, speaking up. "He received a message as we got out of the theater and left straightaway to return home. We brought Lady Southmoor, or whatever her name is, in our carriage."

Zayne suddenly let out a loud groan, causing Eliza to swing her attention to him, unable to help but notice the distinct trace of panic flashing in his eyes. "What is it?" she asked.

"We forgot about Theodore. He's breaking into their house."

17

*H*amilton felt Eliza's hand tremble in his as they made their rather harried good-byes to Mrs. Murdock, who appeared completely delighted by what had transpired. She was currently whispering somewhat loudly to his mother that, given the scandal that had just occurred in her house, her ball would most assuredly be talked about for months. He hid a grin and pulled Eliza through the throng of guests and out into the night, where they stood for a moment, waiting for their carriage.

"I must say, this has been an interesting evening," Mr. Watson stated as he strode up to join them, Agatha on his arm. He frowned at his daughter. "You have a lot of explaining to do once we get home."

"The explaining will have to wait, Father," Agatha said. "I'm going with Eliza."

Hamilton watched as Mr. Watson narrowed his eyes. "You most certainly are not."

"But . . ." Agatha sputtered.

"Roger," Mrs. Watson interrupted, "you can't refuse her this. Whether you approve or not, Agatha is somehow involved in the matter, and it would hardly be fair to exclude her from learning the outcome. Why, even I admit it's incredibly exciting, very cloak and dagger."

Mr. Watson blinked and turned to Hamilton. "I will allow you to explain to my daughter why it would hardly be safe for her to accompany you on what appears to be another madcap adventure."

"I don't recall issuing Agatha an invitation to join me," Hamilton said, earning a glare from Agatha in the process.

"Of course Agatha and Eliza won't be joining Hamilton and Zayne," Gloria said, taking a place next to Mr. Watson. "They'll be returning home with me where we'll await word from my sons regarding Mr. Wilder."

"I'm going with them," Eliza declared.

Hamilton had known this was coming. "It wouldn't be safe."

"It wouldn't be safe for Sally," Eliza corrected. "Did you see how intricately dressed her hair was this evening? She must have spent a good deal of my money to create such an effect, and I do believe it's my right to disassemble it, considering I paid for the style."

"That's why you're going directly back to the house. The last thing we need is for you to end up in jail again, and I'm quite certain disassembling another lady's hair falls under the category of assault." He ignored her immediate sputters as he peered down the road, releasing a breath of relief when he spotted his carriage. He turned to Mr. Watson. "Since Zayne and I need to attend to something immediately—and I do apologize I can't explain what that something is to you at the moment, as it is rather urgent—would you be so kind as to extend my mother and Eliza a ride home?"

"Think no more on the matter, Mr. Beckett," Mr. Watson said. "I would consider it an honor as well as a means of discovering what I actually have been participating in this evening. I almost felt as if I'd taken to the stage."

Hamilton grinned as he took a step toward his carriage, but before he had an opportunity to climb in, a man suddenly rushed up the drive, waving frantically at him.

"Mr. Beckett, sir, wait."

"What is Matthews doing here?" Gloria asked.

"Matthews?" Mrs. Watson repeated.

"He's our messenger, and I fear something dire must have occurred if he felt the need to track us down here," Gloria explained.

"Thank goodness I found you," Matthews said as he came to a panting halt beside Hamilton and thrust a folded piece of paper into his hands. "An urgent message was delivered to the house, and the boy who delivered it claimed it to be of utmost importance and that it must be dealt with at once."

Hamilton shook open the note and scanned it before raising his head. "Theodore's landed in jail."

"It couldn't have happened to a nicer man," Agatha remarked.

"Agatha, what a thing to say," Mrs. Watson proclaimed. "Why, from what I've seen and heard of Mr. Theodore Wilder, well . . . oh, look, it's our carriage," she said as she sent a wary look to Mr. Watson and then practically rushed to the carriage that had pulled up behind Hamilton's. She disappeared into the depths without even allowing the driver to assist her inside.

Hamilton could hear Mrs. Watson's mutters coming out of the open window and he distinctly heard "ogling" and "couldn't help myself" until the voice stopped and silence settled over everyone.

"Cora, I'm shocked" was all Mr. Watson appeared capable of getting out before he moved to his carriage and simply stood by the door, seemingly unable to decide how he should proceed.

Hamilton watched as Agatha shook her head, released a snort, and moved to join her father. "I would not be too concerned, Father, if I were you. Mr. Wilder is indeed a most handsome gentleman, but all ladies learn soon enough that his personality leaves much to be desired."

Hamilton winced when Mr. Watson's eyes suddenly narrowed.

"I was unaware you were acquainted with a Mr. Wilder," he said.

"I met him in Central Park," Agatha admitted.

"You had a rendezvous with the man?" Mr. Watson bellowed.

"Please, I would not 'rendezvous' with Mr. Wilder if someone paid me," Agatha scoffed. "I only met him because he was looking for Mr. Beckett, and as I had accompanied Zayne to Central Park, well, Mr. Wilder tracked us down."

"You had a rendezvous with Mr. Zayne Beckett?"

"Daddy, you're becoming overly upset for absolutely no good reason. I did not have a rendezvous yesterday with Mr. Beckett. I went to Central Park to impart some interesting news to Eliza." Agatha's mouth suddenly snapped shut.

"You were supposed to be at the orphanage yesterday," Mr. Watson said.

"I *was* at the orphanage. I stopped in Central Park after I left the orphanage *and* after I made a brief stop at church."

"You were not given permission to go anywhere except the orphanage, not even church. You certainly didn't have permission to associate with our former governess."

"Eliza wasn't really our governess, Daddy."

"I afforded her a salary, which made her our governess, and you haven't called me 'Daddy' in years. Are you, by chance, attempting to soften me up?" Mr. Watson asked.

Hamilton was fairly certain that was exactly what Agatha was trying to do, but the loud clearing of a throat pulled his attention back to the situation at hand.

"Do forgive me for interrupting this riveting conversation, but it is past time Hamilton and I were on our way," Zayne said. "I hardly believe Theodore will appreciate wallowing in jail for any length of time."

"Quite right," Mr. Watson exclaimed. "It would be a true shame if poor, handsome Mr. Wilder was left rotting in jail." He held open the carriage door and gestured to Agatha, Eliza, and Gloria. "Come along, ladies. Mr. and Mr. Beckett need to get on with their business, and you, Agatha, have some more explaining to do."

Before Agatha could get a single protest out of her mouth, Hamilton's attention was distracted by Zayne, who'd taken Theodore's note from him and, for some reason, was frowning. Zayne lifted his head.

"Did you read all of this?" he asked.

"I skimmed it," Hamilton admitted.

"He wants us to bring Eliza," Zayne said.

Hamilton took the note from Zayne and read it again. "What possible reason could he have for requesting Eliza's presence?"

"I suppose we'll have to ask him once we reach the jail," Eliza said as she strode over to his carriage. "Best not to linger; Theodore is waiting."

"I never said I was agreeable to his request," Hamilton said.

"Honestly, Hamilton, it's not as if he's still in danger, and there must be a completely logical reason why he wants me at the jail," Eliza said as her eyes grew round. "What if he learned the whereabouts of my fortune?"

"What fortune?" Mr. Watson asked.

"I'll explain everything to you once we reach my house," Gloria said as she accepted Mr. Watson's hand up into the carriage. She turned and smiled. "I do hope you and Mrs. Watson will agree to stay with me until we discover the ending to this drama."

"Don't mind if we do," Mr. Watson said before he nodded to Agatha. "Well, in you go."

Agatha's expression turned mulish. "I cannot allow Eliza to go off to jail in the company of two unmarried gentlemen. Think of her reputation."

"I believe it would be prudent for me to think of yours," Mr. Watson grouched.

"Really, dear, Agatha does have a point. I'm not comfortable allowing Lady Eliza to traverse the streets of New York without a chaperone," Mrs. Watson said, sticking her head out the window and smiling at Agatha before smiling at Zayne and then disappearing once again.

The entire world had gone mad.

"But Agatha is younger than Lady Eliza," Mr. Watson muttered before he released a huff of obvious resignation. "Since it appears I am decidedly outnumbered, Agatha, you may go, but you have to promise me you'll stay in the carriage once you get to the jail."

"Thank you, Daddy, and I promise," Agatha said before she stepped forward to kiss her father soundly on the cheek and then moved to Eliza's side. "Shall we get on our way?"

Hamilton found himself in the unusual position of having to admit defeat. He helped Eliza and then Agatha into the carriage before climbing in himself and taking a seat opposite the two ladies.

Both ladies, to his annoyance, were sporting very satisfied smiles.

He'd never had a chance against them.

He waited until Zayne took a seat next to him before rapping on the carriage ceiling. As they rolled into motion, the words "stay in the carriage" drifted through the window.

Hamilton caught Agatha's gaze. "I don't think your father trusts you very much."

"He'll come around. Tonight's the first night I've seen the man who used to be my father."

"Perhaps he's remembered what's really important in life," Zayne said.

Agatha smiled. "Speaking of important, I must say I was very pleased to hear you mention God when you were yelling at Sally, Eliza. May I hope you've mended your bridges with Him?"

"I don't know if I would go that far," Eliza admitted. "It was all rather odd, now that I think on it. For some reason, the words simply popped out of my mouth."

Agatha nodded. "God does have a way of coming back into a person's life without one realizing it, but it's clear by the expression on your face you're still not comfortable discussing the matter, so we will turn to another interesting aspect of the evening." She patted Eliza on the knee. "Tell me, what happened with you and Hamilton before I so rudely interrupted you? I must say neither of you were looking very pleased."

Hamilton watched as a glimmer of temper entered Eliza's eyes before she waved Agatha's comment away with one little flick of her wrist. "That was of little consequence."

Her blithe remark rankled. "I don't believe extending you an offer of marriage was 'of little consequence.'"

"I don't remember hearing an offer of marriage," Eliza said.

"I am fairly certain you did, seeing as how I was there at the time."

Eliza lifted her chin, sent him a glare, and then turned to look out the window, not saying another word.

"Am I the only one confused?" Agatha asked, causing Eliza to shift her attention back to her.

"Hamilton did not extend me an offer of marriage," she said with a sniff. "What he did do was infer I would make an excellent mother."

"Which you would; Piper and Ben completely adore you. I

have yet to understand why you took issue with that particular inference," Hamilton said.

"I hardly appreciate the fact that you were considering marrying me to provide Ben and Piper with a mother."

Now the pieces of the puzzle were beginning to fit together. Hamilton smiled. "We have obviously suffered a misunderstanding, Eliza. Perhaps you did not hear me when I stated that I hold you in high esteem."

Zayne let out a snort. "You've obviously forgotten how to handle a woman."

"Yes, thank you, Theodore Wilder," Eliza scoffed as she directed a glare at Zayne. "For your information, I don't need to be 'handled.'"

"So you rejected his suit?" Agatha pressed.

"There was no 'suit' to reject. I told you, he never proposed."

"It was a simple mistake," Hamilton explained. "I was nervous and unable to think clearly."

"Be that as it may, I will state one more time: I'm not in the market for a husband."

"But you like Hamilton," Agatha said.

"I do," Eliza admitted, "but I have every intention of returning to England, so there is little need to continue this conversation."

Silence settled over the carriage as they rolled through the streets of New York.

❦

"What do you think is taking so long?" Agatha asked.

Hamilton looked at his pocket watch and shook his head. "I'm not certain, but I never thought we'd have to wait in the carriage for over an hour."

"You could go check on things," Agatha said.

Hamilton arched a brow. "And leave the two of you alone? Not likely. If it has escaped your notice, we are currently waiting outside a jail, hardly a respectable place to leave two ladies unattended."

"I'm armed," Agatha muttered.

"Of course you are," Hamilton muttered right back, "but I'm not leaving."

At that moment, the door opened and Zayne jumped in, an almost unrecognizable Theodore right behind him. His hair was matted with blood, one of his eyes was swollen almost shut, and there was not one inch of his face that wasn't bruised.

"Mr. Wilder," Eliza exclaimed, breaking the silence, "what happened to you?"

"Got taken by surprise," Theodore admitted as he lowered himself rather gingerly to the seat. "I thought I'd been incredibly careful scouting out the house, but turns out I was wrong. Although the servants were all in their quarters, and the few guards Mr. Hayes had left behind were patrolling the outside perimeter of the house, I neglected to realize there was someone else lurking in the shadows: one Eugene Daniels."

"What was he doing there?" Hamilton asked.

"No idea. I was not able to question the man, as he was rather intent on smashing my skull."

"He hit you over the head?" Eliza gasped.

"He did. I think it might have been a vase, but I'm not certain. The impact knocked me unconscious, and it wasn't until I finally came to that I realized who'd attacked me. Eugene was standing a few feet away from me, apparently unaware of the fact that I'd awakened, and he was speaking to two of the guards. I only heard the last part of the conversation, which concerned the guards disposing of me, and, after Eugene ordered my disposal, he left."

"Then why are you still among the living?" Agatha asked.

"Lucky for me, one of the guards was a petty criminal I pay occasionally for information. He recognized me and convinced his partner I would make it worth their while if they assisted me. They carted me out of the house and took me to jail."

"Why would they take you to jail?"

"That part I'm a little fuzzy about, but I think they thought jail was the safest place for me."

"That's telling," Zayne said.

"Exactly," Theodore agreed. "If men of the criminal persuasion think jail is the best option, I have to believe Eugene Daniels is one nasty piece of work."

"But why were you arrested and thrown into jail?" Agatha asked with a frown. "I find it hard to believe two criminals would encourage the police to arrest you."

"I don't think their intention was to see me arrested," Theodore said, "but unfortunately, when they dropped me off at jail, they were recognized as wanted men. All chaos erupted as police swarmed us, and I was thrown into a cell along with the two criminals who'd saved me."

"But what happened to them?" Eliza asked. "It hardly seems fair that they should linger in jail while you're free."

"I left bail for them with the night clerk," Theodore said with a smile, the action causing him to wince. "They wanted to stay the night for safety reasons."

"Another telling action," Zayne muttered.

"Too right it was," Theodore said with a nod.

"What now?" Hamilton asked.

Theodore released a breath. "I have to go back. I need to see if a ledger I found is still in Mr. Hayes's desk."

"You're in no fit state to go gallivanting around New York," Eliza protested.

"I'm fine, Lady Eliza," Theodore growled.

Apparently, Eliza did not appreciate his tone of voice. She tilted her chin. "You'll get arrested if you go back, and I thought I gave you permission to address me as Eliza."

Hamilton swallowed a snort.

Women were strange creatures. One minute they were scowling at a man and tilting their adorable noses into the air, and the next, they were giving him permission to address them informally.

He shifted his gaze to Theodore and found the man had apparently rediscovered his charm, as could be seen by the twinkle in his one good eye.

"Thank you, Eliza. I wasn't certain if that request was still valid after our last, somewhat tumultuous, discussion. May I say you and Miss Watson are looking quite delicious this evening? I beg your pardon for not mentioning that sooner."

"This is hardly the time for excessive compliments," Zayne said, sparing Hamilton the necessity of setting Theodore straight.

"There was nothing 'excessive' about my compliment," Theodore returned with a lopsided smile that made him grimace.

Hamilton reminded himself it was not acceptable to enjoy another's physical discomfort. He cleared his throat. "Are you certain it's wise to return?"

"I won't be alone," Theodore said. "I sent out word to a few of my contacts, and they're in the carriage right behind us. They are men who are perfectly willing and able to defend me if Eugene is still on the premises."

"You do realize Bartholomew and Sally are most likely there also, don't you?" Eliza asked.

Theodore shrugged. "I'm one of the leading private investigators in New York, and I still have a few tricks up my sleeve. I'll be able to get past them without them even knowing I'm in their house."

"Like you did a few hours ago?" Zayne asked.

"I'll have a better grasp of the full situation this time," Theodore said. "No one will be able to take me by surprise."

Zayne frowned. "But why did you send word for us to bail you out of jail? You were able to summon your associates; surely one of them would have been more than up for the task?"

"He needed me," Eliza said, drawing Hamilton's attention and causing him to swallow a grunt. He'd forgotten all about the reason Eliza and Agatha were in the carriage with them.

"You're right, Eliza," Theodore said. "I have yet to actually see Bartholomew Hayes, and I need you to positively identify him for me. That way I can have the man carted off to jail, if, in fact, I can get my hands on that ledger again, and hopefully, I'll be able to get you the results you want by learning where the man has stashed your fortune."

"What did you see in this ledger?" Eliza asked as her tone turned breathless.

"I can't say just yet," Theodore said, "because I was only able to take a quick look when I ransacked Mr. Hayes's desk. Luckily, I dropped the hidden desktop back into place before I was knocked out, so Mr. Hayes shouldn't be aware that I know his hiding place."

"What information did your 'quick look' give you?" Eliza pressed.

Theodore blew out a breath. "Again, I really can't say. I don't want to get your hopes up, but we should find answers soon, and look . . . we're almost there."

Hamilton drew in a sharp breath. "We're almost where?"

"I took the liberty of giving the directions to Mr. Hayes's residence to your driver," Theodore said.

Hamilton narrowed his eyes. "It's too risky. I won't allow it."

"My men will watch Eliza every second, and there's no need for her to even get out of the carriage. If I find a man I believe is Bartholomew, I'll bring him to Eliza."

"I thought you said you would be able to slip past him without his even being aware of your presence," Hamilton said.

Was it his imagination or was Theodore looking a bit wary?

"I really don't plan on not having a confrontation with the man," Theodore finally admitted.

"We need to turn the carriage around," Hamilton snapped, reaching up to rap on the ceiling, but stilling when Eliza shook her head.

"I do believe time is of the essence here, and if we do not get to Bartholomew's house soon, he's more than likely to flee into the night, never to be seen again," Eliza said. "This is why I came to New York. We have to see the night through to completion."

Hamilton looked away from her and settled his sights on Theodore, angrier with the man than he'd been with anyone in a very long time. "I won't have her in danger."

"You have my word," Theodore said as the carriage rolled to a stop and he looked out the window. "I'll be back."

"I'm not sitting here while you risk your life," Zayne said. "You can use all the help you can get." He turned to Hamilton. "You should stay with the ladies."

"Hamilton can go with the three of you," Agatha said. "I have my trusty pistol, and I'm more than capable of defending Eliza and myself if the situation warrants it. We'll be fine."

"I want to go with them," Eliza said, a determined expression on her face. "This man ruined my life, and I deserve to be there when he's taken down."

"Out of the question," Theodore snapped. "This is gentlemen's business, and I will not waste a minute of my time arguing the matter with you. Stay here." He sent Eliza a glare and then jumped out of the carriage.

"I swear he just sounded as if he were talking to his dog," Eliza grouched, but to Hamilton's relief, she made no move to exit the carriage.

"Are you going to stay with the . . . ?" Zayne's voice trailed off when Theodore suddenly reappeared, his body blocking the door.

"Get them out of here," he ordered before pulling out a pistol and slamming the door shut.

"What happened?" Hamilton demanded through the window.

"There's a body on the sidewalk," Theodore said.

"Let's go," Hamilton barked when Theodore stepped away and patted the side of the carriage. The sound of the driver flicking the reins came to him, and he breathed a small breath of relief when the carriage rocked into motion.

"There was a body?" Eliza whispered.

He couldn't help himself from reaching over and pulling her to his side of the carriage, gesturing for Zayne to move out of the way as he settled Eliza by his side and hugged her to him. He glanced at his brother and noticed Zayne doing the exact same thing with Agatha.

"Maybe it wasn't really a body," Agatha said. "Maybe it was a delivery package."

"You and I both know it wasn't a delivery package, and I swear, if Theodore makes it out of this one, I'm going to wring his handsome neck," Hamilton said as fear mixed with anger swept over him. "What could he have been thinking?"

"He was simply trying to do what you hired him to do," Eliza said softly.

Hamilton felt Eliza snuggle closer to him and was amazed when some of his anger simply disappeared. When she placed her hand on his knee and patted it in a soothing manner, he found he had the strangest urge to propose to her again, even though the rational part of his brain told him this was hardly the proper moment. Before he could contemplate the thought further, Eliza began to speak.

"You really shouldn't be upset with Theodore, Hamilton. It's true he lacked a bit of judgment tonight, but I'm certain he's angry enough at himself for making such a mistake. I think our time would be better spent saying a prayer for his safe return. And perhaps all of us should say a prayer for the unfortunate soul who lost his or her life tonight."

Hamilton placed his finger under her chin and tilted it up so he could meet her gaze. "I thought you'd shut the door on God."

"Maybe it's time I reopened it."

Hamilton considered her for a moment and then bowed his head, thinking that Eliza was not the only one ready to reopen the door. He closed his eyes and began to pray.

18

*E*liza didn't have the strength to tug her hand out of Hamilton's grasp. There was something decidedly comforting about having his warmth seep through her skin, and even though she was still incredibly put out with the gentleman, she wasn't prepared to abandon his comfort just yet.

She shifted her gaze out the window, but instead of seeing the rapidly passing scenery, images of the night flashed before her eyes. It had been such a trying evening. First, she'd dealt with New York society and Hamilton's insulting offer of marriage, followed by the whole Sally fiasco, and to top matters off nicely, there was now a dead body to consider.

She wanted nothing more than to seek out the comfort of her bed and make it all disappear, but unfortunately, she knew that wasn't going to be feasible anytime in the near future.

The carriage began to slow, and Eliza saw the Beckett house

appear out of the darkness. She pressed her face to the cool glass of the carriage and spotted Gloria scurrying down the walk.

Before anyone could move, Gloria pulled the door open and poked her head in. "You've given us quite a fright," Gloria proclaimed. "Mr. Watson was just about to head off to jail."

Eliza felt Hamilton release her hand, and she tried to appear nonchalant when Gloria's sharp eyes landed on her. She sent the woman a small smile and struggled from her seat, waiting until Gloria took a step backward before she allowed Hamilton to help her down. She moved to Gloria's side, took her by the arm, and began walking toward the house.

"Mr. Watson would have been upset if he'd gone to the jail," Eliza said, "seeing as how we weren't there in the end."

Gloria stopped so abruptly that Eliza lost her footing and had to clutch onto Gloria's arm to avoid a nasty spill.

"Don't tell me you decided to pay a call on Lord Southmoor," Gloria snapped.

"*I* didn't decide to do anything of the sort," Eliza said. "It was entirely Theodore's idea." She tried to prod Gloria forward only to discover the woman was digging in her heels.

"Where is Mr. Wilder?" Gloria asked, craning her neck as she peered behind her.

"He's not with us," Hamilton said, stepping up to join them, Zayne and Agatha in his wake.

"You couldn't get him released from jail?" Gloria asked.

"Oh, we got him out of jail all right, but then . . ." Hamilton paused. "Let's go inside so we only have to tell the tale once. I'm sure Mr. and Mrs. Watson will wish to be included."

Gloria looked as if she wanted to argue, but finally released a dramatic sigh, shrugged out of Eliza's hold, and stomped her way up the walk and into the house, her voice carrying back to them on the breeze.

"I think I hear my father yelling," Agatha muttered.

"We should let Hamilton and Zayne go first," Eliza suggested when she looked up and discovered Mr. Watson standing in the doorway, his frame illuminated by the soft gas light hanging over the door.

"I say, Mr. Beckett," Mr. Watson railed. "I thought you could be counted on to keep my daughter and Lady Eliza out of trouble. What's this I hear about you going somewhere else after you departed from the jail?"

"Mr. Wilder felt it was imperative we travel immediately to Bartholomew Hayes's house," Hamilton said, "but you're absolutely right, Mr. Watson. It was inexcusable for me to allow the ladies to travel there with us. I can only extend to you my most abject apologies."

"It's not as if you had any choice in the matter," Eliza said, sweeping past everyone to make her way down the hallway and into a cheery parlor. For a moment, the warmth in the room from the blazing fire in the fireplace and the elegance of the delicate furnishings artfully spread around the space struck her as odd. It was so completely different than the cold of the night and the taste of death in the air only a short time before.

She shook herself out of her thoughts and joined Mrs. Watson on the settee, turning to watch as Hamilton, Mr. Watson, Zayne, and Agatha entered the room. Hamilton set his sights on her and strode across the floor, plopping down beside her and blatantly ignoring her hiss of protest at the fact that she had to practically sit on Mrs. Watson's lap to allow him enough room on the small settee. "There are other chairs to be had," she muttered under her breath.

Hamilton quirked a brow, and then had the nerve to smile at her. "I prefer the comfort of sitting next to you."

Eliza chanced a glance to Mrs. Watson, who appeared to be trying her best not to grin. Eliza was about to get up when Mrs. Watson rose from the settee and resettled herself in a chair right beside Gloria. "There, problem managed," Mrs. Watson said before she exchanged a smug smile with Gloria. Eliza rolled her eyes and began to scoot away from Hamilton, her progress coming to an abrupt halt when Agatha dropped down on the settee, taking her mother's place.

"Is there something wrong with all the other chairs in this room?" Eliza said.

"I thought we could lend each other support," Agatha said. "My father is bound to become distressed when he learns all the pesky particulars of the evening."

"Which particulars?" Mr. Watson asked as he settled himself into a chair beside the fire, Zayne taking the chair right next to it.

"Again, Mr. Watson, I must apologize for not demanding that Theodore turn the carriage around," Hamilton said.

"Honestly, Hamilton," Eliza said, "you're taking entirely too much responsibility for what transpired. There was no possible way you could have realized there was a body waiting for us."

It took a full thirty minutes to calm Mr. Watson down after that telling remark. Tea was summoned and then consumed as Eliza listened with only half an ear as Hamilton and Zayne tried their best to explain what had happened. She couldn't seem to concentrate on the matter at hand. Her thoughts were spinning every which way, and all she really longed for at the moment was a quiet place to sort everything through to satisfaction.

For some reason, she had the strangest feeling her fate would be decided as soon as Theodore returned. She blinked out of her troubling thoughts when Mr. Watson rose from his seat.

"This certainly has been one of the most interesting evenings I've ever had, but I do believe it's time we took our leave," Mr. Watson said.

"We can't leave now," Agatha retorted. "We need to wait for Theodore."

"It might take Mr. Wilder hours before he has an opportunity to leave the scene of the crime," Mr. Watson argued.

"Roger," Mrs. Watson interjected. "Honestly, dear, you're being unreasonable. I wouldn't be able to get one wink of sleep with matters so unsettled. Besides, neither of us could take to our beds with Agatha so determined. You know it would only be a matter of time until she figured out a way to get back here on her own."

Mr. Watson sent one loud huff in Agatha's direction, but then returned to his seat as conversation resumed.

The sun was beginning to peek through the curtains when the sound of approaching footsteps caused Eliza to swing her attention to the door.

Theodore strode into the room, more disheveled than ever, heavy lines of fatigue apparent around his one good eye. The other eye was now completely shut with an unusual shade of blue and green ringing it.

"The door was unlocked," he growled, sending Hamilton what Eliza could only assume was a glare.

"We were expecting you, and I sent the butler to bed hours ago," Hamilton returned.

"Anyone could have breezed in here and you would have been easy pickings," Theodore said as he stalked over to the tea tray, poured himself a cup, sunk into the only available chair, and took a large gulp. "Bartholomew's dead; someone shot him."

Although Eliza had been determined to seek justice against the man, she'd never wanted him dead. She cleared her throat and felt tears sting her eyes. "What of Sally?"

"Gone . . . and there was no sign of Eugene," Theodore said.

"But . . . why would someone shoot Bartholomew?" Eliza asked.

"As to that, I believe a few of the discoveries I made tonight will help explain," Theodore said, setting down his empty cup before he struggled out of the chair and made his way back to the door. He called out to someone, and a rather disreputable-looking gentleman entered the room and deposited an armful of books on the table. The man gave a short bow and left the room. Theodore moved to the table and picked up one of the books, turning to Eliza and sending her a lopsided smile. "I found more than one of Bartholomew's account ledgers."

She'd been right; her fate *was* to be decided this evening.

"And?" she pressed.

"We now have everything we need to access Bartholomew's accounts," Theodore said, "and there's more." He gestured to two more disreputable-looking gentlemen who were struggling to carry a ratty old chest into the room. With a resounding thud, they dropped it by Theodore's side and made a hasty retreat.

"Is that what I think it is?" Eliza asked slowly.

"It is, and I must admit, modesty notwithstanding, it was quite a stellar feat for me to be able to sneak it away after the authorities arrived. I certainly didn't want it to be taken as evidence."

"It seems a little small," Eliza said slowly.

Theodore nodded. "That's only half your money, but don't despair just yet. We'll return to that subject in a minute." He fumbled in his pocket and withdrew a folded piece of paper. "I found this on Bartholomew's body. It's addressed to you."

Eliza took the paper and unfolded it. She drew in a deep breath and began to read it out loud:

Dear Lady Eliza,

I do not have much time, but I just discovered that you are in New York and took that as a sign to settle matters between us. There are no words to express my deep remorse for what I've done to you and your family. I have no excuse except to state I'm a weak man, and I've allowed others to influence my decisions.

By the time you receive this, I will be long gone, but I've left my account ledgers for you in a false bottom in my desk. These ledgers will give you the information you need to restore the majority of your funds back to you. I say majority because I'm not strong enough to leave you everything.

There is so much more I wish to say to you, but time is running short. I've been told Mr. Wilder was disposed of, but even I've heard about that gentleman's reputation, and I fear Eugene is incorrect in believing the man is dead.

I leave you with one piece of advice, my dear: beware of Mr. Daniels. The man is mentally unbalanced, and I cannot predict what he will do when he discovers what I've done.

Your father did not deserve to have his reputation besmirched. He was a just and honorable man and I can only hope God will forgive my transgressions, as they are many, and that He will watch out for you and see you happy.

Your servant,
Bartholomew Hayes

Eliza looked up. "Am I to assume it was Eugene Daniels who murdered Bartholomew? And did he do so because of this trunk?" she asked.

"No, I think Eugene Daniels murdered him because of this," Theodore said as the two gentlemen returned and placed another chest beside the first one before abruptly quitting the room again. "That's the rest of your money."

"Eugene and Sally fled with nothing?" Eliza asked.

"So it would appear," Theodore said, "but perhaps it would

be for the best if I started at the beginning." He took his seat and released a breath. "Now then, from what I've been able to piece together, Eugene apparently sent Bartholomew a note summoning him home after I was caught snooping around his house. The rest of my story is sheer speculation, but here's what I believe happened. When Bartholomew discovered what Eugene did to me, I think he panicked and realized events were spiraling out of control, especially after Sally arrived home from the ball and apparently told him you were in town. I discovered traveling trunks with gentlemen's clothing stuffed in them, and the office was in complete disarray, leading me to conclude Bartholomew was intent on fleeing."

"And then?" Zayne prompted.

"I imagine an altercation broke out, considering Bartholomew's dead, but I have no clear idea what brought that on, except to think Eugene discovered Bartholomew trying to leave Eliza part of the fortune and decided that wasn't acceptable. Hence the bullet."

"Where did you discover the chests?" Zayne asked.

"One was pushed halfway into a closet in Bartholomew's room, and the other was turned on its side by the back door. I can only guess the chest in the closet was the one intended for Eliza. Bartholomew certainly wouldn't have wanted to hide it in a place we wouldn't find." He smiled a rather sad smile. "If you look on the envelope, Eliza, he was starting to address the letter to you and had gotten as far as putting Hamilton's address on it, so Sally must have told him where you could be found. I imagine writing that letter was one of the last things Bartholomew ever did."

"I still don't understand why those chests were left in the house," Agatha said.

Theodore grimaced. "The body was still warm when I touched it, leaving me to assume our arrival disrupted their escape. They were decidedly outnumbered, so they did the only thing they could. They fled, leaving the money behind."

"Do you believe Eugene and Sally will come looking for their missing chest?" Zayne asked.

"I do," Theodore said.

Eliza frowned. "Wouldn't it be easier for Sally to simply try to get the money Bartholomew left in the bank?"

"I doubt Sally or Eugene could access those accounts, seeing as how Bartholomew appeared to be a somewhat astute gentleman, at least in regard to financial matters. To be on the safe side, I've already sent word to the bank managers to freeze all of Bartholomew's accounts and to alert the authorities if Sally shows up there," Theodore said.

"She won't be happy about that," Eliza mused.

"Indeed," Theodore agreed, "which leads me to my next order of business. You must make immediate plans to depart New York, Eliza. You won't be safe here until Sally and Eugene are apprehended, and I certainly can't tell you when or if that will happen."

Agatha released a snort. "She can't just up and leave, Theodore. Who would look out for her and where would she go? Honestly, that's a ridiculous idea. Besides, haven't you made the claim more than once that you're a first-rate private investigator? I would think someone with your stellar recommendations should be able to protect her."

"Normally, I would agree with you, Miss Watson," Theodore said as he sent her a glare, "but this is an unusual situation to be sure. Eugene and Sally have been left with nothing, and desperation leads people to do unimaginable things. I cannot say with certainty I would be able to keep her safe."

As Theodore's words echoed in the suddenly silent room, Eliza realized he was right.

Sally and Eugene had proven themselves ruthless, and . . . who could say they would only direct their attention to her?

People she'd grown to care about were now in danger because of her money, and she knew she was going to have to leave to ensure their safety, no matter how difficult the decision was. She took a deep breath and slowly released it.

"I'll go back to England," she whispered.

"Out of the question," Hamilton said as he leaned forward and caught her gaze. "You have no one to see to your well-being over there, and besides, perhaps we are jumping to a wrong conclusion."

Eliza frowned. "What do you mean?"

"We're assuming Sally and Eugene have been left with nothing, but I know perfectly well Eugene made a tidy sum from stealing business from me. There is no saying he'll pursue you, given the risks involved."

Theodore cleared his throat. "I hate to be the bearer of more bad news, but before I went to Bartholomew's today, I actually spent a bit of time investigating Eugene. From what I learned, that man was not actually in the railroad business; he passed off any deals he stole from you, Hamilton, to other competitors."

"How in the world did you learn that?" Agatha asked.

Theodore sent her a grin. "If you must know, I am in contact with many individuals who occasionally skirt the law, and they always have quite helpful information to pass along to me when prompted. Unfortunately, I was unable to discover why Eugene was targeting Hamilton's business, but I do still have men looking into the matter."

"You'll have to introduce me to some of these individuals," Agatha said. "They'd be helpful . . ." Her voice trailed off as she shot a look to her parents and then looked up at the ceiling and began whistling under her breath.

"To continue," Theodore said as his grin widened and he seemed to understand he was not to address Agatha's statement,

"I think we should return to Eliza's situation and decide where she will be the safest."

"England is an ocean away," Eliza said. "I doubt Sally and Eugene would follow me there, given the fact that tickets are so dear to purchase, and it's become clear they value money."

Hamilton shook his head and gestured to the two trunks. "I have a feeling that what is in those trunks would be worth crossing an ocean to obtain."

"We forgot all about the trunks," Agatha said. "I, for one, am dying to see what is inside." Her mouth dropped open. "What if it's nothing but books or rocks or something of little value?"

"I assure you I did not lug those chests over here because they're filled with rocks," Theodore said, and Eliza couldn't help but grin at his annoyed tone of voice.

"You already looked in them?" Agatha asked.

Theodore arched the only brow that seemed capable of moving in Agatha's direction and didn't bother to say a single word.

Agatha arched her brow right back at him before turning to Eliza. "Do you mind if I take a peek?"

"Be my guest," Eliza said.

Agatha rose and strode to the trunks, bending down to fiddle with one of the clasps before she flipped the lid open and then took a step back, her eyes wide. "Good heavens, Eliza, I know you claimed your fortune was vast, but I wasn't expecting this."

Eliza got to her feet and moved to Agatha's side before she glanced down at the stacks of bills, mixed with gold coins, and sent Agatha what she knew had to be a weak smile.

Agatha bit her lip and moved to the other chest, pushing it open and peering into the depths. She straightened and put her hands on her hips. "You could feed a small country for a very long time with the amount of money and gold stuffed into these chests."

"Don't forget the jewels," Gloria said as she brushed past

Agatha and bent over the chest, straightening with a glittering diamond necklace in her hand.

"You know, I guess I never realized Bartholomew made off with so many of my family's jewels," Eliza said, accepting the necklace from Gloria. "This belonged to my aunt Teresa. I forgot all about it." She looked up to find Hamilton watching her with that all-too-familiar trace of annoyance on his face. She blew out a puff of air. Now was hardly the time to have to deal with another one of his unexpected bouts of, well, grumpiness. She presented him with her back when Agatha suddenly laughed.

"I can't believe my family employed you as a governess," Agatha said. "You're incredibly wealthy, and I shudder to think how much more money you have stashed in those accounts of Bartholomew's."

"There might not be anything left in them," Eliza said. "Sally was apparently enjoying living the life of an aristocrat, and for all I know, she might have spent the rest of my money on gowns and other frivolous things."

Theodore began shaking his head even as a somewhat gruesome smile stretched his misshapen lips. "I glanced through the account ledgers, Eliza. There's quite a bit of money in those accounts."

Eliza thought she heard Hamilton release a disgusted sounding snort, but still wasn't ready to address his surliness. Instead, she settled for sending Theodore a smile. "I don't know how I'll ever be able to thank you. Since I now have my funds restored, you must send me the full bill. It wouldn't be fair to allow Hamilton or Zayne to pay for your services, as I was the one who truly benefited from them."

That was obviously the wrong thing to say, considering Hamilton let out what sounded like a grunt and moved to her side, glaring down at her. "I told you I would be responsible for Theodore's bill."

"But that was before I had any money," Eliza said.

"I find your offer insulting," Hamilton snapped.

Eliza discovered she was quite done with his ever-changing moods and less than pleasant demeanor, let alone the fact that he'd not once proclaimed any great affection for her, except to state he held her in "high esteem." She lifted her chin and squared her shoulders. "I find your entire behavior insulting, which makes saying what I must say next incredibly easy."

Hamilton narrowed his eyes. "And that would be what exactly?"

"I'm going home."

19

The next day, Eliza found herself strolling down Broadway, entwining one arm with Agatha's while using her other hand to keep a firm grip on Ben, who had the unfortunate propensity of bolting away from her at the slightest provocation. Piper chatted incessantly by Agatha's side, touching on a variety of topics, including the color of the sky and the unusual fashions she spotted on the street.

"May we please go on the El one more time?" Piper asked.

Eliza nodded, trying to keep her mind on the conversation and firmly away from the fact that, in just two short days, she would not have another opportunity to take Piper on her beloved El. Piper caught Eliza's nod and beamed up at her.

One of the two guards walking a few steps behind them let out a loud groan, which caused Piper to spin around on her little heel.

"We've only ridden the El two times today," she said.

"Two times too many," the guard returned.

Piper's lip began to tremble.

"To the El it is," the guard said with a sigh.

Piper's lip miraculously stopped quivering, and she flashed a grin at the guard before turning to Agatha. "Why didn't Grandmother join us today?"

"Your grandmother had a very late night last night," Agatha explained.

"So did you and Miss Eliza," Piper pointed out. "I think Grandmother's mad at both of you."

"If that's what you thought, why did you ask the question?" Eliza asked.

Piper shrugged. "Because sometimes grown-ups slip and tell me things I'm not supposed to hear when I ask questions."

Eliza laughed. "You are incorrigible."

"What's that mean?"

"Trouble," Agatha supplied. "But, if you must know, your grandmother isn't mad at me, only Eliza."

That was nothing less than the truth. Gloria was not pleased with Eliza at the moment, because she wanted her to change her mind about leaving and Eliza was not willing to oblige her. When Gloria had apparently realized her arguments were falling on deaf ears, she'd barricaded herself in her private suite, and Eliza knew perfectly well the woman was spending her time plotting. She shuddered to think what dastardly plan Gloria was going to put into action when she least expected it.

"Is Daddy mad at you?" Ben asked, speaking up.

Eliza pretended she didn't hear the question, quickly distracting Piper and Ben with the sight of a large bird flying overhead. She certainly wasn't going to admit to the children that their father was furious with her at the moment, and that he, like Gloria, wasn't even speaking to her. He'd made a very dramatic statement when he'd slid a one-way steamer ticket under her door before vanishing from the house. He'd also included a scrawled note stating he'd found a handful of guards who'd agreed to take on the job of seeing her safely back to London and staying with her until she found protection of her own.

She'd been more than annoyed by the steamer ticket, but perhaps a little touched that he'd hired men to watch her. Before she'd had an opportunity to track the man down, a solicitor by the name of Mr. Jackson showed up at the house and demanded all of her attention. Her annoyance with Hamilton faded yet again when she learned he'd been the one to send Mr. Jackson to the house, and her mood improved significantly when the solicitor explained that her finances were in wonderful condition and he was quite able to arrange the transfer of her money to any bank of her choice back in England. For some reason, that knowledge did not give her the pleasure she'd once thought it would.

"Thank you for all the toys you bought us," Piper said, interrupting Eliza's less than cheery musings. "Why did you get us so much?"

Guilt was the reason, although Eliza couldn't very well admit that to Piper. She and Hamilton had at least agreed that the children shouldn't be told of her departure just yet. She didn't want them to spend the remaining time they had together in tears, and truth be told, she knew she was not emotionally ready to say her farewells to them just yet. It was better this way. She could enjoy their company without sadness.

"I wanted to do something nice for the two of you," she finally said.

"Our toys won't get stolen while we go on the El, will they?" Piper asked.

"Since we left them in the carriage with an armed guard, I sincerely doubt anyone will attempt to make off with them," Agatha said.

"I think Theodore might have gone a bit overboard posting three guards to watch us," Eliza said dryly.

"I hate to tell you this, Eliza, but we have more than three guards at our disposal," Agatha said as she gestured with her hand. "Those men ahead of us have been trying to be discreet, but I noticed them an hour ago, and the same goes for the men lagging behind us. If my math is correct, we have around ten guards watching over us, and I don't think Theodore can take all the credit for our protection. I've come to the conclusion Hamilton's involved as well."

"He is remarkably diligent when it comes to his children," Eliza muttered.

Agatha rolled her eyes, but Eliza was spared one of Agatha's lectures when Piper let out a squeal and pointed down the street.

"Ooh, did you see that horse?"

Eliza squinted into the distance but only caught a glimpse of a white horse disappearing down an alley. Something nudged the back of her mind, but before she could contemplate exactly what that something was, a voice distracted her.

"Lady Eliza."

As the voice washed over her, recognition set in and fury descended.

"Who is that man?" Ben asked as he peered around her leg. "Why is he smiling at you?"

"He's an arrogant gentleman who is mistaken to think I welcome his smiles," Eliza managed to get out.

Ben suddenly tugged free from her hand and ran toward the man as fast as his short legs could carry him. Before Eliza had the presence of mind to react, Ben opened his mouth and clamped his teeth firmly onto the leg of Lawrence Moore, the Earl of Wrathshire.

A howl of outrage escaped Lawrence's lips.

"Umm, Eliza, don't you think it might be prudent to fetch Benjamin from that gentleman's leg?" Agatha asked in alarm.

"Give him another moment," Eliza said even as she strode forward, her temper burning hot when she realized Lawrence was trying to shake Ben off his leg.

"Don't hurt him," she snarled as she reached them and carefully pried Ben away from Lawrence. "He's only a baby."

"With teeth like a shark," Lawrence grouched, leaning down to rub his leg.

Eliza scooped Ben up into her arms and glared at her ex-fiancé. "What are you doing here?"

"I've come to take you home." He sent her what he must have assumed was a charming smile. "Aren't you happy to see me?"

"Not particularly."

"Now, Eliza, there's no need to scowl at me like that. It's hardly becoming," he said.

"I have every reason to scowl at you, Lawrence, and I really don't care if you find it 'becoming' or not," she snapped, shifting Ben in her arms, which drew Lawrence's attention.

"Who is that child?" he asked.

"This is Master Benjamin Beckett and that is his older sister, Piper," Eliza said with a nod in Piper's direction.

"And she is . . . ?" Lawrence questioned, sending a smile in Agatha's direction.

How was it possible she'd never noticed the way Lawrence leered at other women even when he was in her presence? To think she'd almost married the man. Perhaps Agatha had been right and her loss of fortune had saved her from a life of misery.

"She's my good friend, Miss Agatha Watson."

"Lord Wrathshire, I told you all about Miss Watson on the ride over here," a woman proclaimed as she strolled up to join them and stopped at Lawrence's side. "The Watson family is the family Lady Eliza stayed with when she first arrived in town, although for some odd reason I simply do not understand, she was passing herself off as their governess."

Eliza tilted her head and considered the woman for a moment. "Forgive me, but do I know you?"

The woman tittered, and the sound set Eliza's teeth on edge. "We've never been formally introduced, Lady Eliza, but I was at the Watsons' dinner party when you wore that hideous gown and monopolized Mr. and Mr. Beckett throughout the entire meal. I readily admit I was confused regarding the amount of attention they gave you, but it finally made sense when the truth came out."

Recognition set in. Standing before her was none other than the notorious Mrs. Hannah Morgan, who if memory served her correctly, was on the lookout for a new husband. "You're Mrs. Morgan," Eliza said.

"Indeed."

"Why were you passing yourself off as a governess?" Lawrence asked, drawing her attention.

"I needed the funds."

"So you weren't just pretending?" Lawrence questioned, not allowing Eliza a moment to answer before he continued. "Are you still working as a governess?"

"She got fired," Agatha proclaimed.

"Fired?" Lawrence sputtered.

"It was on account she and I ended up in jail," Agatha said. "But, to be fair, that was all a big misunderstanding."

"I never heard a word of this," Mrs. Morgan breathed.

"We've attempted to keep the matter hushed up," Eliza said.

"But where did you go after you got fired?" Lawrence asked.

"The Beckett family very kindly offered me assistance. I've been staying with them," Eliza said before her eyes narrowed. "But you would have to know that already; how else would you have learned where to find me?"

"I did know you were staying with the Becketts," Lawrence said. "You weren't very difficult to find, once I let it be known

I was looking for Lady Eliza, but . . . didn't Mrs. Morgan just mention something about two gentlemen by the name of Beckett whom you apparently sat with at some dinner party?"

"Mr. Hamilton and Mr. Zayne Beckett, to be specific," Mrs. Morgan supplied with an all too innocent smile.

"Surely you're not staying with these gentlemen?" Lawrence asked, his eyes widening in horror when Eliza nodded. "That is most unseemly."

"There is nothing 'unseemly' about it," Eliza argued.

Lawrence considered her for a moment before he smiled. "Well, no matter. It's all water under the bridge at this point, and I've come to help you sort everything out." He leaned forward and lowered his voice. "I have a surprise for you."

"You have a surprise for me?" Eliza repeated slowly.

"You didn't think I'd travel all this way with nothing to offer, did you?"

"I have no idea what possessed you to travel across the ocean. It's not as if we parted on the best of terms."

"Nonsense," Lawrence argued, "we hardly parted on disagreeable terms."

"You broke off our engagement the moment you discovered my fortune was gone."

"I did no such thing," he said with a haughty lift of his chin, the motion causing Eliza to grit her teeth. She'd forgotten that Lawrence had a tendency to posture. She squared her shoulders.

"That's exactly what you did. I distinctly remember asking you for a small loan to see me through until my affairs could be sorted out, and instead of considering my request, you ended our engagement."

"You took me by surprise," Lawrence said, a hint of petulance in his voice.

"Imagine my surprise when I realized the only reason you wished to marry me was because of my extensive dowry."

"That's not true at all," Lawrence blustered. "I only needed a bit of time to mull the matter over, and when I finally mulled it to satisfaction, you were nowhere to be found."

"It's not as if I left your house and boarded the first boat to America," Eliza returned. "It took me a few weeks to make my preparations. Are you suggesting it took you that long to 'mull' over the situation?"

"Have you always been this difficult, or is this an unfortunate habit you've managed to pick up in America?" Lawrence questioned, ignoring her accusations.

Eliza counted to ten and found that was not enough time to control her emotions. She added another ten and then opened her mouth. "You mentioned a surprise?"

"I don't know if you deserve it."

"Oh, Lord Wrathshire, give the poor lady her surprise," Mrs. Morgan said with a beaming smile in Lawrence's direction.

"May I inquire, Mrs. Morgan, exactly how you came to be involved with my ex-fiancé?" Eliza asked.

"Ex-fiancé?" Mrs. Morgan practically purred.

"Lord Wrathshire and I are no longer engaged," Eliza said.

"That is simply not true," Lawrence snapped.

Eliza arched a brow and wiggled her hand in front of him. "I don't see a ring."

Lawrence blanched. "Where is it?"

"I sold it," Eliza said. "I needed the funds, and since you're the one who broke the engagement, etiquette demands I may keep the ring and do with it as I see fit."

"It was a family heirloom."

"Not anymore."

"Well, no matter," Lawrence said with a nod. "We'll simply track it down once we return to London. You do remember where you sold it, don't you?"

"I do, although I don't know if that man will still be skulking around the streets in the same location. He had a somewhat peculiar look to him."

"You sold it to a man on the streets?" Lawrence hissed.

Eliza nodded.

Mrs. Morgan cleared her throat. "I believe we're beginning to attract attention with our raised voices. Perhaps it would be best if we discontinued this particular conversation and returned to the more pleasant one of how I came to be with Lord Wrathshire."

"This should be interesting," Agatha muttered, and Eliza had to bite back a grin at Agatha's arched brow.

"I was on my way to pay my respects to Mrs. Beckett when I happened upon Lord Wrathshire getting out of his carriage," Mrs. Morgan said. "We began a polite conversation, and I soon realized I could be of assistance to him because, for some unknown reason, the Beckett servants were less than forthcoming regarding your whereabouts."

"Eliza's life is in danger," Agatha explained.

"You must tell me all the details," Mrs. Morgan exclaimed.

"No," Eliza argued, "we're not delving into my personal business."

"I don't see why not," Lawrence retorted. "If your life is truly in danger, then as the man in your life, I certainly deserve to know the details."

"You're not the man in my life, and we were speaking about how Mrs. Morgan came to meet you," Eliza said, turning her back on Lawrence and giving Mrs. Morgan a nod.

"Well," Mrs. Morgan continued, "fortunately, I spotted a maid slipping out of the house, and when she recognized me, she told me you could be found shopping. I couldn't very well leave Lord Wrathshire to find you on his own, so I escorted him here."

"How fortunate for us you were able to find us," Eliza said

before she turned to Lawrence and narrowed her eyes. "How did you get to New York?"

"Oh, well, that's where the surprise comes into play," Lawrence said. He moved to the right and pointed to a gentleman standing a short distance away.

Eliza frowned as she took a step forward. The man was oddly familiar to her, but she couldn't quite place him. She took another step forward, her gaze lingering on the gentleman's burnished copper hair, which, she saw, he wore a trifle longer than fashion currently allowed. Her eyes skimmed over his face, taking in the darkness of his skin, as if he'd spent an excessive amount of time in the sun. Her eyes widened when she got to the man's eyes. They were the exact same shade as hers. Her mouth dropped open in shock.

"Grayson?" she sputtered, finding she was unable to move.

"Hello, Liz."

Eliza could only stare at her brother, her mind completely numb. She blinked. "You're supposed to be dead."

"Apparently I'm not, as I seem to be standing here conversing with you."

"You've been gone for over six years," she whispered. "Father had you declared dead."

"I'm sorry about that. . . . Well, not sorry Father had me declared dead, but sorry that you *believed* me dead."

"We wouldn't have believed you were dead if you'd only bothered to send us a note," Eliza bit out. "Why didn't you send us a note?"

"Eliza, this is hardly the proper moment to get into all of this," Lawrence said. "We're standing in a crowded street, which is hardly conducive to an intimate conversation."

Eliza ignored his statement, keeping her gaze locked on her brother. "You should have let us know you were alive. Father

242

spent hours praying for your safe return, and then he mourned you for years."

"I never meant to cause him anguish, but you know perfectly well I never got along with Father, and he is the reason I left home in the first place," Grayson said.

"You abandoned your responsibilities," Eliza said.

"I was young, and I never asked to be the only son of a titled aristocrat. I wanted to experience life before being forced to assume such a mundane existence."

"And did you experience life?" Eliza snapped.

A haunted look flashed into Grayson's eyes before he blinked and the look disappeared. "I did."

"You left me with a heartbroken father. I was the only one left to hold his hand when he died."

"For that I'm deeply sorry."

"Your apology is not enough," she hissed.

"Do you want me to bite him?" Ben asked solemnly.

"Yes," Eliza said.

Ben looked at Grayson and shook his little head. "He's not bad, Miss Eliza, just sad."

Leave it to a baby to point out the obvious.

Eliza sent Ben a smile. "I didn't really want you to bite him, darling. He's my brother."

"I thought you said you didn't have any family," Piper said slowly.

"What nonsense is this?" Lawrence blustered. "Of course Lady Eliza has family. She has me, and we're to be married as soon as we return to England. I have already procured a special license, and arrangements are being made as we speak."

"That was a bit presumptuous, Lawrence," Eliza said. "I find myself curious, though. Where did you procure the funds to pay for this wedding?"

He beamed back at her. "Did I forget to mention that? How

remiss of me. Your brother has very kindly offered to pay for the event." He leaned forward and lowered his voice. "He has returned to England an incredibly wealthy man."

Eliza narrowed her eyes as she shifted Ben in her arms. "Let the biting commence."

20

Anger caused Eliza's stride to increase even as she realized her brother was matching her step for step. She jostled Ben around in her arms, tripped on an uneven piece of sidewalk, shook off Grayson's arm when he tried to steady her, and pressed forward, shooting him a glare as she did so. "Explain to me exactly how Lawrence was able to convince you we were still engaged."

"How was I to know the man was lying?" Grayson asked.

"Oh, let me think, probably from the outlandish explanation he must have given you explaining why I traveled to America without him."

"I did not give him an outlandish explanation," Lawrence argued as he trotted up between them, his breathing a bit labored obviously due to the fact that he rarely participated in anything as remotely strenuous as a brisk walk.

Eliza came to a stop and sent Lawrence a glare, becoming

distracted when Ben patted her cheek and sent her a smile. She returned the smile and set him on his feet before she took his hand and began walking, this time at a more leisurely pace, not bothering to dignify Lawrence's statement with a reply.

"Lawrence told me the two of you had a bit of a row," Grayson said.

"You honestly believed I would cross the Atlantic over a little bit of a row?"

"I suppose I didn't think the matter over sufficiently," Grayson muttered.

Eliza rolled her eyes and nodded to Lawrence. "How exactly did you become acquainted with my brother?"

A shifty expression crossed Lawrence's face before a placid smile quickly replaced it. "I heard tell of a mysterious gentleman who'd come to town. From what I learned about him, I thought it sounded as if he might just be your long-lost brother."

"That's complete nonsense," Eliza snapped. "You most likely learned the gentleman was incredibly wealthy and went to acquaint yourself with him on the chance he had an unmarried daughter."

"That was a low blow indeed," Lawrence sputtered.

"I do have a daughter," Grayson admitted before Eliza could direct another scathing remark to Lawrence. "Not that she's even remotely ready for marriage, given the fact that she's two."

"And she's Chinese," Lawrence proclaimed.

"You've been to China?" Agatha suddenly asked as she huffed into place beside Grayson, Piper by her side.

"Where else would he acquire a Chinese daughter?" Lawrence asked.

Eliza swatted Lawrence on the arm. "Be quiet." She looked at her brother. "This is my very good friend, Miss Agatha Watson. Agatha, this is my brother, Mr. Grayson Sumner, more formally known as the Earl of Sefton."

"Mr. Sumner will do just fine, Miss Watson," Grayson said as he stopped and bowed. "I never did put much store in titles."

Agatha eyed Grayson with a long, considering look. "Why did you let Eliza think you were dead?"

"It's a riveting tale," he replied, "but this is hardly the time to get into it. Besides, I thought we were talking about Lawrence."

Eliza nodded. "We were, and I must admit I'm still confused. May I assume Lawrence sought you out and then convinced you of his intention to marry me after he discovered your true identity?" She drew in a gulp of air and continued before Grayson could reply. "And then, did the two of you simply hop on a boat with the intention of fetching me home?"

"It did go something like that," Grayson said.

"Did it ever occur to you to seek out Spencer to verify Lawrence's story?"

"I didn't want many people to become aware of the fact that I'd returned."

"Spencer is family."

"Barely, he's what, our second cousin or some such nonsense?"

"You should have sought him out to discuss the situation, considering you're the true Earl of Sefton and you don't appear to be dead."

"I have no intention of reclaiming my title," Grayson said. "You must realize my daughter will never be accepted within London society. I won't put her in a situation where she'll grow up an outcast."

"You can't simply decide you're just not going to be the Earl of Sefton," Eliza said with a snort.

"I don't see why not," Grayson countered. "It's worked out rather well for me so far, and besides, Spencer is more than capable of managing the estates, and I hardly believe he'll be thrilled to discover I'm alive. It will be easier all around if I never return."

"That's ridiculous," Eliza snapped. "Although, you might have a point about Spencer, but . . . we can certainly compensate him for managing the estates while you've been away, and quite frankly, I never believed he enjoyed assuming the title. He absolutely loathes London society, as does his wife, and he'll be thrilled to hand over all that pesky responsibility to you once the two of us return to town. Add in the fact that I'm more than willing to share some of our recovered fortune with him, and I do not believe we have a problem."

"You're forgetting my daughter."

"And you're forgetting the true nature of London society," Eliza countered. "Wealth can go far in causing people to overlook such details."

Eliza was distracted when Lawrence suddenly took her arm and beamed down at her. "That is wonderful news regarding your fortune, darling," he said.

"Not for you," Eliza said with a sniff before she shrugged out of his hold. "Now, we really need to postpone this conversation because we've almost reached our destination. I've promised the children one last ride on the El, and as they've been more than patient with all of this, I have to make good on my promise."

"You could take them another day," Mrs. Morgan suggested as she sidled up next to them.

Eliza blinked. She'd completely forgotten all about Mrs. Morgan, but the woman's comment caused a slice of pain to travel through her heart. She would not be able to take the children another day, which meant she wasn't going to deprive them of her time. She wanted to savor each and every minute she had left with them.

"You're more than welcome to join us," she said with a nod to Mrs. Morgan.

"I'm not riding on that rickety elevated train," Lawrence scoffed.

"Then you may stay behind," Eliza said coolly.

Lawrence mumbled something under his breath before he fell into step as they all began strolling in the direction of the train platform.

"Would your daughter not enjoy this outing?" Agatha asked.

"Ming is back at the hotel with her nannies," Grayson explained. "She's only two, and I must admit she's a bit cranky at the moment. We've been traveling for what seems like months, and I fear this latest trip to America has been a bit overwhelming for her."

"Did you only recently return from China?" Agatha asked.

"Indeed. I barely stepped foot into England before I became acquainted with Lord Wrathshire, and the next thing I knew, I'd been convinced to purchase tickets to America, and off we sailed."

"It's no wonder the child is cranky," Eliza replied. "She needs a more stable environment."

"That hasn't been a choice of late."

Eliza couldn't help but notice the despair lingering in the depths of her brother's eyes, but before she could question him about it, they arrived at the platform. She bought tickets for everyone, including the guards who'd been following them the entire time, and then waited as the train ground to a halt in front of her. She took Ben up in her arms, grabbed hold of Piper's hand, and sailed through the door, taking the nearest seat and smiling when Agatha took the seat next to her. Grayson sat behind them, and Lawrence was forced to sit with Mrs. Morgan, although, he really didn't appear to be bothered with the seating arrangements in the least, considering Mrs. Morgan was obviously doing her best to be charming.

The train moved away from the station, and, although Eliza spent the ride trying to devote her attention to Piper and Ben, a disturbing thought kept running through her mind.

Her brother was alive, and she'd not even made a point of welcoming him back.

Tears flooded her eyes, and a sigh of relief escaped her when the train finished its loop and pulled back into the station. She helped Piper and Ben down to the platform and turned to find her brother watching her. She stepped to his side.

"It is so good to see you," she said before Grayson pulled her into his arms and held her tightly for a long moment.

"I'm sorry," Grayson whispered into her hair. "I never meant to hurt you."

"That was disgusting," Lawrence exclaimed, ruining the moment. "It was filthy on that train, and I don't even want to mention our fellow passengers."

Eliza stepped out of her brother's embrace and sent Lawrence what she could only hope was a cool look. "I told you there was no need for you to go. I'm certain Mrs. Morgan would have been more than delighted to keep you company."

Mrs. Morgan smiled and nodded, causing Eliza to stifle the urge to roll her eyes. A thought flashed to mind. Perhaps Mrs. Morgan could be a diversion where Lawrence was concerned. If memory served her correctly, the woman was wealthy in her own right, and from what little Eliza had discerned about her, she had the feeling the woman would not be opposed to assuming the role of Lady Wrathshire.

"May I suggest we make our way back to the Beckett house? There's still much left to discuss, and I, for one, would love a cup of tea before we continue our conversation." She looked to Mrs. Morgan. "You're invited too, of course."

"You are so kind," Mrs. Morgan purred before she latched on to Lawrence's arm. She sent him a wide smile. "Shall I ride back to the Beckett house in your hired carriage?"

Lawrence blinked. "Of course," he said, turning to Eliza. "Will you join us?"

"My carriage is parked just down the street, and besides, it's not a very long journey from here. You'll be fine with Mrs. Morgan for company," Eliza said.

Lawrence sent her a glare before he took Mrs. Morgan by the arm and stalked away, leaving Eliza with the surprising desire to laugh. Poor Lawrence didn't stand a chance with the cunning widow, and truth be told, she was fairly certain they deserved each other. She turned to find Grayson smiling at her.

"Don't you think Mrs. Morgan would make a wonderful countess?" she asked.

"Ah, I thought I remembered that particular look," Grayson said. "You're scheming in order to get Lawrence out of your life."

"Exactly," Eliza agreed as she took Ben from Agatha and waited for Agatha to take Piper's hand before walking back to the carriage. Grayson took Ben from Eliza so she could climb up and then surprised her when he insisted on holding him.

"He's almost asleep, Liz, and I have a far larger lap to settle him in than you do," Grayson said as he took his seat and snuggled Ben close to him.

Eliza scooted over to make room for Agatha and Piper and then tapped on the roof. As the carriage rolled into motion, Eliza's attention returned to Grayson, who was absently brushing the hair out of Ben's face. "Fatherhood has changed you."

"You have no idea," Grayson muttered.

Agatha leaned forward. "Tell me all about China. I've always longed to go there."

"It's not a place I would recommend," Grayson said with a trace of bitterness in his voice. "I only stayed because I landed in a rather lucrative situation."

"What kind of 'situation'?" Eliza asked.

Grayson sent a pointed look toward Piper and didn't respond.

"All right then," she said. "Tell me about your daughter."

"There's not much to tell."

"Does she have a mother?" Eliza asked.

"Of course she has a mother," Grayson muttered. "Be kind of difficult to explain if she didn't."

"Am I to assume her mother was your wife?" Eliza pressed.

"You shouldn't assume anything," Grayson said before he sighed. "If you must know, I address Ming as my daughter for lack of a better word."

Eliza tilted her head. "So . . . she's not really your daughter?"

"I'm all she has," Grayson said softly.

"She's your daughter in all the good ways," Piper said, drawing everyone's attention.

"Well said," Grayson replied. "Now, why don't we talk about something pleasant?"

Eliza found she was unwilling to drop the subject just yet. "You weren't married?"

"I never said that, but again, this is hardly the appropriate time to discuss the matter. It's very complicated, somewhat sad, and not anything a child should hear."

"I'm five," Piper proclaimed.

"Which is certainly old, but your brother is not nearly old enough to hear the story," Grayson said.

"He's asleep," Piper pointed out.

Grayson smiled at Piper, a smile that took Eliza straight back to their youth. Grayson had always been a wild and irresponsible boy, but she'd loved him all the same, and a feeling of happiness settled over her as she vowed right then and there that she was never going to lose him again.

Eliza blinked out of her thoughts when Piper, seemingly realizing Grayson was not going to give in to her demands, turned to look out the window and then gave a squeal of delight.

"We're here, and look, Daddy and Uncle Zayne are waiting for us on the front stoop, and isn't that your friend from England getting out of that carriage?"

Eliza peered out the window and swallowed a sigh. "How did Lawrence and Mrs. Morgan get here before we did?"

"I suppose they were able to travel faster seeing how they didn't have an armed escort impeding their progress," Agatha replied as the carriage door opened and Zayne popped his head in, his eyes going directly to Grayson.

"Who are you?" Zayne asked.

"Zayne, this is my brother, Grayson Sumner, or more officially, Lord Sefton. Grayson, this is my good friend Mr. Zayne Beckett."

"Good friend?" Grayson questioned.

"Brother?" Zayne asked at the same time.

"I'll explain to the best of my abilities after we get into the house," Eliza said. "Would you be so kind as to carry your nephew? He fell asleep on the way home, and I have no desire to wake him just yet. The poor little dear is exhausted."

Zayne looked as if he wanted to say something else, but then blew out a breath, took Ben from Grayson, and stepped aside to allow everyone room to exit the carriage. Eliza watched as Piper hit the ground and dashed to Hamilton's side.

"Daddy, Daddy, guess what? We went to the El, bought toys and . . . we found Miss Eliza's brother."

"Extraordinary," Hamilton exclaimed before he turned, narrowed his eyes, and stalked up to join Eliza and Grayson. "May I assume you're Eliza's brother?"

"I'm Grayson Sumner. And you are?"

"Hamilton Beckett," he replied, giving Grayson's hand a perfunctory shake before he continued. "I thought you were dead."

"It was a general consensus to be sure," Grayson replied. "My sister has been more than vocal voicing her protests over my regrettable lack of correspondence with her."

"As she should," Hamilton returned. "You left her alone."

"She had me," Lawrence proclaimed from behind them.

"And you are?" Hamilton asked, his voice turning silky smooth in a split second.

"That man said he's come to take Miss Eliza home," Piper said before Lawrence could speak.

"Did he?" Hamilton asked softly, his eyes turning dangerous. Eliza watched Hamilton eye Lawrence, his expression darkening with every passing second. To give Lawrence his due, he was an incredibly attractive man, but compared to Hamilton, he didn't measure up well in the least.

Honestly, what was she thinking? Now was hardly the time to become distracted from the situation at hand.

"My goodness," Gloria said as she barreled out of the door and came to a sudden stop, causing Mrs. Watson to plow into her back. "Whatever is going on out here and who are all these people? Oh, hello, Mrs. Morgan. What an unusual surprise."

"Mrs. Beckett, how wonderful to see you," Mrs. Morgan gushed. "I have heard the most interesting gossip swirling around town."

"I can't say I'm surprised," Gloria replied. "Our lives have been quite interesting of late."

"Indeed," Mrs. Morgan said. "We must talk all about it."

"I don't believe now is the right moment," Gloria said firmly as her gaze swept over Lawrence and then Grayson. "Mrs. Watson, have you ever seen those two gentlemen?"

"I have not," Mrs. Watson replied.

"Mother, what are you doing here?" Agatha asked.

"As you didn't offer to include me in your shopping expedition, I decided to check on Gloria," Mrs. Watson exclaimed absently, her eyes on Grayson. "You must be one of Lady Eliza's relations. I can see a marked resemblance."

"I'm her brother," Grayson said.

"This is certain to complicate matters," Mrs. Watson said.

"Complicate matters?" Eliza asked.

"Nothing to concern yourself with, my dear," Mrs. Watson muttered before turning back to Gloria. "It would seem as if we might need to alter our plans."

"What plans?" Eliza questioned.

"Never mind," Gloria replied with a smile in Grayson's direction. "I'm delighted by the fact that someone in Eliza's family has finally arrived to take the girl in hand. She has become somewhat stubborn, and I'm sure you'll be able to talk some sense into her. I'm Mrs. Gloria Beckett."

Grayson bowed. "I'm Mr. Grayson Sumner at your service, Mrs. Beckett."

"Charming," Gloria proclaimed with a smile before turning to Lawrence and quirking a brow.

"I am Lord Wrathshire, Lady Eliza's intended."

"Another complication," Mrs. Watson declared.

"Hardly," Gloria replied, her eyes never leaving Lawrence's face. "May I suggest we repair to the house before we attract unwanted attention?"

Everyone turned to follow Gloria into the house except Lawrence, who stepped in front of Eliza, blocking her path as his eyes narrowed. "You neglected to mention the little fact you're sharing house space with gentlemen who are remarkably young. For some reason, I pictured Mr. and Mr. Beckett as elderly men who were extending you a kindness."

"Don't forget handsome," Eliza couldn't resist adding, catching Hamilton's eye as he waited for her by the door. She sent him a grin.

"This is most unseemly," Lawrence snapped. "Your reputation is at stake."

"My reputation is no longer any of your concern."

"As your future husband, I would have to disagree. You have not been behaving in a very virtuous manner, from what I can discern, and I must say you will have a bit of explaining to do to Reverend Michaels before we marry. I am most certain he will want a full confession of all the sins you have committed on your trip, and I really must insist on hearing them also."

Eliza rolled her eyes. "I have not committed any grave sins, Lawrence, but I'm amazed you would attempt to drag religion into this situation. It's not as if you've ever been a man of strong faith."

"Is everything all right?" Hamilton asked as he appeared at Eliza's side.

"I am having a discussion with Lady Eliza, and I would appreciate it if you would allow us some privacy," Lawrence said. "What we have to say to each other is none of your concern."

"Everything regarding Eliza concerns me."

"On my word, sir, your manner of addressing *Lady* Eliza is far too familiar."

"We've become good friends," Hamilton said.

"I am her dearest friend," Lawrence stated.

"You abandoned her in her hour of need."

"How could I have known she would get it into her head to track that scoundrel across an entire ocean on her own?" Lawrence blustered.

"If you truly knew her, you would have realized she would act exactly as she did."

Lovely warmth spread over Eliza at Hamilton's words. It would appear the man understood her more than she'd realized. Before she could respond, Lawrence sent her a scowl.

"I do not care for the direction this conversation is heading. For some reason, this gentleman seems to be under the misapprehension he knows you better than I do. You need to set this Mr. Beckett straight and explain to him that we've been promised to each other from practically the moment of your debut."

Eliza felt the distinct desire to scream. Honestly, she'd never realized the gentleman was so tenacious. She drew in a breath and then slowly released it, finding it did nothing whatsoever to cool her temper. "We're no longer promised to each other, Lawrence. If you will recall, you broke that promise when you abandoned me."

"I find myself curious to hear exactly what your explanation is regarding why you abandoned Eliza," Hamilton said, breaking back into the conversation.

"I don't owe you an explanation," Lawrence said.

"Were you in need of a wealthy wife?" Hamilton pressed.

"That was a requirement," Lawrence muttered. "If you must know, my family estates are extensive and quite expensive to maintain."

"You could have sought out employment if you needed additional funds."

"I don't have time to seek out employment," Lawrence said with a curl of his lips. "I am responsible for managing vast amounts of land that, while profitable, certainly do not bring in enough funds to sustain my pleasant life."

"So, in order to maintain your high standard of living, you abandoned Eliza when she no longer was able to bring added wealth to your family?"

"Exactly," Lawrence agreed, obviously pleased Hamilton was finally catching on. "I had already spent part of her promised dowry on new additions to one of my country estates. You would not believe the problems that occurred when it became known her father had squandered all of his money. Creditors began pounding down my door, and I had no choice but to begin looking for another wife."

"You spent my money before we were even married?" Eliza hissed.

"There is no need for your outrage, my dear. Our engagement was well known, along with the fact that your father was to bequeath substantial funds to you. I did nothing wrong."

"Did it ever occur to you to offer Eliza some manner of assistance when Mr. Hayes disappeared with all her money?" Hamilton asked. "If you weren't able to extend her a loan, the very least you could have done was travel with her to search for Mr. Hayes."

"I could hardly offer to leave England," Lawrence scoffed. "It was the height of the social season."

And to think she'd almost married this fool.

She chanced a glance to Hamilton and found him watching Lawrence as if he'd never seen anything like the gentleman in his entire life. Disgust, annoyance, and a surprising trace of amusement all jostled to take up space in his eyes, and for some reason, her temper faded to nothing as a laugh escaped her lips.

"Honestly, Eliza, this is hardly the time to allow your warped sense of humor free rein," Lawrence snapped. "I am beyond disappointed with your behavior, and quite frankly, you'll be fortunate if I do not change my mind about marrying you." He sent her a glare and turned on his heel, marching into the house.

"Shall we follow him?" Hamilton asked.

"I suppose we don't have another choice."

Hamilton offered her his arm, and Eliza knew it would be churlish to refuse his offer. For some reason, she wasn't nearly as annoyed with him as she'd been over the past few days, and she had the sneaky suspicion it was because she didn't actually want to be annoyed with him. She was honest enough with herself to admit she still held him in affection, but her life seemed to be spiraling out of control, and she had no idea how to set matters right or even allow Hamilton to know she just might have made a grave error in regard to him and his ridiculous offer of marriage.

Not that she wanted to marry him, or at least she didn't think she did, but she would not be opposed to returning to this country at a later date, once the danger had passed, if only to see if something, well . . . interesting could develop.

Her musings were interrupted when she realized they'd somehow reached the parlor, and she frowned as she glanced around. "What happened to Piper and Ben?" she asked.

"Miss Jamison took them outside to play," Gloria said. "She very wisely discerned that our conversation was not going to be appropriate for tender ears." Gloria smiled. "Piper grumbled the entire way out of the room."

"I bet she did grum . . ." Eliza's words died on her tongue as the sound of rushing feet met her ears. A feeling of dread swept over her when one of the guards burst into the room and stumbled to a stop.

"The children are gone."

21

*C*haos erupted as everyone bolted for the back door and raced into the garden.

"They went over the wall," Miss Jamison yelled from her position on the ground, a guard bending over her.

Hamilton spun in midstride and ran for the wall, Zayne a step behind him. Eliza reached the wall before either of them and took a running leap, but failed to get over the wall when an arm snagged her around the waist. She was pulled to the ground and turned to find Hamilton shaking his head at her.

"You can't come," he rasped as Zayne cleared the wall and disappeared over the side.

"I can help," she sobbed.

"Eliza, please, there isn't much time." The despair and panic in Hamilton's eyes brought Eliza up short. His children had been snatched, and he couldn't waste precious time arguing with her. She gave him a short jerk of her head.

"Summon Theodore," he said before he jumped over the wall.

Eliza simply stood there for a moment, her mind completely numb. She blinked when Grayson sprinted past her and dove over the wall, his action breaking through her stupor. She took a deep breath, wiped the tears off her cheeks, and set her sights on Gloria, who was bending over Miss Jamison. She managed to take all of three steps before she was jerked to a stop, one of the guards holding on to her arm.

She narrowed her eyes. "What are you still doing here?"

"My orders were to protect you. I need to get you out of the open."

"I don't need protection," she snapped. "Piper and Ben are babies. You should be searching for them." She shrugged out of his hold and continued over to Miss Jamison, kneeling by the poor woman's side. "Are you hurt?"

Miss Jamison struggled to a sitting position, raising a shaky hand to her head. "They just appeared out of nowhere," she said. "One minute the yard was empty, and the next, it was filled with men. I was knocked off my feet and the guards were attacked."

Eliza lifted her gaze and realized there were two men lying on the ground, one of the remaining guards bending over them.

"They're not dead, are they?" she called.

"Just knocked out, Lady Eliza. I've sent one of the servants to summon a physician."

Eliza nodded and turned back to Miss Jamison. "What happened next?"

"Two men snatched Piper and Ben and took them over the wall. It was as if they'd been waiting for us. I couldn't stop them." Tears ran unchecked down Miss Jamison's face.

"Of course you couldn't stop them," Eliza said. "You were decidedly outnumbered, and we're fortunate you weren't seriously harmed. Do you remember how many men there were?"

"I think there were seven, maybe eight. It all happened so quickly."

"Hired thugs, from the sound of it," Agatha said, dropping down beside Eliza. "Did you hear them say anything?"

"No, but one of them did leave a note. He dropped it on top of me before rushing away. I gave it to that man over there."

Eliza lifted her head and settled her attention on a guard who was speaking with another man a short distance away, a piece of paper in his hand. She scrambled to her feet and rushed over to them.

"What does it say?" she demanded.

"I'm sorry, but I can't divulge the contents to you. You might compromise the situation."

"I beg your pardon?"

"You're mentioned."

Eliza held out her hand and waited impatiently as the guards exchanged looks.

"You'll need to wait until Mr. Wilder arrives," one of the guards said, stuffing the note into an inside pocket of his jacket.

"I'm not above retrieving that," Eliza snapped.

"Eliza," Theodore called as he ran across the lawn to join her. "I got here as quickly as I could. I was on my way here when one of my men ran into me." He skidded to a stop and eyed her warily. "What are you doing?"

"I'm contemplating bodily harm because your man won't allow me to read a note the abductors left."

Theodore swung his attention to the guard and arched a brow.

"We thought it best to withhold the information from her." The man retrieved the note and passed it to Theodore, who read it quickly and released a sigh.

"Is it from Eugene?" Eliza asked.

"And Sally," Theodore admitted.

"They want me?"

Theodore shook his head. "They want the contents from the two chests."

"What chests?" Lawrence asked, coming to a stop by Eliza's side, his breathing once again labored.

"The chests that contain part of my fortune," Eliza replied absently. "They can have it."

"Eliza," Lawrence gasped, "you can't simply hand over your money to a bunch of criminals."

"Of course I can," Eliza said, her temper flaring when Lawrence stepped in front of her, causing her to brush past him in order to speak to Theodore. "How do we get the money to them?"

Theodore frowned. "Eliza, I know you're distraught at the moment, but I must point out that it's not always wise to give in to these types of demands. There's no guarantee they'll return Piper and Ben after they receive the ransom."

"Now, there is sound advice," Lawrence proclaimed, earning a glare from Eliza before she looked back at Theodore.

"They won't hurt them," Eliza said. "Sally always had a soft spot for children, and I can't see her allowing Eugene to discard Piper and Ben."

"Are you certain you want to go through with this?" Theodore asked.

"I'll do whatever it takes to get the children home."

"Are the chests at the bank?" Theodore asked.

"No, they're in Hamilton's safe. At least, one chest is. We combined the contents because I thought it would be easier to take one chest back to England rather than two." She spun and headed for the house. "Are you coming?" she asked over her shoulder.

"Don't we need to wait for Hamilton to get into the safe?" Theodore asked.

"Hamilton gave me the combination," she said.

"It seems you are far too familiar with Mr. Beckett," Lawrence sputtered.

"It's none of your concern how 'familiar' I am with Hamilton," Eliza returned as she set her feet to motion and ran toward the house, Theodore running beside her. Agatha met them at the door.

"Where are you going?" Agatha asked.

"To get into Hamilton's safe," Eliza said. "It's in his room."

"How do you know that?" Agatha asked.

"I've been in there. And yes, Gloria acted as chaperone when Hamilton showed the safe to me."

Eliza dashed through the main floor and hurried up the steps, making her way down the hallway and then into Hamilton's room. She moved to the wall, shoved aside the board that blended into the wood, and then made short shrift of unlocking the safe and pulling the door open. She turned and gestured to Theodore. "I'm going to need a hand with this."

Theodore motioned Eliza out of the way and grabbed the handle of the chest, releasing a grunt as he heaved and pulled the chest free of the safe. "I have no idea how you're going to get this back to England, even if you do have guards traveling with you. It's bound to draw attention."

"She wouldn't even have thought about going back to England if you hadn't put the idea in her head," Agatha grouched.

Theodore narrowed his eyes. "If you will recall, Miss Watson, England is her home, and I was only concerned with keeping her safe. By the clear disgruntlement in your voice, may I assume you have doubts regarding that decision?"

"She's only taking your advice to run away from Hamilton," Agatha replied with a sniff. "It really has nothing to do with her safety."

Theodore's eyes widened. "I do beg your pardon, Eliza. I did not realize you had affection for Hamilton, although, I can certainly understand why you'd want to flee. Love is a fickle creature, and Hamilton is a brooding sort. I would run too."

"Hamilton is not brooding," Eliza argued, "and I'm not running away."

Theodore sent her one of his condescending smiles. "Aren't you?"

Why in the world was she even arguing with the man? It was clear he possessed the emotional range of a wet mop, and besides, she'd actually been reconsidering the whole departing-the-country business. Before she could formulate a suitable reply, Hamilton suddenly rushed into the room, Zayne right behind him.

"Any sign of the children?" Eliza questioned, finding the answer in Hamilton's face.

"We lost them," Hamilton said. "There were horses waiting beyond the wall, and the men dispersed in all directions. Our men are still searching the streets, but Zayne, your brother, and I thought it best to return home to see if there was any news."

"Eugene left a note," Eliza explained. "He's demanded the chest."

"He wants your money?" Hamilton questioned, his gaze flickering to the chest resting on the floor.

Eliza nodded. "He can have it."

"I don't think I can allow you to do that," Hamilton said slowly.

"I don't see why not," she replied, grabbing on to the handle as she nodded to Theodore. "We're wasting time." She straightened when Theodore made no move to assist her. "What?"

"There's a huge amount of money in that chest," Hamilton said.

"Do you honestly think I care?"

"They are not your children," he said softly.

"They're as good as."

Hamilton moved so quickly Eliza didn't have a moment to draw a breath. One minute she was standing next to the chest, and the next, she was firmly enveloped in Hamilton's arms, his strength engulfing her.

"I don't know what I did to deserve you," he whispered into her hair, his voice raspy. "I don't want you to leave me when this is done."

Eliza felt him stroke her hair as his warmth surrounded her, and she drew comfort from his closeness. "I'm not going anywhere," she finally whispered into his shirt.

"I say, Mr. Beckett, this is beyond reproach," Lawrence raged as he stalked into the room. "I demand you release my fiancée at once."

Eliza felt Hamilton stiffen, but instead of releasing her, he shifted her to his side and kept his arm around her waist before he swung his attention to Lawrence. "She isn't your fiancée."

"She will soon be my wife once we return to England."

"Over my dead body," Hamilton bit out.

"Gentlemen," Zayne interrupted, casually insinuating himself between Hamilton and Lawrence, "while this is a riveting conversation to be sure, we have a bit of a crisis at the moment, and I must insist you cease this argument until a more appropriate time. We have to keep our attention centered on finding Ben and Piper."

"You're right, of course, Zayne. I apologize. I fear my anxiety has gotten the best of me," Hamilton said with a nod in Lawrence's direction.

"Too right it has," Lawrence replied with a sniff.

"Are you certain about the chest?" Hamilton asked.

Eliza nodded. "I've never been more certain about anything in my entire life."

Hamilton brushed her cheek ever so softly with his finger before he moved away from her and looked at Theodore. "Where do they want the chest delivered?"

"At an abandoned warehouse up north," Theodore said. "We

have three hours to get it there, and Eugene demanded we not bring extra men, not that we'll pay attention to that part of the note. I'll send men ahead of us to discreetly watch the area and hopefully track Eugene back to the children once he picks up the chest."

"Won't that increase the danger for the children?" Eliza asked.

"We can't neglect this opportunity. It may be the only chance we have of recovering Piper and Ben," Theodore said.

"You will keep an eye on the money?" Lawrence asked.

"I don't care about the money," Eliza snapped.

"We'll still try to retrieve it, Eliza," Theodore said. "You wouldn't want these criminals to benefit from their deed, would you?"

"I don't want anyone putting themselves in danger over that chest," Eliza stated. "If we get Piper and Ben back, and Eugene and Sally end up with my money, it won't bother me in the least."

"You really are an incredible woman," Hamilton said.

Eliza resisted the urge to melt into a puddle at his feet. Her emotions were swirling every which way, and yet she knew now was not the time to sort through them. Nothing was settled between them, but that would have to wait until Piper and Ben were returned. She released a breath. "I'm not that incredible, Hamilton. I've simply come to realize there is something more important in life than money."

"We're going to have a long discussion when this is over," Hamilton promised.

Eliza smiled. "I imagine we will."

Zayne cleared his throat. "Shouldn't we be off?"

Hamilton nodded before he looked at Theodore. "Zayne and I will accompany you?"

"Certainly," Theodore agreed before he glanced at Eliza and Agatha. "You two need to stay here."

"We could be of assistance," Agatha said.

"There is no place for women in a situation like this," Theodore said.

Agatha opened her mouth to argue, but Eliza interrupted what she knew would be a lengthy tirade. "Agatha, we need to let them get on their way. Piper and Ben are out there, scared and alone, and we will be a comfort to Gloria if we stay."

"I'll feel better knowing you won't be in danger," Hamilton added.

"I don't believe I'm personally in danger; they don't want me, just my money. It does seem to be a recurring circumstance in my life," Eliza added with a pointed look to Lawrence.

"I don't want your money," Hamilton said. "In fact, I'll do my best to return the exact amount you're handing over, if we're unsuccessful in reclaiming your chest. I simply don't have enough time at the moment to convert the money from my accounts."

"You're that wealthy?" Lawrence questioned.

"I might not have as much total wealth as Eliza, but I can cover what's in that chest."

"And we have your word on that?"

"Lawrence, enough about the money," Eliza said. "It's not as if it's my entire fortune. I have more money in my accounts, although I do plan on sharing it with Grayson and my cousins."

"Your brother has no need of your funds," Lawrence scoffed. "From what I learned back in England, the man is one of the richest in the country."

"Thank you, Lawrence, for spreading that personal information around," Grayson remarked as he entered the room. "Gloria is waiting for everyone in the parlor, and I told her I'd come fetch you." He sent Eliza a small smile before turning to Lawrence. "What say you and I return to the hotel for a bit? I need to check on my daughter, and you need some time away from my sister." Not giving Lawrence an opportunity to reply, Grayson took him by the arm and hurried him out of the room.

It was lovely to have a big brother again.

"Let's go," Theodore said as he took hold of one side of the chest and Zayne took hold of the other before they struggled out of the room.

"You'll keep an eye on my mother?" Hamilton asked softly.

Eliza nodded, fighting back the tears she would not allow Hamilton to see.

"Thank you," Hamilton said, surprising her by pulling her into his arms and holding her tightly.

"You'll stay safe?" she managed to ask once he released her.

"I'll do my best," he said before sending her a small smile and then striding from the room.

"Coming?" Agatha asked from the doorway.

"I'll be there in a minute. I just need a few moments to myself."

Agatha nodded and left the room, closing the door behind her.

Eliza moved to the window and stood there for a moment, watching Hamilton and Theodore wrestle the heavy chest into a waiting carriage. She leaned her forehead against the glass and felt tears slip down her cheeks as the carriage pulled away and then disappeared from view.

Her thoughts were jumbled and confused as she tried to reason everything out. How could this have happened? How could God allow children to be taken? Anger began to burn through her as she stalked over to a chair and sat down.

Images of Piper and Ben whirled through her mind, her thoughts becoming more and more tangled. She dropped her head into her hands.

"I don't know what to do," she said out loud.

Trust.

She lifted her head and peered around the room.

"Trust?" she whispered, brushing the tears from her face. Was it honestly as simple as that? She thought of Agatha's remark concerning how fortunate she'd been to have her money stolen from her. It had forced her out of her pampered, privileged life, and it had forced her to acknowledge the fact that Lawrence was hardly a man who could make her happy.

Had it been God's plan all along? Had He created a way to allow her to become a better person? Had He given her an opportunity to discover love?

She blinked.

"Do I love Hamilton?" she asked the room, straining her ears to hear a response, while already knowing the answer. The room remained silent and she blew out a breath.

"This is a ridiculous conversation," she muttered, getting to her feet. "You sound like a crazy woman talking to yourself."

Trust.

"Stop it," she whispered, rubbing her forehead with her hand. The word kept tumbling around and around her mind until it changed.

Trust in me.

She looked up at the ceiling. "Are you trying to tell me something?"

Silence met her question. She sighed, took a deep breath, and bowed her head.

"Please, God, help me. I know I have not trusted you for a very long time. I've suffered disappointments and heartache, and I've wrongly blamed you. I know I have no right to ask anything of you, but I desperately need your help, and I want to believe in you and all the grace you give. Please, show me what to do."

As Eliza stood there, her head bowed, a feeling of peace settled over her, and her mind stilled. She stayed there and allowed the feeling to swirl around her. She closed her eyes, and an image immediately flashed to mind. Her eyes sprang open. She raced out of the room and scrambled down the stairs, calling for Agatha at the top of her lungs.

"What is it?" Agatha demanded from the bottom of the steps.

"I know where they are, and we're going to rescue them."

22

"I really must protest," Gloria said as Eliza moved to her wardrobe and began rummaging around, searching for appropriate clothing to wear.

Eliza ignored Gloria, snatched up a pair of trousers, and threw them at Agatha. "Put those on," she ordered, turning back to continue her search. "Ah, there they are," she exclaimed, pulling out another pair of pants.

"Why in the world do you two need to wear pants?" Mrs. Watson asked when Agatha stepped out from behind the privacy screen and tugged her skirt over the pants in question.

"You never know when you might become parted from your skirt," Agatha said.

"As if that happens on a regular basis," Mrs. Watson sputtered.

"Eliza lost her skirt when we broke into Bartholomew's home," Agatha returned. "Lucky for her, she'd had the foresight to put on a pair of trousers; otherwise, I shudder to think of the ogling she might have had to endure if she'd ended up in jail in only her undergarments."

"Indeed," Eliza agreed, slipping behind the screen and returning a moment later, twisting her own skirt into place. "Ready?"

"Before either of you step foot out of this house, I need to understand exactly why you think you know where Piper and Ben have been taken," Gloria said.

"That's a bit difficult to explain," Eliza said slowly.

"Try," Gloria said.

Eliza bit her lip. "You're going to think I've lost my mind, but this morning, Piper pointed out this very pretty horse, and that horse flashed through my mind a few minutes ago."

"A . . . horse?" Gloria repeated.

"Exactly, but it's not just any old horse Piper saw this morning. I have cause to believe it's the one Hamilton told me about a few weeks ago, the one that used to belong to Mary Ellen."

Gloria's eyes widened. "Are you talking about Diamond?"

Eliza smiled. "Yes, I think Diamond was being ridden this morning in the city, and I also think it was either Sally or Eugene riding her."

"You're right, you have lost your mind," Gloria muttered, exchanging a look with Mrs. Watson before addressing Eliza again. "I find it hard to believe Sally or Eugene would risk detection by taking to the streets on a horse that is so easily identifiable."

"We know they're somewhere close, Gloria, given the fact that they orchestrated the abduction," Eliza said. "Besides, it wasn't as if whoever was riding the horse was parading down a main street. I saw the horse disappear into a residential area."

"And you think, what, that Sally and Eugene live on that particular street?" Gloria asked.

Eliza nodded. "That's where we'll find Piper and Ben."

"I travel on residential streets all the time, but I don't live on all of them," Mrs. Watson pointed out before she tilted her head and looked at Eliza. "Tell me, why are you so certain about this?"

"Well, now, don't get all strange on me, but I have come to the conclusion God told me," Eliza said and couldn't help but smile at the three incredulous faces gaping back at her. "I know it's difficult to believe, but I can't explain it any other way. You see, I was standing in Hamilton's room, and I was really angry—angry with God, to be exact. I couldn't understand how He could have allowed this to happen. Anyway, as I was thinking the situation through, an unusual thought kept coming to mind, and when I finally listened, well, that's when I remembered the horse."

"Unusual thought?" Agatha asked.

"I kept thinking 'trust' over and over again." Eliza blew out a breath. "I know it's odd, but there you have it. I think God was, in a not-so-subtle way, reminding me that I need to trust Him again, and I need to trust my own judgment."

Eliza looked around and found everyone still gazing at her with amazingly blank expressions on their faces until Gloria suddenly stepped forward, gave her a quick hug, and then patted her cheek. "Well, what are you waiting for then? You need to go rescue my grandbabies."

Eliza released a relieved breath. "Thank you, Gloria. Give me a minute to write down directions to where I think I saw that horse, and thankfully, it is not far from here. If Hamilton and Zayne arrive back at the house before Agatha and I return, you'll need to give it to them." She moved to the dresser, snatched up a pen, and quickly jotted down directions. She straightened and handed the paper to Gloria. "I don't remember the exact location, but I wrote down a few of the surrounding shops. We can always pray Agatha and I will be successful, but if something were to go wrong, we might need assistance."

"You will be careful?" Mrs. Watson asked.

"Please, how dangerous can it be?" Agatha returned. "We're

only dealing with a murderer and a woman who enjoys imper-
sonating the aristocracy and stealing fortunes."

"How silly of me to worry," Mrs. Watson replied weakly.

Eliza and Agatha moved together down the stairs and climbed
into the Watsons' carriage.

"I can't believe my mother actually allowed me out of the
house," Agatha commented as she settled into the seat.

"I know," Eliza agreed. "Even Gloria went along with it with
relatively little resistance, and"—she let out a groan—"they're
going to follow us."

"Surely not."

"I'm afraid they are," Eliza said, pointing out the window.

Agatha leaned forward. "Is my mother actually *running*
toward the carriage?" She got off the seat, shoved her head out
the window, and yelled at the driver to pick up the pace. The
carriage began to move at a fast clip as Agatha drew in her head.
"We won't lose them, you know," she said as she retook her seat.

"They might be able to keep up with us while we're in the
carriage, but we can outrun them once we get out," Eliza said.

"That'll go over well," Agatha muttered with a grin before
she suddenly sobered. "So tell me, what do you think happened
to you?"

Eliza knew exactly what Agatha was asking, even though
her question was rather vague. "I think God sent me a message,
or cleared my mind so that I was able to realize and remember
what I'd seen this morning."

"Meaning the horse?"

Eliza nodded. "I know this is going to seem unusual coming
from me, as you are the woman of strong faith, but I think God
is watching over us and wants us to find Piper and Ben. I think
you've been right all along, and He has some plan for me."

"I'm glad you finally realize that," Agatha said.

The carriage turned onto Broadway, and Eliza kept her focus

on the passing buildings. "Here, stop here," she called to the driver when she recognized a shop.

She scrambled out of the carriage and waited for Agatha, taking her arm and pulling her across the street.

"Good grief, Eliza, you're about to take off my arm," Agatha complained as Eliza tugged Agatha into a shop and peered out the window from behind a display of hats.

"May I assist you with something?" a voice laced with suspicion asked, causing Eliza to jump.

"My dear woman, you scared me half to death," Eliza remarked, forcing what she hoped was a pleasant smile on her face.

"Is there a reason you're skulking in my window display?"

"Uhh . . ." Eliza began, "you see . . . umm . . . we're attempting to evade someone."

"May I assume this someone is an overly amorous gentleman?" the woman asked.

"Well . . ." Eliza sputtered.

"No need to go into all the pesky details," the woman said with a wave of her hand. "Would you care to use the back door to make a speedy escape?"

"That would be most appreciated," Agatha said.

Eliza fell into step beside Agatha as they followed the woman through the shop and out a door that led to a dirty alley.

"Was there anything else you needed?" the woman asked.

"You haven't noticed an unusual white horse in this neighborhood, have you?" she asked.

"I saw a beautiful white horse being ridden down the street just this morning," the woman replied.

Eliza's heart began to race. "Do you happen to know where this horse is stabled?"

"I'm sorry, I do not, although you could check with Mel. He boards horses for a fee, and if anyone knows where that horse is, he would. His stable is three streets up that way," she said as she pointed down the alley.

"Thank you, you've been very helpful," Eliza said before grabbing Agatha's hand and hustling her down the alley. They reached the main street, and Eliza pulled Agatha to a stop, leaning forward to peer around the building.

"What are you doing?" Agatha asked.

"I'm looking for your mother and Gloria."

"I keep forgetting about them," Agatha said.

"Yes, well, I haven't, and the last thing we need is for them to meddle in this particular business. They are mothers, and as such, you know they'll balk if they feel we're putting ourselves in danger." She straightened. "I don't see them. Let's go."

She moved into the street and set her sights down the road, increasing her stride with every step she took.

"This seems almost too easy," Agatha muttered.

"I don't think it's going to be easy once we actually locate the right house," Eliza admitted. "We'll need to get past Sally, maybe Eugene, and you know there are going to be some guards watching over Piper and Ben."

"I didn't think about that," Agatha whispered.

"We'll be fine," Eliza said with a nod.

It didn't take long to locate the stable in question, and to Eliza's delight, a beautiful white horse was standing docilely in her stall. It took only a few coins to the stable hand to learn the address of the owners, and then Agatha and Eliza were off once again.

"I can't understand how anyone could have thought that horse would go unnoticed," Agatha said. "What if this is a trap?"

"Eugene and Sally don't realize we know about the horse," Eliza replied. "I'm telling you, we're on the right track. It's all a matter of trust at this point."

"This coming from a woman who completely turned her back on trust," Agatha said.

"I've changed," Eliza said simply, pointing to a handsome townhouse. "I think that's the place."

"Funny, him residing here," Agatha mused.

"What's funny about it?"

"Well, remember when all this started, when we first became friends?"

"Of course I remember, Agatha. It wasn't that long ago."

"Quite right, but the reason we went to Bartholomew's house was because he was to attend a dinner at Eugene Daniels's house, but I know this was not the house, because, although it's nice, it is hardly impressive enough to host a dinner party for New York society."

"He must have abandoned that house," Eliza said.

"If he has the money to purchase multiple dwellings, why in the world is he so intent on securing your fortune?"

"People like Eugene can never have enough money."

"He reminds me of your Lawrence."

"He's not *my* Lawrence."

"I didn't mean to offend you," Agatha said. "You're the one who used to be engaged to the man, but at least you seem to have no remaining feelings for him."

"Of course I don't have feelings for him. He's an arrogant fool."

"You would have never discovered that if you hadn't come to America," Agatha said. "And you wouldn't have found a man who truly cares for you and whose affections you return."

"I'm not going to discuss Hamilton at this particular moment."

"Are you still planning on returning to England?"

"I'm not certain."

"You're thinking about staying," Agatha said with a smug smile.

"Again, not the right time to discuss this," Eliza repeated, moving into the shadows in order to study the townhouse, which was now only one house away.

"I don't see any guards," Agatha said.

"That doesn't mean they're not there."

"What if it's the wrong house?"

"Then you and I will most likely end up in jail once again."

"The house is completely dark."

"No, the windows are simply blocked with drapes. I can see a sliver of light coming out of that window on the bottom floor."

"Let's find a different window," Agatha said.

"We should try the back," Eliza said.

It took Eliza and Agatha a good five minutes to locate the back gardens, as they had to first find an opening between the closely built townhouses, and then find the correct house.

"They all look alike," Agatha complained as she landed beside Eliza after scaling a stone wall and dropping to the ground. "I don't want to sound like a big baby, but I think that dog managed to take a huge chunk out of my skirt when he latched on to me."

"Good thing that was the wrong house."

"Good thing? The mutt almost had me for supper."

"True, but that little boy came to your rescue and if it hadn't been the wrong house, the barking would have brought everyone out to see what was causing so much noise," Eliza said as she scanned the house and then pointed. "Look, there's a window and . . . a handy tree."

Agatha looked up and her eyes widened. "The window's on the third floor."

"It most likely won't be locked, then," Eliza said. "Who would imagine someone breaking into the third floor? It's crazy."

"Exactly," Agatha muttered.

"We should take off our skirts." Eliza quickly unfastened the waistband and allowed her skirt to fall to the ground. "It will make it easier to climb that tree."

"Did I mention you're a bit smaller than I am?" Agatha asked as she followed Eliza's example and dropped her skirt to the ground.

"What does that have to do with anything?"

"These pants leave very little to the imagination."

"It's not as if anyone will see. Our plan is to rescue the children and get out of there unnoticed."

"You honestly think we can get Piper and Ben down this tree?"

"Good point," Eliza said before she brightened. "We'll take them out a lower window."

Eliza grabbed on to a branch and began to climb, a grin stealing over her face when she heard Agatha muttering behind her.

"What's the matter?"

"Split a seam."

Eliza's grin widened as she continued to climb, realizing that this was certainly an unusual moment to be amused. She reached the window and pushed on it, releasing a sigh of relief when it opened. She swung from the branch and pulled herself through the window, Agatha following a few seconds behind.

"Did you hear that?" Agatha whispered.

"Hear what?" Eliza whispered back.

"My pants ripped again."

Eliza stifled a laugh and cautiously edged her way through the room, using her hands to guide her way.

"A lamp would be helpful," Agatha muttered.

Eliza finally located the door and eased it open, turning her head so she could hear more clearly.

The beautiful sound of Piper's voice immediately came to her.

"If you yell at my brother one more time, I will make you very, very sorry," Piper was saying.

"Then tell the little monster to stop biting me," Sally returned.

"They're alive," Agatha whispered, fumbling with the waistband of her pants.

"What are you doing?"

"I'm trying to get my pistol out."

"Good thinking."

"Thank you," Agatha said. "I brought one for you. I took it from Hamilton's gun case."

"How do you use this thing?" Eliza asked, accepting the gun Agatha offered her.

"Don't tell me you can't shoot a gun."

"Just explain the basics, and I'll do my best not to shoot you by mistake."

"There's a comforting thought," Agatha mumbled. "Perhaps you should give the gun back to me."

"I will not. They have no idea I don't know how to operate it."

"Fine, then just hold it away from you, but don't wave it around, don't pull the trigger unless our very lives are at stake, and if you do pull the trigger, make sure the gun is pointed at the bad people."

"There's no need to be snippy. . . ." Eliza's voice trailed off as Ben's cry sounded down the hallway. Eliza threw caution to the wind as she raced toward the sound of his voice, the gun swinging wildly as she ran. She burst into the room, the gun in front of her, her eyes taking in the scene in a single glance.

She couldn't say who was more surprised to see her: Sally, who was attempting to pry a screaming Ben off of her, or Piper, who was gaping at Eliza as if she couldn't believe her eyes.

"Let go of him," Eliza snarled, "or I swear I will shoot you right here on the spot."

"I'm trying to," Sally snapped, "but the little beast won't stop biting me."

"Mama," Ben sobbed as he caught sight of Eliza and ran to her as fast as his legs could carry him. She scooped him up with one arm, keeping the gun firmly trained on Sally with the other.

"You came," Ben wailed, nuzzling her neck with his face. She could feel wetness from his tears, and fury washed over her.

"How could you dare take these children?" Eliza began, her temper increasing steadily as Ben clung tightly to her arm.

"How dare you ruin my life?" Sally returned.

"You ruined your own life, Sally. There was never any need for you to steal from my family. My father paid your husband well."

"He did not pay him well enough to provide us with the type of life I wanted."

"You're the daughter of impoverished parents. That you cannot appreciate the sacrifices they must have made to provide you with an adequate education is truly revolting. You were able to become a governess, and as such, you were able to meet and marry Bartholomew, which elevated your status significantly."

"I wanted a title and wealth to go with it."

"Then why marry Bartholomew?"

"He did provide me with a title and wealth, albeit through somewhat unorthodox means."

"You stole my title and my wealth," Eliza snapped.

"You were in no danger of losing your title. As for your wealth, you were engaged to an esteemed member of society. I hardly thought you would miss the funds."

Eliza realized the conversation was getting them nowhere. She forced aside the words she longed to vent and took a deep breath. "Why did you kill your husband?"

"Bartholomew's death was an unfortunate accident."

"He accidently got in the way of a bullet?" Agatha asked as she strode into the room and joined Eliza.

"He should have listened to Eugene's counsel instead of letting his regrets get in our way," Sally said.

Eliza tilted her head. "Just out of curiosity, how does Eugene fit into all this?"

"That is none of your business."

Agatha moved forward and smiled as she cocked her pistol. "We're making it our business."

Sally eyed the door, obviously thought better of making a run for it, and released a dramatic sigh. "If you must know, Eugene is a distant cousin of mine. He sought me out a few years ago when he visited England, and it was he who convinced Bartholomew to delve into a bit of embezzlement and split the proceeds of that embezzlement between us." She let out a small sigh. "Bartholomew balked at first, but he agreed to the plan because I longed for a better life. We made arrangements to meet up with Eugene here after my husband took all there was to take from Lord Sefton's estate." A brief glimpse of what appeared to be pain flashed through Sally's eyes. "He never could refuse me anything." Her gaze hardened. "I was happy here until you arrived and destroyed everything."

"You can have the chest," Eliza said. "I only want the children."

"Now, that does pose a dilemma," a male voice drawled from the doorway, "because, you see, I've decided to keep the children as well."

23

*A*ny thoughts on how we can get out of here?" Agatha whispered five minutes later.

"Not a one," Eliza whispered back, struggling to loosen the bindings that were securing her hands behind her back. "I can't believe we were overpowered by those thugs so quickly."

"There were five of them," Agatha said before she blew out a breath. "Do you think maybe you misunderstood God's intentions? Perhaps we weren't supposed to search for Piper and Ben on our own."

"I didn't misunderstand," Eliza argued quietly. "If we hadn't found them, they would be terrified at the moment instead of receiving comfort from our presence." Eliza caught Piper's gaze and sent her a wink, which Piper returned.

"But still," Agatha muttered, "it might have been prudent to bring reinforcements."

"What are you two discussing?" Sally asked, leaving her spot by the door to saunter closer to them.

"We were contemplating how you'll handle residing in jail," Eliza said.

"You silly girl," Eugene drawled, coming back into the room and stopping next to Eliza as he sneered down at her. "By the time anyone finds your body, Sally and I will be long gone from here."

"Body?" Agatha mouthed in horror.

"Unfortunately, you'll have to be disposed of too, my dear," Eugene said, swinging his attention to Agatha.

Eliza cleared her throat, determined to delay Eugene and his dastardly plans for them for as long as possible. "Why do you want to keep the children? You hardly seem the fatherly type."

"They're a part of my dear Mary Ellen," Eugene said.

"So you were acquainted with Mary Ellen," Eliza said.

"How did you reason that out?"

Eliza shrugged, the motion causing her to list to the side. She struggled back into an upright position. "It seemed too much of a coincidence—her death, your involvement with the Beckett business ventures, and then there was the horse."

"What about a horse?" Eugene asked.

Eliza smiled. "Come now, Eugene, it really wasn't well done of you to bring that particular horse back to town. Diamond is very distinctive, and she's what led me here to you."

Eugene's face turned purple as he spun around to confront a now visibly nervous Sally.

"You dared to take out the horse?"

"I only rode to the market. You couldn't very well expect me to walk, and you did take our only carriage. Besides, Diamond hadn't been seen for over two years. It was ludicrous to think anyone would recognize her."

"But someone obviously did," Eugene hissed. "I thought I'd

made myself very clear in regard to Diamond. No one is to ride her except me."

"I remember riding my mother's horse once," Piper said, drawing Eugene's attention away from Sally. "I was really little, and my mother held me in front of her and took me around the park."

Eugene beamed at Piper, causing a tremor of fear to course over Eliza. She could only watch helplessly as he leaned over the little girl and brushed her hair away from her face.

"My adorable little girl," Eugene began, "you will be allowed to ride the horse whenever you like, seeing as Mary Ellen's blood resides in your veins."

"I don't like blood," Piper said, pulling back her head as her eyes narrowed. "You're not a very nice man, and I want to go home right this very minute."

"I'm afraid that won't be possible, pumpkin," Eugene replied with a rather frightening smile. "I've decided I want you to live with me. I loved your mother very, very much, and you should have been my daughter."

"I already have a father," Piper replied, her expression turning mulish.

"I will take over that role, and Sally will become your mother."

"That boy called Eliza 'Mama' when she came into the room," Sally said, her eyes glittering as she stared at Ben. "I don't think he'll come quietly."

"He's only a child, Sally, hardly difficult to manage," Eugene said, switching his attention from Piper to Ben. He leaned over and put his face right in front of Ben's. "Sally is going to be your mama now, child, and I will be your daddy. Doesn't that sound delightful?"

Eliza watched as Ben's body tensed, and before she could get a single word of warning out of her mouth, he launched himself straight at Eugene, clamping onto the man's face with his little teeth.

A roar of pain erupted from Eugene's mouth as he forcefully pried Ben off him and threw him to the ground. Eliza screamed and struggled to get free when she saw Eugene's fists were clenched. She knew he was more than capable of retaliating, knew he would have no qualms about using those fists against a small child. To her horror, Ben had picked himself off the floor and looked as if he was thinking about giving Eugene another bite.

"Ben, no," Eliza yelled.

Ben drew in a ragged breath, turned his head, and then, to Eliza's relief, ran to her side and jumped into her lap, his trembling arms snaking around her neck as he buried his head against her shoulder.

"Leave him," Eugene spat when Sally moved to retrieve him, wiping a smear of blood off his face. "He obviously has more of his father in him than his mother. He will stay behind. The girl will suffice."

Piper suddenly gave a rather wicked grin. "I bite harder than my brother."

Eugene glared at her for a moment and then shrugged. "Fine, join your brother. I have no further use for you."

Piper scampered across the room and plopped down by Eliza's side. Eliza blinked and then stilled when she realized Piper was pressing something that felt very much like a knife into her bound hands. She swallowed a laugh. Eugene had no idea who he was dealing with, and she had the strangest feeling they would be all right. She decided then and there her best plan of attack would be to keep him distracted as she tried to free her hands.

"You were in love with Mary Ellen?" she asked, sawing at her hands as discreetly as possible.

"I was," Eugene said, his voice softening in a split second. "We met at a dinner party here in town, and I quickly realized she wasn't happy with her lot in life. She deserved more than her husband was willing to give her, and I was perfectly happy to shower her with affection. I adored her."

"But . . . something interfered with your affections," Agatha said.

"Her husband," Eugene snarled. "I have come to believe he was threatening her, which is why she refused to run away with me."

"May I assume you and Mary Ellen shared a close relationship?" Agatha asked.

Eliza had the distinct impression Agatha was taking over the task of distracting Eugene in order to allow her time to cut through her bindings. "If you're asking if we shared an intimate relationship, the answer is no," he said. "Mary Ellen was a true lady; she wouldn't even consider the idea, although I must admit I derived satisfaction from the fact that her husband believed her to be unfaithful. I knew his jealousy would one day force her into my arms."

Eliza stilled and looked up. "But your plans were ruined when she had that unfortunate accident."

"Yes, of course. That accident kept us from being together forever."

The truth hit Eliza square in the face. "You killed her," she breathed.

Eugene's face turned white. "I loved her."

Eliza ignored his comment as the pieces of the puzzle began to tumble into place. "That's how you got information on Hamilton's company," she muttered. "Mary Ellen gave it to you." She lifted her head. "You were blackmailing her, weren't you?"

"You've lost your mind," Eugene raged.

"Explain the horse," Eliza demanded. "How did you come to have her?"

"I found her," Eugene said.

Eliza arched a brow.

Eugene glared at her for a moment before his shoulders suddenly sagged. "You don't understand. I didn't have a choice."

"Murder is always a choice, Mr. Daniels," Eliza said, realizing by the faraway expression in Eugene's eyes that he wasn't listening to her.

"She wouldn't leave him, and that angered me. She tried to end all communication with me. That's when I was forced to resort to blackmail, although, at the time, I didn't actually want the information on the Beckett company. It was simply the only thing I could come up with on the spur of the moment."

"You blackmailed Mary Ellen into giving you information you didn't even want?" Agatha asked.

"Blackmail is tricky," Eugene said. "As I said before, I settled on Hamilton Beckett's business because it was an impulsive decision, one I made for the sheer purpose of keeping Mary Ellen in my life. I had no idea the lady would turn obstinate, forcing me to . . ." His mouth snapped shut.

"Kill her?" Eliza finished for him when Eugene remained silent.

"I learned she was still fond of her husband," Eugene spat. "On the last day of her life, she came to me and handed over a two-year plan she'd pilfered from her husband's office. After she gave it to me, she told me she was finished, that she wanted nothing else to do with me and that if I didn't leave her alone, she would confess to her husband what she'd done." His eyes took on an insane glint. "I couldn't very well allow her to live after that."

"Cover your ears," Eliza whispered to Piper and Ben, who immediately did what she asked.

Eugene continued as if he hadn't noticed her distraction. "I hit her . . . hard . . . and she fell to the ground, begging me to leave her alone. I was consumed with rage. I advanced on her, hitting her until she was quite dead. I put her on her horse and took her down by the Hudson River. I stood there for an hour, waiting for her to fall off, but the stupid horse would not cooperate until I threw a rock. I thought that was the end of it, but the horse followed me, and I took it as a sign I was meant to keep her, a lingering reminder of my gullibility. I knew perfectly well the horse was very distinctive, so I spirited Diamond away to a farm in the country. Only recently did I bring her back to town. I was going to have Bartholomew claim he'd purchased the animal, but we all know what became of him."

"Why did you decide to seek revenge against Hamilton?" Eliza asked.

"Because I realized her husband was the real reason she'd rejected me, not because she held him in affection, but because he'd most likely threatened her. I set out to ruin the man, not realizing he was too wealthy to bring to absolute destitution. I had to settle for knowing I was a thorn in his side."

"But why have Bartholomew steal all my money?" Eliza asked, biting back a yelp as the knife finally broke through her bindings and nipped her skin. She carefully slipped the knife into Agatha's hands, all the while keeping her attention on Eugene's face.

"My dear, deluded girl, your fortune had nothing to do with the Mary Ellen business, it was simply a means to an end. I always dreamed of great wealth but . . . I must admit it is odd how you became involved with the Beckett family."

"Almost like fate," Hamilton snarled from the doorway, a pistol pointed at Eugene, Gloria by his side with her own pistol at the ready.

Eliza jumped to her feet, scooped Ben up on her shoulder, and grabbed Piper's hand, her eyes darting around for the quickest route of escape.

Hamilton rushed to her side, bloody and bruised, and Eliza had never been so happy to see someone in her entire life.

"This way," he ordered as he snatched Piper into his arms, spun on his heel, and headed back to the door.

"Run, Eliza," Mrs. Watson bellowed as she flew past Eliza to join Gloria. "Get the children out of here."

"Go," Agatha yelled, finally free of her bonds and wrestling a gun away from Sally.

Eliza nodded and sprinted after Hamilton, the sound of gunfire making her jump. They thundered down the hallway and arrived at the stairs, Hamilton suddenly putting Piper down when he was confronted by a large man wielding a knife.

"Find the servants' stairs," he yelled as a sickening thud met Eliza's ears. Before she could even take a step to grab Piper, Hamilton spun around again, picked Piper up, and grinned as the thug lay motionless at his feet.

"Impressive," she breathed.

"Thank you," Hamilton returned as they raced back the way they'd come, Piper yelling instructions as to where to find the other set of stairs.

It didn't take them long to reach the bottom. Hamilton paused at the door and carefully opened it to check if the coast was clear.

"Did you find them?" Zayne yelled as he brought down a vase on top of a man's head, causing the man to crumple to the ground.

"I did, but I had to leave Agatha, Mother, and Mrs. Watson all alone up there."

Zayne didn't bother to reply as he rushed past them and raced up the stairs.

"We're going to have to skirt the edges of this room, Eliza," Hamilton said. "From what I can tell, the police have arrived and there's a bit of a brawl going on at the moment. Think you're up for it, or should we try another route to escape?"

"Who is to say another route won't be filled with only thugs?" she muttered.

"Forward it is," Hamilton said as he gestured for her to follow him.

Eliza pressed Ben's head into her shoulder as they dodged fighting men and finally reached the door. Hamilton snagged her hand and pulled her out of the house. Eliza stumbled when her eyes took in the chaos erupting on the front lawn. Police officers swarmed around the house, and there were men lying in the middle of the street, their hands bound behind their backs.

"Over here," Theodore called as he appeared around the side of a carriage and stepped over the form of an unconscious man. "You'll be safe in my carriage."

They ran to his carriage, and Hamilton shoved Piper inside before he turned to take Ben from Eliza, gently setting his son on the seat.

"You didn't put me down that nicely," Piper complained, causing Hamilton to grin at his daughter.

"I do beg your pardon, Piper. I assumed you were made of sterner stuff."

"I am, but you didn't have to throw me in here."

Eliza was surprised when a laugh escaped her throat. She climbed into the carriage and sat down, scooping Ben into her lap.

Hamilton joined them and shut the door, peering out once to ascertain there were guards watching over them before turning his attention back to Eliza.

"Thank God all of you are safe," he muttered, his eyes welling with tears.

Eliza blinked back tears of her own. "But how did you know where to find us?"

"We were following Eugene's men, and only knew you were here when we saw Mrs. Watson and my mother out on the street. I had only just brought my horse around the corner when my mother, of all people, came rushing up to me."

Eliza sat forward and reached for the door. "I completely forgot about your mother. We have to go back. She's still in there."

"My mother is perfectly capable of handling herself, and she'd kill me if I let you out of the carriage. Besides, Zayne went to help her, remember?"

"Grandmother had a gun," Piper said, speaking up.

"So did Mrs. Watson," Eliza added.

"Do you think they shot that bad man?" Piper asked.

"It probably didn't come down to that," Hamilton explained. "Theodore sent one of his associates to summon the police right after we left the warehouse, and clearly, Theodore's associates are incredibly competent, because police were arriving before we even entered the house. I have no doubt they will take Eugene and Sally in hand." He took a deep, steadying breath. "Are you two all right?" he asked, looking at Piper and Ben.

Piper nodded. "You would have been very proud of us, Daddy. We barely cried at all, and I know Ben promised never to bite anyone again, but he did bite that Sally person, and he left a big mark on that man's face, but I don't think he should get into any trouble about that, because it was very brave of him."

"It was very brave of him, and he certainly isn't in any trouble," Hamilton said, leaning forward to pick Ben off Eliza's lap and settle him against his chest. "It sounds as if both of you were very brave," he said, inhaling deeply as he placed his face against Ben's hair. "This is a scent I will never take for granted again," he said softly.

"Ben called Miss Eliza Mama," Piper said, an almost wistful expression crossing her face.

Ben lifted his head. "She is too my mama now. She came to save me and that makes her my mama."

"Miss Agatha came to save us too," Piper pointed out.

"Miss Agatha doesn't get to be our mama because she doesn't love Daddy," Ben proclaimed, popping his thumb into his mouth and gazing across the seat at Eliza.

"Yes, well, this is a subject Miss Eliza and I will need to discuss in private," Hamilton said, the look in his eyes causing every single hair on Eliza's neck and arms to stand to attention. She absently brushed the hair down on her arms and finally got up the nerve to meet Hamilton's gaze.

If anything, the gleam in his eyes had intensified. She cleared her throat, remembering there were two small children in the carriage with them. "Did you manage to hear anything Eugene was saying?"

Hamilton grinned, apparently perfectly aware of the fact that she'd deliberately changed the subject, but then sobered and tilted his head. "I did hear some of it, at least the part regarding Mary Ellen." He released a sigh. "It appears I was wrong about my wife, and I must say, it's a relief to learn she wasn't unfaithful to me."

"I'm glad you were able to hear that," Eliza said. "I know it's been weighing heavily on you these past years, and at least now you know the truth. I'm thankful I was able to get him to talk, even though I readily admit my purpose with that was to simply distract him."

"You shouldn't have been there to 'distract' him in the first place," Hamilton grouched.

Before Eliza could respond, Piper interrupted.

"If Miss Eliza hadn't been there, Daddy, Ben and I would've been scared."

"You weren't scared with Miss Eliza and Miss Agatha there?" Hamilton asked.

"No, Miss Eliza had that same crazy look in her eyes when she pulled that nanny's hair. I knew we'd be fine," Piper proclaimed.

"Well, I guess I won't be able to lecture her, then."

"You should kiss her instead."

Eliza's mouth dropped open at Piper's suggestion. A tingle of something delightful washed over her, but it disappeared in a flash when the carriage door whipped open and Theodore poked his head in.

"You'll be happy to learn I retrieved your chest and . . . Am I interrupting something?" he asked.

"Daddy was about to kiss Miss Eliza," Piper proclaimed.

Theodore grinned. "I'll come back later."

"Theodore, he wasn't going to kiss me," Eliza sputtered. "You don't have to leave."

"Go away, Theodore," Hamilton drawled.

Eliza gulped as Theodore laughed and firmly shut the door.

24

I can't believe you just sent Theodore away," Eliza said.

"He didn't go far. He's standing right outside the door," Hamilton said.

"Are you going to kiss her now, Daddy?" Ben asked, pulling his thumb out of his mouth.

"No, I'm not going to kiss her right this moment, especially with you two looking on. It hardly lends itself to a proper atmosphere."

"But if you kissed her, she would have to marry you," Piper said.

"Where do you come up with these ideas?" Hamilton asked.

"Grandmother," Piper said with a grin.

"That certainly explains a lot," Hamilton grumbled before he set Ben down next to Piper and moved to join Eliza on the opposite seat. He took her hand and brought it to his lips. "I need to thank you for giving me back my children. You were remarkable tonight, and I will be forever grateful."

"I don't need or want your gratitude," Eliza managed to get out, finding it difficult to even think with his hand still holding hers and the heat from his lips pulsing through her fingers.

"What do you want?" he asked softly.

Before Eliza had an opportunity to answer, the door flung open and Gloria jumped in, wiggled her way between the children, and reached out to pull Piper up on her lap as she released a long, relieved sigh.

"What a night," she exclaimed, pressing her lips to Piper's forehead. "Are you all right?"

"Grandmother, you're squeezing me too hard," Piper complained, although she was grinning from ear to ear. "Did you shoot anyone?"

"She did," Mrs. Watson said before Gloria could respond, climbing into the carriage and peering around before scooping Ben up and taking his spot, settling him into her lap before turning back to Piper. "Although, I must admit, I don't think she intended to shoot the man. It was not her fault Agatha knocked that Eugene fellow directly into the path of your grandmother's bullet. From what I could tell, Gloria was simply trying to frighten the man into surrendering."

"Is he . . . dead?" Eliza whispered.

"Of course not," Agatha said as she allowed Zayne to help her into the carriage. She looked around and then gestured to Eliza with her hand. "Scoot over."

"Where would you suggest I 'scoot'?" Eliza asked.

"You can sit on Hamilton's lap," Agatha said.

Eliza didn't have a chance to protest. Hamilton sent her a grin, and the next thing she knew, she was snuggled on his lap, his hand resting on her waist. She felt her cheeks flame and looked around for a distraction. "Why do you have that coat tied around you?"

Agatha plopped down on the seat and rolled her eyes. "My

pants split all the way down the back when I tried to tackle Eugene."

"They were quite delightful pants while they were still intact," Zayne remarked cheerfully as he squeezed his lanky frame into the carriage and nodded to Agatha. "Scoot over."

"There's no room," Agatha said, "and you shouldn't have been noticing my pants."

Zayne took Agatha's hand, pulled her to her feet, took her spot on the seat, and pulled her into his lap. "This is cozy," he remarked to no one in particular.

Eliza grinned. She couldn't help but notice that Agatha was certainly not protesting about sitting on Zayne's lap. Her gaze darted to Gloria and Mrs. Watson, and her grin widened as she watched them exchange delighted smiles.

"So what happened?" Hamilton asked, drawing her attention. "Have all the miscreants been apprehended?"

"I am pleased to say everyone has been rounded up, and I've been told they will soon be residing in jail," Zayne said as he sent Eliza a smile. "I do believe any lingering danger to you, my dear, is now at an end, and you will be able to return to England without fear. That is . . . if you're still intent on returning home."

Eliza felt Hamilton's body tense. She drew in a deep breath and slowly released it. "I believe I have reconsidered."

"You're not going back?" Gloria asked as her expression turned hopeful.

"I think I belong here," Eliza said quietly.

"She's going to be our new mama," Ben said.

"Ben's a little ahead of himself," Hamilton said.

"Everyone, out," Gloria suddenly barked, and Eliza could only watch in amazement as everyone tried to get out of their seats at the same time, and with a lot of jostling and sly grins, they hurtled one by one out of the carriage until the only people left were herself and Hamilton.

"That was fast," she muttered.

Hamilton laughed. "My mother is nothing if not determined."

Eliza realized there was absolutely no reason for her to remain on Hamilton's lap, and besides, she really wanted to see his face at this particular moment. She was not exactly certain what he was going to say to her, but she knew, deep in her heart, whatever he was about to say would most likely change her life forever. She struggled off his lap and took a seat on the opposite side of the carriage, listing ever so slightly to the right when the carriage set to motion. She steadied herself and then looked at Hamilton, the breath leaving her in a split second when she caught his gaze.

There was something incredibly warm in his eyes, something that almost seemed like . . . love.

Hamilton leaned forward, took her hand in his, and smiled. "There is much I need to say to you, Eliza, but allow me to begin by stating that I know I blundered badly with you before, when you thought I wished to marry you because I needed a mother for my children. At the time, I have to admit, I thought exactly that. I was not ready to commit myself to a woman; I didn't have an ounce of trust in my body. Tonight you provided me with answers I've been seeking for years. You were able to extract information from Eugene, which put my mind to rest, and I can finally move forward. I know Agatha has been the one to say all along that God has a plan for the two of us, but I must say I do believe she's right. I can only hope you'll allow me another chance."

Eliza felt tears begin to well in her eyes as hope swirled through her. "Are you asking me to marry you?" she managed to get out.

"I am asking you to marry me, but I wish to be very clear. I don't want you as my wife because you'll make an excellent mother for Piper and Ben, although I have no doubt you would be exceptional in that role. I only want you to accept my proposal if you can assure me that someday you'll be able to trust me and, perhaps, love me as I have grown to love you."

"You love me?" Eliza whispered.

"How can I not?"

He loved her.

Mr. Hamilton Beckett, the most wonderful, compelling gentleman she'd ever known, loved her. She took a deep breath, ignored her racing pulse, and felt a smile spread over her lips when she realized she'd been quiet longer than she'd thought, because Hamilton was watching her now with worry in his eyes. She squeezed his hand.

"I would marry you even if you only wanted a mother for your children," she began. "I can't imagine living without Piper and Ben, but as you said before, I need to be clear. I can assure you I trust you completely, and I can also assure you I have loved you from almost the moment I set eyes on you. It takes a very special man to see beyond a hideous puce gown to the woman beneath."

"Is that what that color is called?" Hamilton asked softly before he rose and then took a seat right beside her, his fingers tightening on her hand. "You love me?"

She nodded and smiled. "I must admit that I do, with all my heart."

"And you want to marry me?"

Eliza laughed, feeling happier than she ever had in her life. "I would love nothing more than to marry you and live with you here in New York."

"You will not miss England?"

"There is nothing for me there," she said. "You have stolen my heart completely, Mr. Beckett, and I believe it is now yours forever."

His gaze intensified, and he leaned forward, causing Eliza to take in a sharp breath of air.

He was going to kiss her.

Finally.

She leaned into him, but before his lips could touch hers, the carriage began to slow and then came to a stop, causing Hamilton to release a snort.

"Horrible timing," he muttered as he pulled away and gestured out the window. "It would appear we have arrived home and . . . we have an audience."

Eliza raised her head and couldn't help but grin. Gloria, Agatha, Mrs. Watson, Zayne, Piper, and Ben were standing on the sidewalk, each one of them beaming at the carriage.

"They'll be so excited," she said.

"Yes, they will," Hamilton agreed. "We'd better not keep them waiting. From the way my mother is bouncing up and down, I'm afraid she's about ready to storm the carriage."

Eliza laughed and waited as Hamilton opened the door and jumped to the ground before he turned back and offered her his hand. She took it, stepped out beside him, and was suddenly pulled from his side and enveloped in a warm hug from Gloria.

"So?" Gloria prompted. "Am I finally going to get to plan a wedding?"

"I give you leave to plan whatever type of wedding you'd like," Eliza said.

Gloria squeezed her hard, took a step back, wiped tears from her face, and nodded. "Lovely, I will get right to work." She turned to Mrs. Watson. "I do hope you'll assist me, Cora. I have come to rely on your expert advice."

Mrs. Watson wiped a few tears of her own away and smiled. "But of course, Gloria. I would love nothing more than to assist you. Perhaps someday you'll be able to return the favor."

Gloria and Mrs. Watson sent pointed looks at Zayne and Agatha, who both cheerfully ignored them as they moved to hug Eliza and then Hamilton.

A thought suddenly occurred to Eliza after Agatha released her. "What happened to Theodore?" she asked.

"He made a hasty retreat once it started getting emotional," Agatha said with a roll of her eyes. "I saw him almost running away from the carriage right after everyone decided Hamilton had something of importance to tell you. He's obviously not a gentleman who is accustomed to dealing with situations of a romantic nature."

"We'll have to take him in hand," Gloria proclaimed, causing Eliza to grin.

"He'll enjoy that, but at least it will keep you out of my business," Zayne muttered, earning a swat from his mother in the process.

"Did anyone hear anything else regarding Eugene and Sally?" Hamilton asked.

Eliza was a little taken aback to realize she'd almost forgotten all about them.

"Theodore was going to have them taken to jail, after a physician takes out that bullet from Eugene's arm," Zayne said with a glance at Gloria. "I have a feeling those two will spend the rest of their lives behind bars."

"I feel somewhat sorry for Sally," Eliza said. "I hate to think of the woman wasting the rest of her life."

"She aided in the murder of her husband," Zayne pointed out.

"I don't think she did," Eliza said. "I think Eugene was solely responsible for Bartholomew's death."

"Well, we have no say in what happens to her," Gloria said. "She broke the law, and the courts will decide her fate."

"I suppose you're right," Eliza agreed, unwilling to spend another minute of her life contemplating Sally's situation. She looked down and found Piper grinning up at her, looking as if she were about to burst with questions. She lifted her head. "Would it be possible for me to have a few moments alone with the children?"

"Good heavens, dear, I should have thought of that," Gloria said before she took Mrs. Watson by the arm and sent Eliza a nod. "Here we've been rambling on and on, and poor Piper and Ben have been made to wait. We'll see you in the parlor whenever you're ready."

Eliza watched as Gloria, Mrs. Watson, Agatha, and Zayne traveled up the walk and disappeared into the house before she turned to Piper. "I do apologize, Piper. You should have been the first to hear the news."

"Are you going to marry Daddy?"

Eliza grinned and nodded, but before she could get another word out of her mouth, Lawrence suddenly appeared in the doorway. He set his sights on her and stalked forward, a distinct expression of surliness on his face. He came to a stop directly in front of her. "Where in the world have you been? I had your brother bring me back here over an hour ago because I needed to speak with you concerning our return trip to England, and you were nowhere to be found."

Eliza's patience with the man was beginning to wear thin. "I do apologize for the fact that you were inconvenienced, Lawrence, but I find it truly telling you would believe I would want to talk about a return trip to England when Piper and Ben were missing. Honestly, I have come to think I never truly knew you, and if you must know, while you were cooling your heels in Hamilton's house, I was out attending to the little matter of rescuing the children. They're fine, by the way, in case you neglected to realize that."

"I have no idea why you concerned yourself with this matter in the first place," Lawrence snapped, ignoring everything else Eliza had said. "There were plenty of qualified people searching for them. You should have conferred with me before going after them."

"She's my mama," Ben proclaimed as he sidled up next to her

and snagged her hand. She smiled down at him, but her smile faded when Lawrence opened his mouth.

"She most certainly is not," Lawrence hissed.

"She's going to be," Piper said. "She's marrying Daddy as soon as Grandmother makes the arrangements."

Eliza let go of Ben's hand and took a step toward Lawrence. "Perhaps we should discuss this in private," she said, brushing past him to stride up the sidewalk and into the house.

Lawrence fell into step behind her. "I cannot get out of this country fast enough."

"You'll be on a boat in a day and a half," Eliza said as she increased her pace and stalked into the first available room, which happened to be the drawing room. "You'll be happy to learn I'm giving you my steamer ticket so you can return to London without having to spend any money purchasing your own ticket."

He frowned. "How will you get back?"

"I'm not going back."

"That's ridiculous; you belong in England. You possess an esteemed title."

"I have no need of that title anymore," she said softly.

"But . . . you have to marry me," he sputtered.

"I can't marry you, Lawrence. I don't love you."

"I don't love you either, but that doesn't mean we can't marry. We used to rub along quite nicely together."

"While that certainly sounds enticing, the whole 'rubbing along together' idea, I'm afraid it doesn't appeal to me anymore. I deserve better."

"And you believe that Beckett man is better?"

"I do."

"He only wants you for your money."

"You're confusing him with you," Eliza said. "You only wanted me for my money. You never knew the real me or even wanted to learn about me."

"But I've come all this way to fetch you home."

"I'm sorry, but I can't go back. My place is here."

Grayson stuck his head in the door. "Am I interrupting?"

"Yes," Lawrence barked.

"Sorry," Grayson said, striding into the room. "I wanted to check on my sister."

"She's being impossible," Lawrence grouched.

"She does have the tendency to behave that way at times," Grayson said cheerfully before he sent her a grin. "Mrs. Beckett just informed me of your exciting news. I must say I am happy for you, Eliza." He turned back to Lawrence. "Did you hear Eliza's getting married?"

"I might have heard something to that effect," he mumbled.

Grayson nodded. "Good, but that's not why I came in here. I think I have a solution to your financial problems."

Eliza resisted the urge to laugh as Lawrence went from sulky to pleasant in a split second.

"I'm listening," Lawrence said. "What is your solution?"

Grayson reached into his coat pocket and pulled out a ticket. He handed it to Lawrence, who turned sulky once again.

"Eliza told me she was going to give me hers."

"That is for Mrs. Morgan," Grayson said. "I have a feeling the two of you would suit admirably, and from what I understand, she's wealthy in the extreme. You may take my carriage to travel to her residence. Mrs. Beckett was kind enough to give my driver directions to her house. I have to believe Mrs. Morgan will be delighted to see you again and will be only too willing to take on London high society."

"Mrs. Morgan?" Lawrence mused as he tapped the ticket in his hand for a brief moment and then strode for the door, not even bothering to speak to Eliza again before he disappeared.

"Incredible," Grayson said with a laugh. "I don't think he was very distraught over your upcoming nuptials."

"I don't think Lawrence is capable of that particular emotion," Eliza said.

"Mind if I come in?" Hamilton asked, drawing her attention.

"Please do," Eliza said.

Hamilton stepped into the room, carrying a little girl in his arms, Ben and Piper tagging along at his side. "I thought you might enjoy meeting your niece."

Eliza shot a look to Grayson. "This is your daughter?" she asked, remembering his confusing statement about calling the girl his daughter "for want of a better word."

"This is Ming," Grayson said. "And we'll talk more about her later, but yes, I consider her my daughter."

Eliza looked at the dark-haired girl in Hamilton's arms and couldn't resist her. She stepped to Hamilton's side, held out her hands, and found her heart melting when Ming leaned toward her and allowed Eliza to scoop her up. "Aren't you a little darling?"

Ming Sumner patted Eliza's face before she stuck her thumb in her mouth and buried her head against Eliza's shoulder.

"She's a little shy," Grayson explained.

Ming lifted her head. "Down."

Eliza grinned and set Ming down, her grin widening when Ming and Ben, watched over by Piper, scampered around the room. "Yes, I can see she's incredibly shy."

"I've decided to stay in America," Grayson said.

"I figured that out when you gave Lawrence your ticket," Eliza said.

"Why would you give Lawrence your ticket?" Hamilton asked Grayson. "I thought Eliza was going to give him hers. You haven't changed your mind, have you?" he asked, turning to Eliza.

"Of course not," Eliza said, stepping to his side and allowing herself a small sigh of satisfaction when his arm went around her. "Grayson gave his ticket up so Mrs. Morgan could join Lawrence."

"That was a wonderful idea," Zayne said as he strolled into the room, Agatha by his side.

"Why do you say that?" Agatha asked.

"Mrs. Morgan has been known to pursue every available bachelor in the city. I've always felt a bit sorry for her, and she'll be thrilled with an estate to manage and a title to flaunt."

"My dears, I really must insist you go and change out of those pants," Gloria exclaimed as she bustled into the room. "Mr. Watson just arrived, and we don't want the poor man to have an attack. He's already reeling from discovering his wife helped bring down Eugene and Sally."

"Did you tell him you shot Eugene?" Agatha asked.

"Did you tell him you're planning on writing an article regarding tonight's event for the newspaper?" Gloria countered.

"I've yet to actually speak with my father," Agatha said with a smile.

"You're writing an article for the paper?" Eliza asked in delight.

"I am. My editor from the *New York Tribune* was standing on the street outside Daniels's house, watching the chaos and taking notes. When he actually recognized me and remembered who I was, well, he decided I would be better equipped to write the story since I had inside information. He wants me to present him with a full article that he promised to run on the front page. I really must get busy, as he wants the article turned in later tonight. Would you mind if I took my leave?"

"Of course not," Eliza replied, "but you might need to secure another ride. I have a feeling your parents are going to want to stay for a while."

"I'll see you home," Zayne volunteered, "but you're going to have to get out of those pants."

"Why?" Agatha asked.

Zayne began to whistle under his breath.

A feeling of peace descended over Eliza as Hamilton pulled her close to him. She watched the children as they giggled and played, none the worse for their ordeal, and then her gaze switched to Grayson, the brother who had been returned to her. She felt Hamilton's lips graze the top of her head and could do nothing to stem the tears that suddenly blinded her.

He loved her and wanted to marry her.

She blinked to clear her eyes and looked up to find Hamilton smiling back at her.

"Happy?" he asked softly.

"Indeed."

EPILOGUE

~∽~

Three weeks later, Eliza stood by a window in the church, watching a light snow fall. She turned as Piper raced into the room, Ben and Ming at her heels.

"It's snowing," Piper proclaimed.

"I see that."

"It makes the day more beautiful, like God is sending you kisses."

"What a lovely thought," Eliza said, bending to kiss Piper on the forehead.

"Are you ready to go?" Agatha asked, beautiful in a gown of shimmering blue. "I think Hamilton's getting a bit anxious."

"Can I call you Mama now?" Piper suddenly asked. "I know it's not time, but Ben calls you that, and I just wanted to know if it would be all right if I did the same."

"Of course you may call me Mama," Eliza said, blinking back yet another round of tears at how lovely her life had turned.

"You are the best daughter a mother could ever hope for, and I love you more than you will ever know."

"Don't start crying," Piper ordered. "You'll ruin your look."

"Who is crying?" Gloria asked, bustling into the room and coming to a sudden stop when she got a look at Eliza. "Oh, you are so beautiful," she wailed, dissolving into tears.

"She is indeed," Mrs. Watson agreed, dabbing her eyes with a handkerchief.

"Why is everyone crying?" Ben asked.

"That's what families do at happy events," Agatha told him.

"Come on, everyone out," Grayson said, holding open the door as he caught Eliza's eye.

"Grayson, Ben wants Ming to walk down the aisle with him," Eliza told her brother.

"Are you sure?" Grayson asked.

"She's part of our family, and besides, I've learned not to argue with Ben when he really wants something."

Grayson cleared his throat as he watched Ben grab on to Ming's hand and tug her to their place in line before turning back to Eliza. "This is what you want, isn't it?"

Eliza smiled. "I'm not changing my mind, Gray. I love Hamilton."

"Good, because I think he's perfect for you."

As Grayson walked her down the aisle a few moments later, Eliza's breath caught in her throat when she got her first glimpse of Hamilton. He was more handsome than ever in his formal attire, and she still found it hard to believe he was soon to be hers.

Hamilton took her hand when they reached the end of the aisle. Grayson placed a kiss on her cheek and stepped back. The hair stood up on the nape of Eliza's neck when Hamilton leaned forward and smiled at her.

"You're beautiful," he whispered and then surprised her by sending her a wink.

She couldn't help it; she grinned.

The minister beamed at them as he had them repeat their vows, and with every word spoken, Eliza's grin grew wider. Hamilton returned it and much to her delight, they were soon pronounced man and wife.

"You may kiss the bride," the minister encouraged.

"Finally," Piper said loudly, causing everyone to laugh.

When Hamilton's lips claimed hers, Eliza realized her life was complete, just as she realized God had never deserted her. He had shown her the way back from despair and given her a precious family to call her own along with a precious gift . . . the gift of love.

ACKNOWLEDGMENTS

The journey to publication is a fascinating one and filled with people who deserve my sincerest thanks.

- To Bethany House, for giving me the opportunity of a lifetime.

- To my extraordinary editor, Raela Schoenherr, for having such an amazing eye for detail and for imparting suggestions in the kindest possible way.

- To Paul Higdon and John Hamilton, for capturing Eliza perfectly with such a gorgeous cover.

- To my agent, Mary Sue Seymour, for plucking me out of the slush pile and pointing me in the right direction. You've become a friend.

- To the Marketing Department at Bethany House, for their diligence in promoting my book.

- To my sister, Tricia Gibas, for thinking everything I write is wonderful, even when it's not.

- To Rachel Kortmeyer, whom I know I bore endlessly with my talk of all things writing, but who still remains my friend.

- To Karen Bohland, for the "Fabio" tip.

- To my critique partner, Kimberlee Gard, for always being cheerful and enthusiastic.

- To Carol McMinn and the rest of the ladies at the Parker Library, for knowing where to find the answers I need.

- To my son, Dominic, for simply being my son.

- To my husband, Al, for all the support and love and for not becoming too annoyed when I interrupt him in midsentence on a regular basis because a plot suddenly flashes to mind and I have to discuss it right there and then. You have all my love.

- And, of course, to God, who makes everything possible.

DISCUSSION QUESTIONS

1. Why do some people distance themselves from God, as Eliza did, when their lives are not going as planned?

2. Mr. and Mrs. Watson are relentless in their pursuit to obtain a husband for Agatha. Is their behavior justified? Should parents put pressure on their children to get married, get a job, have children, etc.?

3. Hamilton was very affected by his wife's behavior and subsequent death. Do you think he was truly able to come to peace with what happened to her? Have you ever had to come to terms with poor treatment from a friend or significant other?

4. Agatha has been forced to assume a man's name in order to publish her articles. How would you feel about having to pretend to be of the opposite gender to be taken seriously in a profession?

5. Eliza gave up a life as an English aristocrat to be with Hamilton. Will she have regrets? Would you give up your current life to do something completely different?

6. Hamilton and Eliza's friends and family continue to bring up the possibility of a relationship between the two of them. Did you or do you have friends who played or want to play matchmaker for you? Do you appreciate this or does it frustrate you? Why or why not?

7. Mr. Theodore Wilder is a man of his time and frequently frustrates the forward-thinking women in this story. Does he have any redeeming qualities?

8. Mr. Watson seems somewhat heartless at the beginning of the story. What caused him to change?

9. Does Lawrence deserve Mrs. Morgan?

10. Eliza rediscovers God in the midst of great anger. Why do you think He came back to her then? Is this something that has ever happened to you?

Jen Turano, author of *A Change of Fortune*, is a graduate of the University of Akron with a degree in clothing and textiles. She pursued a career in management for nine years before switching to full-time motherhood after the birth of her son. When she's not writing, Jen can be found watching her teenage son participate in various activities, taking long walks with her husband and dog, socializing with friends, or delving into a good book. She is a member of ACFW and lives in a suburb of Denver, Colorado. Visit her website at www.jenturano.com.

If you enjoyed *A Change of Fortune*, you may also like...

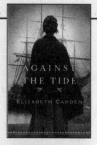

When Lydia's translation skills land her in the middle of a secret campaign against dangerous criminals, who can she trust when her life—and heart—are in jeopardy?

Against the Tide by Elizabeth Camden
elizabethcamden.com

When Lily Young sets out to find her lost sister amidst the dangerous lumber camps of Harrison, Michigan, she will challenge everything boss-man Connell McCormick thought he knew about life—and love.

Unending Devotion by Jody Hedlund
jodyhedlund.com

When undercover Pinkerton agent Ellie Moore's assignment turns downright dangerous—for her safety *and* her heart—what's this damsel in disguise to do?

Love in Disguise by Carol Cox
authorcarolcox.com

mL   9-13